A new Life

in Ventis

Richard Dee

4Star Scifi

Cover by Avalon Graphics

Richard Dee is a native of Brixham in Devon, England. He left Devon when he was in his teens and settled in Kent. Leaving school at 16 he briefly worked in a supermarket, then went to sea and travelled the world in the Merchant Navy, qualifying as a Master Mariner in 1986

Coming ashore to be with his growing family, he used his sea-going knowledge in several jobs, including Marine Insurance Surveyor and Dockmaster at Tilbury, before becoming a Port Control Officer in Sheerness and then at the Thames Barrier in Woolwich.

In 1994 he was head-hunted and offered a job as a Thames Estuary Pilot. In 1999 he transferred to the Thames River Pilots, where he regularly took vessels of all sizes through the Thames Barrier and upriver as far as HMS *Belfast* and through Tower Bridge. In all, he piloted over 3,500 vessels in a 22-year career with the Port of London Authority.

Richard is married with three adult children and two grandchildren.

His first science-fiction novel, *Freefall* was published in 2013, followed by *Ribbonworld* in 2015. September 2016 saw the publication of his first Steampunk adventure *The Rocks of Aserol* and *Flash Fiction*, a collection of Short Stories. *Myra*, the prequel to *Freefall* was published in 2017, along with the first of the *Andorra Pett* series, the adventures of a reluctant sleuth. He contributed a story to the *1066 Turned Upside Down* collection and is currently working on prequels, sequels, and new projects.

For Helen B, it was all her idea!

Escape

Chapter 1

The parade ground was a shambles. A line of bodies lay under a camouflage tarpaulin, booted feet and feminine shoes poking out in turn from its edge. There was the stench of blood and burnt flesh hanging in the air, away to one side the wreckage of a flying machine still smouldered and the carcases of several Drogans lay where they had fallen. Moans of pain could be heard from those still trapped under the collapsed seating; the brightly coloured bunting that had fluttered from it in welcome now seemed to hang in sorrow. The temperature had dropped sharply as the afternoon had worn on and a light drizzle softened the harsh outlines of the wreckage, diluting the red stains on the ground.

A steam crane was trundling slowly across the cobbled square ready to lift the wreckage away and a line of uniformed medics stood behind makeshift tables, prepared to tend the injured as they were revealed, they were already blood stained from their exertions with the accessible casualties.

Men and women milled about aimlessly; dazed and shocked they called out for their loved ones whilst the soldiers had formed into squads and were being given orders.

In the midst of all this chaos Terrance stood; a bewildered expression on his face. He knew that he was at least partly responsible for the carnage. In his eagerness to ensure that there was no obstruction to their view of the flyers he had left the crowd practically undefended.

Cavendish, his superior, had already told him that there would be a reckoning for his actions and he quailed inside at what that might entail.

As far as he could tell, at least half of the government were under the tarpaulin, and several minor members of the royal family had joined them in death. In any other circumstances Terrance would have seen the demise of so many as a chance to move up the ladder, especially if Cavendish had been one of the dead. Now it was just a weight around his neck.

A captain of the camp guards came to him and threw up a salute. "Your orders, sir?" he barked. Terrance felt like his thoughts were held in treacle, he had difficulty in forming them into words, what was he to do? The soldier stood, confidently expectant in front of him.

He realised that he had to try and find Strongman and Grace; he assumed that they had been in the steam lorry that he had lost sight of on the coast road; surely they must have been aided. Perhaps he could still apprehend those who had helped them; they might be persuaded to talk. Any triumph would give him a lever to deflect the criticism that would be bound to follow.

"A prisoner has escaped, and we need to find the men who helped her," he began. "I'm sure that she has gone in a steam lorry down the cliff road, but her accomplices may still be in the camp."

He was interrupted by the arrival of a bloodstained Cavendish; he shoved Terrance out of the way and addressed the soldier in crisp tones, "I suspect the camp has been infiltrated by traitors. Captain, muster the garrison and issue red caps to all the men. Then we can search thoroughly for anyone not wearing one. We should concentrate our efforts by the fence to the south; they would surely head towards the town. Break out the Exo-men and all the vehicles; get those flyers airborne and searching again, we must find them before it grows too dark to search."

"Yessir," the captain threw up another salute and ran back towards the ranks; shouting for his quartermaster.

"I was about to say that," Terrance told Cavendish. "I want to search the road down the cliffs again."

"We have not located her in the camp," he replied, "just her abandoned clothing. We have searched everywhere; she must have been in the lorry that you followed and lost on the road. Along with your fellow, what was he called?"

"Strongman," replied Terrance, stung by the venomous thoughts that the name stirred. How had that naive fool and his band plucked her from under his nose, here of all places?

"It has all the marks of a coordinated rescue," said Cavendish, "well planned and executed. Strongman has found good allies in those soldiers. Of course the Drogans helped but I think that his plan would have succeeded without them. The more important question is, how did they know she was here?"

"I'm unsure," said Terrance, thinking that only the two of them knew. Even Lucy, his secretary in the Ministry, knew nothing of Grace. She knew only of his whereabouts but in any event she would never reveal that, unless it was under duress. He had recognised at least one of the soldiers in the cab of the lorry; he had been with Strongman when he had last seen him in the park. They were connected, that much was certain. Perhaps it would be best not to let Cavendish know too much, it would not help his cause.

Cavendish continued this train of thought. "It's plain that this Strongman had help, we saw it in Metropol City, you recall that I was following him; now it may be that all his helpers were in that lorry. But it's also possible that some of his men will be forced to walk out of the camp."

He stroked his whiskers, it helped him concentrate. "We know that it's fenced and guarded. So where can they go?"

"Maybe they intend to lay low, hide in plain sight until the fuss dies down," Terrance suggested.

"Quite," said Cavendish. "But that is why I have ordered the issue of red caps to all the known soldiers in the garrison, if they try to blend in then we will find them."

"If they do get out," added Terrance, "they cannot leave Northcastle, I have ordered that the Ryde is watched and we can easily secure the town. Apart from the Rail and one road, the only way out is over the hills. Along with those in the lorry, they may not have a safe place to hide; we can search the town and find them all."

Cavendish nodded, so this man had plugged the more obvious holes. "What about the port?" Again Terrance was sure that he had done the right thing.

"I have sent word to halt all movements; only one vessel has left today; it had to make way for the arrival of the mysterious rocks from Aserol on the *Bold Cutter*."

Cavendish changed his tone to one of appreciation. "Again, good thinking," he said, a bit of encouragement was in order; it would disguise his true intentions. "Well done indeed, and which vessel was that?"

Here Terrance was in possession of the facts and spoke confidently, "The *Swiftsure*, Captain Nabbaro. He is a regular visitor; the ship has left for the East. In any event, they would not have had time to get from here to the port and on board. It was due to depart at around the same time as the flyers' demonstration started."

"Find them, Terrance. Investigate this Nabbaro and his ship."

Behind them, there was a growl as the engines on the rank of Exo-men were started. Huge doors swung open on all the buildings around the square and the latest machines of war emerged to join in the hunt. Lines of mobiles and lorries pulled into the square along with the latest invention, a large squat mobile with armoured sides. It was designed to travel over rough terrain, having six pairs of large iron-shod wheels mounted on springs. The wheels were fitted with a system of retractable spikes which could be engaged to grip on boggy ground or help them grip on hillsides. Thick chains drove them, powered by a large steam engine in its belly and smoke belched from its chimney as the engine propelled it. Large gas guns were mounted on its shell.

The machine was so new that Terrance had not seen a working version yet. It clanked and wheezed its way across the surface of the parade ground, throwing cobbles into the air, he hoped that he would not be blamed for the damage, unleashing the experimental machine had been Cavendish's idea. No matter, there were prisoners aplenty to repair such things.

Terrance felt his stomach turn at this desperate display of might; he knew that things had gone very wrong. While he might be personally responsible, he would not be cowed. "Events have gone against us, it is true," he began but Cavendish waved him silent.

"I have given you every chance to deal with them," he said in a cold voice. "You even had the woman hostage here; the whole lot of them appear to have been here today. Yet despite that we are empty handed and surrounded by corpses."

Terrance gazed at the carnage. "This was not all my doing," he replied defiantly. "I cannot control Drogan attacks. As far as I knew there were none in the area; no intelligence on the beasts was ever passed to me."

"Ahh, but you were wrong to remove the defences; that was another error on your part. I really think that I must consider your future, but as it happens, things are working to my advantage."

Privately, Cavendish was euphoric, like all ambitious politicians he had enemies in the government, now that several of them were laid under the tarpaulin, the power of those that remained was diminished and the time was ripe for him and his supporters to make their move.

It would never do to enlighten Terrance of course; he was a dead weight and easily replaceable. Better to let him attempt to rescue matters here before his demise was arranged. Terrance still controlled the Waster mine, source of the mysterious rocks, and had some authority in this camp. It would be better to allow him to relax a little so that he never saw the fatal blow coming. And a well-run organisation such as the Waster mine and all its riches, together with the transport company would be a fine gift. It could be a way of ensuring loyalty in a new protégé. He already had several in mind. It would be best to keep Terrance isolated here, out of the way of his machinations.

Softening his face he said, "Very well then, now is not the time for recrimination; do your best to catch these men, I will not interfere, you are doing the right things. I must return to Metropol City as soon as possible in any case. News of today's events must be carefully handled. The government of Norlandia needs a firm hand, His Majesty must learn of events. There will be funerals to arrange and official mourning to observe. Then no doubt we will again attempt to rid the land of Drogans. I will call you by speaker when I have things under control."

Cavendish walked away towards his mobile, Terrance let out a long breath, Cavendish's changes of mood had him in a spin. However, it looked like he was safe for the time being. His senses had returned, he knew what he must do. The ship with the rocks had arrived; there were things to attend to. He would be safe here, out of Cavendish's reach. He could make himself useful while the storm raged in the city. Mrs Grantham and Lucy would keep him up to date on events.

Behind him, the might of the armies of Norlandia started a search of the camp, buildings were scoured and the ranks of machines swept across the heather, desperate for a sight of what they had been told were a group of foreign saboteurs and terrorists. Their orders were simple, find them and capture them, any without red caps were suspect. They should be captured alive if possible but if not… well never mind.

Chapter 2

At the dockside, Keen and Maloney watched with relief as the *Swiftsure* was pulled clear of the wharf by two tugboats and turned in the basin. Horis and Grace had waved at them and disappeared inside before the gangway was lifted, no doubt they would stay out of sight until Norlandia was a line on the horizon. As the *Swiftsure* picked up speed and moved towards the harbour entrance the remaining stevedores shut the steam cranes down and departed, leaving the two of them alone on the wharf with their load of logs.

"The other vessel will be here shortly," Maloney said. "We need to get away from here before she is alongside, no doubt Terrance will be coming down to see his cargo arrive."

"We had better dump the logs sharpish then," replied Keen. They moved the lorry into the overhang at the front of the cargo shed. Using the steam piston under the loadbed, they tipped the logs into a rough pile, secured them with wedges and set off for the dock gate.

"You made it then?" the customs man remarked as they stopped at the barrier.

"Barely," replied Maloney. He brandished a wad of greasy notes from his breast pocket. "But look, we have the cash to prove it, it's off to the ale house for us now."

The man laughed. "I've to wait till my shift is over, get along with you and have the first ale for me." He waved to his mate and the barrier lifted. They drove the lorry out into the town, behind them the port prepared to receive the *Bold Cutter* and her special cargo.

Less than an hour later, Keen and Maloney arrived back at Mrs

Wring's. They had left the lorry in a quiet side road a good mile away from her residence and had walked the rest of the way. They saw several patrols of soldiers moving up the streets, knocking on doors and searching houses but they stayed ahead of them and were not challenged. Harris, who they had left at the house with all their gear, would be ready for them. Mrs Wring opened the door, grim-faced until she saw them, then she broke into a smile. Her apron was dusted with flour and the smell of cooking wafted around her frame like some precious perfume.

"I thought it was the other soldiers searching, they have been here once already," she announced. "Mr Harris and I sent them packing." Maloney could imagine Mrs Wring in full flow; she would frighten the most battle-hardened man and leave Harris little to do.

"Are there only the two of you?" she continued, peering past them along the street. "Come in, quickly." She ushered them inside and slammed the door. "Into the back parlour, your comrade awaits, he says that he is replete from my pie and good gravy," she said. "Although I do feel that he needs feeding up."

She pushed Maloney and Keen down the hallway. Harris was sat in the parlour, looking well fed and content, he rose to greet them. "Hello, you two," he said cheerfully. "I'm just getting to enjoy my time here, but I fear my belt might need loosening if we stay much longer."

"So," shouted Mrs Wring from the kitchen, where no doubt she was making them char, "was your mission a success?"

"It was," confirmed Maloney as he sat in an easy chair. "We have completed our task and it all went perfectly. We had a little welcome help from the Drogans; they arrived in force and caused a distraction at the right time to help us. Sadly their arrival brought death and destruction, but the lady is rescued and safely away with her man. We got them to their ship and watched it depart. Now we have to await the arrival of the rest of our band and we can leave you here in peace."

"That's good news," said Mrs Wring, amid a clattering of cups. "Though I shall miss your company, it was just like old times with Mr Wring and his mates. And you know, I quite liked the little fellow. You can relax now; I am making char and some food, then you can tell me all the details."

Harris groaned. "More food?" he said. "I cannot eat another morsel."

Mrs Wring peered around the door frame and gave him a suspicious look. "Is my food not good enough?" she asked, one eyebrow raised. Harris wisely declined to comment.

They did as they were told; 'some food' was a huge platter of bread, cheese and pickles which they shared among them, Harris included. They ate and drank in silence for a while.

"When might we expect Sapper and the rest?" Mrs Wring asked.

"They will hike out of the camp," said Keen. "If the town is being searched, then the camp will be too, and more so. Sapper will lay low, and move when he can, we should not expect them before tomorrow night, if then."

She nodded. "I see. We must prepare for more searches I suppose, they will be sore to have lost their captive. I wish Sapper good luck evading them; I hear they test fearsome machines of war in that place."

After they had finished, they moved to easy chairs. Maloney and Keen told of the events at the camp, the rescue and the Drogan attack. She was shocked to hear of all the destruction but doubted that anyone in the general population would ever get to hear of it. And the idea of flying machines fascinated and terrified her in equal measure.

"We know little of all the doings of the state in that place," she grumbled. "Look at the way they treated me and my dear husband. If they can lie about simple things, who knows what else goes on? And flying, well, I'm not sure of that." She shook her head at the idea.

"We expected that the town would be searched," Maloney agreed with her assessment. "It will be a few days before we can safely depart. They may be back here again, once they have looked everywhere and found nothing."

"That will not be a problem, laddie," said Mrs Wring. "I have a good cellar under this building. You may all stay in there, or in this back parlour. Never fear, I have no love for officialdom and will keep you safe."

The next morn, at some early hour, Maloney awoke to two sensations. One was the smell of frying porker, the other the noise of someone hammering on the door. Quickly he roused Harris and Keen, between them they used the back stairs to make their way to the kitchen. Mrs Wring was there, frying and singing. "Hurry along, you two," she said. "Harris can stay with me, the soldiers yesterday saw him so he will be expected. Away the rest of you go, down to the cellar."

The knocking at the door grew louder as she closed the cellar door behind them. Peering through the keyhole Sapper's view was suddenly obscured as she went to the door. She had pulled a curtain over the doorway. They moved down the stairs into the shadows as the front door opened. Through gaps in the floorboards they could hear the conversation.

"What do you want?" asked Mrs Wring aggressively. "Be quick, laddie, my fast-breaker is growing cold."

"Beg pardon, madam," replied a young sounding voice. "I have to search the house for foreign anarchists."

"No you don't," she answered. "Your men searched the house yesterday and found nothing, for sure I would not entertain such overnight, I'm a respectable woman."

The soldier stammered. "I'm sure you are; I have my orders."

"Well you can go and pester someone else," she said. "There is nobody here except me and Mr Harris, my lodger." There was the sound of some remark and Mrs Wring spoke again with a raised voice. "Don't you cheek me, young man. Would you talk like that in front of your family? I'm a respectable widow."

There was the sound of the door slamming and soon the singing resumed.

Ten minutes later the door opened. "You may come out now," she said. "They have got back in their mobile and gone. I am calmed down, the porker is ready and char is brewed."

"I'm glad you were not ranged against me in the jungle," said Maloney. "I may have lost more than one arm."

"They're naught but young boys," she answered. "If you act like their mothers it's enough to dissuade them. And the cheek of it; he was a boy young enough to be my grandson. Daring to ask me if Mr Harris here was my fancy man!"

Harris had the grace to look embarrassed at that while Maloney tried to keep his face straight. Mrs Wring meanwhile served fried porker and eggs together with thick wedges of bread and mugs of char. "Sit and eat," she instructed.

Mrs Wring went to market in the morn but was careful to buy small quantities of provisions. "I laid in a stock whilst you were away," she explained, "most of the local folk know I take guests on occasion. I'm not so stupid as to give you away by purchasing a whole bovine, you know."

And her look was so fierce that no-one doubted her.

They spent the day in the parlour. Soldiers came to the house twice more, each time they were more insistent and each time Mrs Wring sent them packing. There was little to do except wait. Even if he had managed to get out without difficulty, Sapper and the others would not be arriving before the evening. They did not venture out of the house; there was little point in it, for they had their return Rail tickets.

Chapter 3

As the steam lorry drove away, Sapper breathed a sigh of relief. The mission was accomplished; now all that remained was for him and his men to get out of the camp undiscovered. And the Drogan attack had made that a lot easier. Looking around he quickly spotted Wilson and Meek and the three grouped together. But where was Daniel?

"Haven't seen him, Sapper," they both replied to his question.

Sapper looked around, there was a semblance of order emerging, the Drogans were now coming off worse under the twin assault of the flyers and the soldiers. The beasts on the ground were dead or dying and those left in the air suddenly shot away, chased by the flyers. There was a line of soldiers firing gas rifles and behind them more opening ammunition crates and reloading weapons. And over there, under the eye of a sergeant-major, was the unfortunate Daniel. At least he still had the parchment on his lapel, he should be sensible enough to keep his mouth shut.

Just as Sapper was debating his next move there was the noise of a heavy weapon and then the wail of a siren from the direction of the gate.

"We need to go," said Wilson. "They are discovered."

Sapper adjusted his cap; he was of equal rank to the man with Daniel and hoped he could bluster his way through.

Walking over to Daniel he bawled at him. "Private Daniel, what in Bal's name are you doing here?"

The other NCO looked him over, spotting the unfamiliar cap badge and the parchment pass.

"He one of yours?" he asked. "Blasted balloonists, where was his rifle eh? I'll be putting him on a charge; you can get him from the glasshouse tomorrow." Daniel looked suitably shocked.

"I'm sorry to have to tell you," said Sapper, "but you can't have him. He's already on a charge from my captain, I have to get him back over to him before supper." He waved at Wilson and Meek. "We've been looking for him, these Drogans messed us up."

"What did he do then?" asked the other suspiciously.

"Tell him, Daniel," ordered Sapper.

Daniel gulped. "Absent without leave, Sergeant-Major," he said, eyes downcast.

The man was not taken in. "There's no leave here," he said. "Even for the high and mighty balloonists."

Sapper clipped Daniel around the ear. "Tell it true, lad," he urged.

Daniel hung his head. "Well there was a lady in the servery," he started.

A broad smile came upon the face of the man. "Aha," he said. "There's always a lady somewhere, I hope she was worth it, be off with you then, it seems like the threat is over anyways."

"Come on, blast you," said Sapper, grabbing Daniel by the shoulder and dragging him away. When they were out of earshot he rounded on him.

"What was all that about?"

"Sorry, Sapper," said Daniel. "I was looking for the lady like you said and I got grabbed by him."

Wilson was holding four rifles. "Here you are, Sapper, one each. I got them from the throng." He passed the weapons out.

"Right-ho, boys," Sapper decided, "form up and let's head for the fence."

As they hastened away they could hear the roar as mobiles and machinery were prepared for the job of searching, even though it was getting late in the day. Officers called for search parties to find a woman.

They kept going, wanting to reach the safety of the cave and their packs before darkness fell. Their haste meant that they didn't see that all the searchers were issued with red caps and instructions to fire on sight if any were found without them.

They made good time across the country and reached the cave just as dusk was falling. The lack of light had not stopped the search, they heard several flying machines but none passed close to them before they got under cover. And their buzz stopped as night fell. It seemed that they were searching the area around the fence that was their target. The Exo-men kept going in the dark; they could be seen in a line quartering the ground towards the fence, bright gas lamps shining on the heather. And there was another noise, like a large mobile, but it stopped before they caught sight of it.

"We are safe enough here," said Sapper. "Let's have a meal and a sleep; tomorrow we move quickly to the gap."

They retrieved their packs, which were untouched, and spent a quiet night in slumber, taking it in turns to stand guard. There were no flying machines after dark but patrols with gas lights could be seen in the distance. The earth shook from the passage of the Exo-men but none came close to their hiding place. Sapper was of the opinion that the ground around them was too rough for their balance to cope. The search went on but concentrated on the fence, apart from the noise they were not disturbed.

Just after sunrise, they awoke and after a swift fast-breaker from their packs, they set off again for the fence.

They passed a stranded mobile, large and of a type unknown to them, there were soldiers and white-coated scientists clustered around it, one of the huge wheels had come off and was lying on its side a distance away. Two of the large Exo-men were attempting to lift one corner whilst a third was straining to move the wheel. Orders were shouted; the men were engrossed in their task and never noticed the four who slipped past them.

"That's a new kind of mobile," said Wilson. "I've never seen the likes of that before."

"It looks to me as if it's intended for work on rough ground."

"But not perfected yet; we must be important if they're sending out all the new inventions."

"Quiet now, lads," whispered Sapper. "We're coming to the fence. It might get busy; keep sharp."

As they crested the last rise they laid flat. Creeping to the top they could see that the fence was unguarded. And the gap at the cliff edge had not yet been mended.

"Quick march, boys," ordered Sapper. "Through the gap before anyone sees us."

There was about one hundred yards of open ground to cross to reach the fence; with a gully about halfway between it and them. They had just traversed it when they heard a mobile approach. Without thinking they laid flat in the heather, their uniforms blending in.

A mobile with a mechanical gas gun mounted on the roof came into view, travelling up the roadway between the two fences, it was filled with soldiers. It stopped in front of them and several got out, the officer marched to the fence.

In the still air, Sapper could hear the conversation between the soldiers. He officer noted that the fence was damaged, he split his command and sent some back to report and bring materials to mend the breach. There were only six men remaining, as lightly armed as they were. The mobile turned and headed back towards the camp.

"That'll be reinforcements on the way," said Sapper, "we must try and bluff our way through this before they return. Safety clips off and follow my lead." The four rose as one and approached the group at the fence.

"Halt! Who goes there?" the officer shouted, suddenly noticing the men marching toward him. "What's your business?" Beside him his men levelled their rifles.

"We are following the trail of the escaped prisoners," shouted back Sapper.

"Then where are your red caps?" asked the leader of the soldiers, a captain by the look of it. "You have none. You are the enemy we are searching for. Now put your rifles down and stand still."

Sapper looked around him; they had rifles but were caught in open ground, the others' guns were already raised. He made a quick decision. "Down and back to the gully, boys," he shouted and as one the four dropped to the scant cover of the heather and started to crawl backwards. Their jungle training had taken over and they obeyed instantly.

"Fire at will," the sergeant shouted and the air was filled with the hiss and thump of projectiles. The ground in front of them was churned by their impact.

Meek shouted out, "I am struck," and the men on either side of him moved quickly and grabbed a leg each, pulling him back with them to safety. Somehow, no-one else was hit as they arrived in the safety of the gully. They shrank into cover, the earth at the lip was churned by the fire and a continual rain of bullets either thudded into the earth in front of them or whistled over their heads.

Meek was quickly examined, there were two bullet holes in the shoulders of his tunic and he was gritting his teeth, obviously in great pain, yet trying not to speak and give away their position. Sapper gave him a full ampoule of analgesic which dulled his senses. Wilson had a mirror on a small stick which he used to peer over the edge of the gully at the fence.

"Right, lads, we have to move, and before they return. One of us goes left and one right. Daniel, you stay here with Meek. Twenty paces to the sides and prepare to return fire. We can then shoot back from three directions at once."

Quickly, with the experience he had gained in the Jungle Wars, Sapper arranged his limited force. "Must we shoot at them?" asked Daniel.

"I know they're our own countrymen but they started it. We can't wait, now go." The group split up, they moved quickly into position.

Peering over the lip, Sapper saw that a section of the inner fence had been removed and that the soldiers were concentrating their gaze on the place where Daniel and Meek were. He could see the results of their first barrage, it looked like a ploughed field where they had been caught and he wondered how only Meek had been touched in that welter of ordinance.

The remaining soldiers had opened a gap in the fence and split up; four of them formed a skirmish line, fixed bayonets and marched through the gap in the fence. The other two followed, one to the left and one to the right to cover them. Sapper recognised that they were both following the same tactics, it would be what it would be, no time to waste, the mobile would soon be back at the camp.

Sapper blew his whistle. The three survivors rose and fired as one and the soldiers all went to ground. Of the four closing on them, only the sergeant stood again and returned fire. The two on the flanks were untouched. Not bad shooting, Sapper thought, but not enough. The survivors kept up rapid fire and earth flew by his ear as he realised that they had his range. He heard Daniel cry out and there was another shout from his right. Please, no more casualties, thought Sapper. They were stuck again. He decided that they should all move to the left, towards the cliff edge and repeat their attack.

Just as he was about to pass the order, he heard a noise above him. Looking over his shoulder he saw that a flying machine had come. Now Sapper knew that his time was up. He had seen what its gas guns had done to the Drogans; his small band would be easy meat.

From his vantage point high above the fence, Ralf saw the situation clearly, the red-capped soldiers firing at the small band trapped in the gully. He realised that they must have been part of Grace's rescue party. He could not fly past and see them slaughtered. Nor could he assist in the deed.

The leader of the soldiers saw Ralf's approach and was pleased;

half his squad were dead at the hands of what must be foreign agents, now the might of Norlandia would rain down upon them. The three had formed up into a tight group again. "Here comes our saviour, boys," he called. "The brave lads of the flyers, watch them do battle."

Ralf armed his guns, flying in a slow circle over the scene. Taking a deep breath he pointed the nose of the plane down and fired.

Sapper had tried to worm his way under the heather at the base of the gully, they all had, and he braced himself for the impact of the projectiles from on high.

The guns fired, loud above the roar of the engine.

Sapper lifted his face up to the sky, the plane had swung around for another pass, it had obviously missed him on the first attempt. He peered over to his right, Daniel was still in the land of the living, his face lined with pain but he managed a sickly grin and, "Flesh wound," through gritted teeth. Beyond him he could not see Wilson; he feared that there was another injured man there.

The guns spoke again and he realised that the flyer must be on their side. Perhaps it had to do with Grace? He lifted himself up and peered cautiously towards the fence.

The soldiers' position had taken a pounding, that was for sure and no-one moved where they had been. Sapper stood and the plane flew past him. He could see the pilot, who waved and waggled the craft's wings in salute, before turning and flying back towards the camp.

"Come on, lads," he called. "Somehow the flyer was on our side; let's get through the fence before the mobile returns."

Sapper and Wilson picked up Meek, who had sadly succumbed to his wounds. Daniel could still walk; he had been wounded in the upper arm but had staunched the blood with a dressing. Wilson was unhurt; his cry had come from a near miss that had showered him with earth and stones. They set off through the wreckage towards the inner fence. Daniel stooped and removed all the red caps they could find, the three donned them, the rest they put in their packs, that should confuse any pursuers and help the flyer avoid awkward questions.

Then they collected up the bodies, including Meeks, and threw the comrades in death over the edge of the cliffs. Once they had climbed around the broken outer fence they were free of the camp.

Once clear, they headed for the cliff edge, where Sapper had seen a track on his earlier foray. As they started to drop down the path and were out of sight from the fence they heard a mobile arriving and many shouts.

Chapter 4

Dusk was falling by the time they had descended the pathway and joined the road towards the town; they decided to keep going rather than risk being caught in the open. And they had the red caps now, which would help them if they were stopped. Ahead of them were the lights of Northcastle, they could also see the smaller lanterns from the soldiers who searched. Relaxed, they marched on into the town. It was dark as they approached Mrs Wring's house, they had avoided two patrols and were by now tired and hungry.

Mrs Wring opened the door to their knock; she viewed them with annoyance. "Be off with you," she said, "disturbing honest folk at this time of night. You have searched my poor house already today, can I get no rest?"

"Why, Mrs Wring," said Sapper, "you have us wrong, we are not searchers, unless it is for one of your pies." He removed his red cap and held up his lantern.

"Come in, quickly," she said, her face breaking into a broad grin. "Mr Maloney is skulking in my cellar, among the stored cheeses and provisions."

"Not so," said the man himself, he had heard Sapper and come up, followed by Keen. "It's good to see you, Sapper," he said clasping his hand. "But where is Meek?"

"I think we'd better sit down and I can explain," said Sapper. "Mr Meek will not be returning."

Mrs Wring made them char and broke into a pie while each group brought the other up to date on events. Sapper was relieved to hear that Horis and Grace were safe. Maloney, in turn, was saddened to know that one of his command had perished. Mrs

Wring cleaned Daniel's wound with a lotion she possessed, which made him wince, and bound it up.

The role of Ralf the flyer drew a gasp from Maloney. "Grace mentioned in passing that there was one flyer who had offered to help her," he said, "but I paid it little attention, thinking it merely a ruse to gain her affection. Clearly it was not."

"I had to dump all the bodies over the cliff edge," said Sapper. "It hurt me to do it for they all deserved respect and decency; even the ones who fought us were acting out of the best motives."

"Then why, laddie?" asked Mrs Wring, she had joined the conversation and was accepted as one of them.

"It was the red caps that did it," he explained. "The flyer, who must have been the one that Grace told of, he was on our side and killed those ranged against us. I did what I did to hide the evidence and protect him."

Mrs Wring nodded her head. "I see, laddie," she muttered. "My man, rest him, told me of the things he had to do at times, they were not always pleasant but very often necessary."

Now they were all assembled, they began to plan for their departure. They had Rail tickets and civilian clothes left at Mrs Wring's for their journey. They had their army discharge papers which showed that they were no longer military men, merely demobilised seekers of employment.

To avoid being seen as a group, Wilson and Keen left first for the journey back to Metropol City, they carried their packs and a large selection of Mrs Wring's comestibles to sustain them on the Ryde. Harris followed at a distance to ensure that they got through the barriers, there were a large number of soldiers on duty in the town and the Rail terminus, several times the pair were stopped but they were not suspected.

Once the Ryde had left, Harris returned to Mrs Wring's. Daniel's wound was healing, helped by the good food that Mrs Wring provided.

The next day Sapper and Harris went to the terminus, followed by Maloney, who had removed his false arm to alter his appearance. They found that there were fewer soldiers and the pair passed easily onto the platform and the Ryde.

On the third day, Maloney and Daniel made ready to leave Mrs Wring, she was emotional at their departure, wiping at her eyes whilst pretending that she had some speck in them. Again she had prepared enough food, bread, cheese and fresh meat pies for a week's journey, Maloney had his arm fitted and Daniel his arm in a sling. They passed through the town and onto the Ryde with ease.

"That was an adventure and no mistake," said Daniel as they sat eating pie. The Ryde thundered through the countryside, their carriage was deserted. "I would never have thought that I would be shot at by my own side," he continued.

Maloney nodded gravely. "We did the right thing," he said. "Although it was uncomfortable to go against one's own, right has prevailed. Power cannot be abused like that."

Daniel nodded. "Never mind all the niceties, it was good fun!"

A week later Maloney arrived back at the hotel in Aserol. He had seen Daniel safe to the barracks in Metropol City, where the group were reunited. Then he had taken the Ryde to Aserol. He had a lot to do, there were people to warn, and a job to return to, but first he had to see his wife Shirl and explain his absence.

Whilst in the city, he saw that changes were underfoot, the government had new ministers and the place was in mourning. Officially there had been an attack by foreign agents that had caused the deaths in Northcastle, repelled by the brave soldiers of First Minister Cavendish's army. Maloney shook his head as he read the news, the people had no idea, he thought, of what really went on in their own land. The grip on people's knowledge was complete; as was their ignorance of it.

It was not just the government that had changed, when the Ryde pulled into the terminus at Aserol, Maloney saw that the signage referring to the mining company had all been altered, everywhere, on Rail wagons, the yard and the lorries, all references to 'Waster' had been expunged and replaced with 'Morken'.

So it was Morken Mining and Metals now, thought Maloney. Mr Terrance must be in trouble over his handling of events in Northcastle. This sign of the man's fall from grace made Maloney's absence from his home and family seem worthwhile, it was a fitting comeuppance for his treatment of Horis and of Grace.

He walked to his house from the terminus; he had been sat in the Ryde for a long while and wished to stretch his legs. He passed several people who bade him a good day, it was nice to be back among friends. And the weather was far better here, it was not cold, although a breeze blew from the sea, it was warm, the sun shone on his back.

Arriving at his house he opened the door. "Hello, girl, I'm back," he called. His wife, the twin of Mrs Wring, ran across the room and enfolded him in her arms.

"Mr Maloney, where have you been?" she said. She stood back. "Is that another woman's gravy on your shirtfront?"

"It is," Maloney replied with a grin. "Her pie was good but not a patch on yours, I have had adventures, sit and I will tell you all."

Shirl listened to his tale till late at night, alternately laughing and crying. "You are a wonder," she said at the end of it. "You and your men! You were always on the side of the ordinary man against the might of the government."

"And why should I not be?" Maloney answered. "I would stand for any if they were decent and honourable, but when you see injustice, 'tis your duty to oppose it."

Chapter 5

The next morning, Maloney went to the hotel. Sayrah was on duty at the desk, looking as disdainful as ever. "Good day," called Maloney as he strode by, bound for the manager's office.

"Where have you been, Mr Maloney?" she shouted at his back. "Off on another of your adventures eh, whilst the rest of us do your work for you?"

He did not answer, he and the manager had an agreement, he had helped the hotel in many ways, retrieving lost articles and extracting payment from those who had sneaked away. The manager was happy to let him have his absences in return. Sayrah was not as important as she believed herself to be.

"Hail, Maloney," said the man, rising from his desk to clasp his good hand. "How are you, was your mission a success?"

"It was," replied Maloney. "I helped a man retrieve what was his," he said enigmatically.

"Your wife called in and explained your absence," continued the manager. "Of course, your position is still open for you, should you want it."

"Thank you," said Maloney. "I appreciate your help. I can resume my duties tomorrow, but tell me, why does the mine have new owners since I was gone?"

"Well noticed," said the manager. "This is why I value you, you miss nothing. I think it is due to the accident, a backlash against the previous owner. After the collapse things were starting to settle, then, Obley the manager at the Waster was attacked in the street by an angry mob, they blamed him for the collapse, right or wrong. He was hospitalised and sadly expired from his injuries.

About the same time as Mister Cavendish became First Minister, the mine was sold, and new management installed. It had been in the Terrance family for years, as you know. The tale was that they were glad to be rid of it. Now some fellow called Morken owns the place. Out of respect he has left the site of the accident closed. Production from the other shafts has increased overall. Folk say he is a slave-driver. And there is talk of secrets; he has a separate group of miners working on goodness knows what."

"Then no doubt things will carry on as before," Maloney had a good idea of what the secret was, but never said. "After all, Aserol and its happenings are merely a plaything among the great and the good in the big city."

The manager nodded but Maloney had realised what the message was behind the deeds. Cavendish had consolidated his grip on power by removing Terrance and installing his own man in charge of the mine. The cave where the rocks were found may be officially closed but he was sure that the rocks were still being mined and removed.

If Terrance had managed to survive the purge that all new governments made, then he would surely come looking for revenge. That would mean no good for Grace and Horis. And Divid would know where they were, Grace was bound to get in touch with her brother. If Terrance were determined, it would not be hard to locate the pair. Maloney thought for a second, it was a visit he would have to make on his way home.

"Thank you for your understanding," said Maloney. "I will resume my duties in the morning."

With the manager's good wishes ringing in his ears, he left and went directly to Grace's parents' dwelling.

Her father Caln answered the door. "Come in, Mr Maloney," he said. "You are most welcome here." It was Maloney who had looked out for Grace when she had first found employment at the hotel and Caln was grateful.

"How can we help you?" he asked when Maloney was seated and

provided with char.

"I have news of Grace," he began.

Caln took on a serious look. "We have not heard from her in several lunars, neither has her brother," he said. "Pray tell me without delay, is she well?"

"She is in good shape, or at least she was not ten days ago when I saw her last," he said.

"That is a relief," said Permilia, Grace's mother, who had come into the room from the back parlour to join the menfolk. "Since she left us to live with Divid and his wife we see her little enough, and when he said she had gone away we were concerned."

"What has she been doing?" asked Caln.

Maloney hedged. "She has had many adventures," he blandly said. "Myself and others have done our utmost to keep her safe. There might be those who still seek to harm her though. If any such come looking, you must tell them nothing and pass a message to me."

"Did you involve her in one of your schemes?" asked Permilia, her face showing concern for her daughter. "I know of your military shenanigans, tell me now; did you put my girl in any danger?"

Maloney shook his head vigorously. "I give you my word, madam. She became involved innocently in affairs, and once she was we worked to release her. As I said, the last I knew was when I put her safe aboard the *Swiftsure* in Northcastle."

"Northcastle," said Caln, fear in his voice. "That's a dangerous place for a young lady to be in. Why could she be in Northcastle? Was she alone?"

Maloney shook his head. "No, sir. I would not leave her alone; she was with a friend, a respected employee of the Ministry of Coal." He neglected to mention the reason for her being there; he was saved that by Permilia, interrupting Caln's chain of thought.

"You call that safe?" she scoffed. "With my brother and his motley crew of ne'er-do-wells. Who knows where they will go on his wanderings?"

"With Captain Nabbaro is the safest place, trust me." Maloney thought it better not to mention Horis, that should come from Grace herself. Besides which, for all he knew they may have gone separate ways by now. He finished his char. "Thank you," he said, "now I must get back to my Shirl, but first I have to pass the same message to Divid."

"We will tell you if anyone asks," said Caln. "My thanks to you for keeping her safe."

"It was my pleasure," said Maloney. "I haven't enjoyed an adventure so much for a long while."

Maloney's next call was to see Divid; he went only a few streets away to the dwelling that he and his wife shared with Grace. Divid was absent but his wife, Bess, was at home, with a babe.

"Well, Mr Maloney, what a pleasant surprise to see you, come in and take char," she said. "Divid is expected."

A sensible girl, she knew Grace well, the three of them had been friends from their schooldays, and Grace had moved in to help pay their rent when Bess found herself with child. Maloney was on his second mug of char, he was rapidly filling up with the stuff, when Divid arrived, covered in coal dust from his labours.

"Hail, Maloney," he shouted, his voice matching his size. He moved to shake his hand but stopped. "Let me get myself clean first," he said. "Have you news of Grace?"

"Your bath is drawn," said his wife. "Piping hot, as you like it."

"Thank you, my love, I will be but a few moments," he said and in less time than that he reappeared in clean clothes. He sat beside Bess and took the babe in his huge hands, as gentle as a summer breeze he rocked the infant, who slept on, contented.

"Now then," Divid said. "I assume you have news of my sister."

Maloney told him of Grace's whereabouts, this time he mentioned Horis, the name brought a smile to Divid's face.

"I liked the fellow," he said. "He had honesty and a certain innocence about him. More than that, he could drink a vast amount of ale for his size. They will make a fine pair. If I know Grace she will have him bent to her will in no time."

"They are safe on the *Swiftsure*," agreed Maloney. "They will return to Aserol one day, when the fuss is over, no doubt you might go on board and see them then. My worry now is the man who they escaped from. He has lost the mine and may well come looking for revenge."

Divid's face took a serious expression. "I was moved by the old owners," he said, "for daring to question their conduct after the accident. I work at the railyard now, driving my Exo loading the wagons. I can't say that I'm sorry. Things have changed since this Morken took over; the talk in the ale house is of extra work and less safety."

"As I have just said to Caln, keep your eyes and ears open," replied Maloney. "If anyone asks for Grace, tell them nothing and let me know."

"Will we be safe?" said Bess. She took the babe from Divid, as if it were safer with her.

"Fear not, ma'am," was Maloney's comment. "I will ensure that you are."

He had an idea that there might soon be some excitement in Aserol.

The *Swiftsure*

Chapter 6

Meanwhile, the subjects of the manhunt were blissfully unaware of the hue and cry they had raised in Northcastle. The *Swiftsure* ploughed through a low swell, rolling and pitching easily. They were no longer on their way to the Eastlands but now headed to Omnipa in the far south-west of Norlandia. The change of orders had not been expected and the way that they had been delivered had been one last thing to keep Horis on edge.

Having passed between the harbour breakwaters, the *Swiftsure* slowed and a lee was made. The pilot left the wheel-space, escorted down by the duty officer to the approaching cutter. As the cutter came alongside, there was a flashing lamp.

"Why are they signalling?" asked Horis, as he saw the winking light. Hector concentrated as he read the coded message of short and long flashes.

"They have dispatches for us," replied Hector.

Immediately Horis shrank into a corner. "Are we discovered so quickly?" he asked.

"Fear not," said Hector. "It will probably be some mundane message from my agents, a change of orders I expect. They would have been unable to deliver it as we were forced to sail early. If we were required to hand you back for some reason, a warship would be here to make us turn about, not the cutter."

Horis relaxed somewhat as the bucket was lowered and an envelope placed inside it. The duty officer returned with it after seeing the pilot safely away. Hector split the flap and read the note. "As I thought, it is a letter from my agents; there is a change in our itinerary."

"Where are we bound now?" asked Grace, who was unconcerned. Horis realised that he was the only person who had been bothered, this must be normal practice, perhaps all seafarers were used to it.

"We sail to Omnipa," Hector replied. "For a load of exported goods to Tarpitt, thence loading cofé and cacao beans, returning to Norlandian ports."

Horis and Grace exchanged worried glances, this was not what they wanted, if it should be suspected that they were aboard there would be soldiers waiting for them on the jetty in Omnipa. There was plenty of time to get a message from Northcastle to Omnipa overland long before they would arrive. Omnipa had no Rail but there was a garrison and a speaker station for the military.

Hector tried to reassure them. "Omnipa is quiet and out of the way, they only have the mail delivered every fortnight or so, and even that depends on the brigands in the area. If they are active then the place is isolated. Likewise the speakers, as fast as they are laid and connected, so the criminals steal the copper wires and sell them back to the foundry. It is more than likely that they will not have heard any news about you. In fact, this might well work to your advantage."

"How might that be so?" asked Horis, he wanted to be away from Norlandia as soon as possible and stay away until any fuss had died down. How could this diversion possibly be to his advantage?

"Well, firstly, as far as anyone in the port is concerned, we are sailing to the Eastlands, only the sender of the letter knows different. And as they are not in Northcastle, they may not be asked."

Horis could see the sense in that. Hector continued, "Also, if you wish to withdraw funds, Omnipa is as good a place to do so as any, and it might be an idea to realise your assets while you still can."

Horis understood; he could retrieve his money from an

unsuspecting bank. Especially one that had no way to communicate with its head office, except by unreliable post. The longer he left it, the more likely that word would have reached them and he could find that his account had been seized.

"Then it's good that I have my passbook," he said, "in my pocket safe with my other papers. Perhaps you are right."

"I can keep things safer for you on my ship than in any bank," said Hector, "especially under your name. It would not be long before everything was taken on the orders of Terrance."

Horis had already lost his apartment in Metropol City and the few possessions that he had there, to lose the small savings he had would be the last straw.

And with that thought, it was time for dinner. As Horis and Grace entered the saloon there were cheers and applause for them from the assembled crew and officers. They took seats at the top table, next to Hector's place and were soon answering questions about their adventures. Grace's tale of capture and imprisonment brought gasps and mutterings, then when Horis spoke of the rescue there were cheers and more applause. They all remembered his earlier voyage on the ship. Then he had been accompanied by Maloney and Grieve, to a man they were shocked at the turn of events.

"Hector charged you with looking after Grace," the engineer said, as Horis stopped for a drink, "and you did so admirably."

"It was not just my doing," he repeated, several times. "I have Mr Maloney and his men to thank for most of my good fortune." Even so, he basked in the praise.

The cook on the *Swiftsure* had produced another superb repast, after a mixed root soup there was grilled bovine steak with accompaniments, all followed by a rich fruit pie and creamy sauce. The conversation continued, with everyone dissecting the tale, when they got to the Drogans' attack and the appearance of the flying machine there was surprise.

"We never knew of such as these flying machines," said one

of the artificers. "The Drogans must have been alarmed at the intruders in the air; I suspect that they see it as their domain."

The engineers then entered a long discussion about the mechanics of flight and Horis found that he was no longer the centre of attention. Grace pled tiredness from the excitement and excused herself to sleep. Horis also sought to escape but as he made to follow her, one of the engineers produced a bottle of spirit and the toasting began. After a while, and another bottle, Horis began losing his grip on sobriety; eventually he staggered off to the passenger cabins, chose an empty one and fell fast asleep.

When he awoke, he found that he was still fully dressed, his head ached and his mouth was dry, it was not unlike the morning after his adventure in the *Drogans Rest* in Aserol, all those months ago. That had been when he had first met Grace, they had gone to view the harvest celebrations and that had been the start of all his adventures. The morning after that, he had felt wretched, he had still Ministry duties to perform and Terrance to impress. Now, for the first time in ages, he felt relaxed and complete. All of his worries had been assuaged.

He was blissfully happy to be reunited with Grace, the fact that she had suffered on his account made him all the more tender towards her, and after he had made himself presentable and broken his fast they spent the day just walking the deck and holding each other, while they talked of her imprisonment and her treatment by Terrance.

He sensed that she needed to talk, to break the spell it had over her and cauterise the wound. The day was chilly but fresh and the low sun broke through scudding clouds every now and then. Occasional spray splashed the deck as the vessel moved in a short sea, and they laughed as they were damped by the salty water.

"It was so foul," she said, after she had laughed at his protestations of a pounding head, her expression changed as she remembered the cell and the desolation; she shook while Horis held her. She spoke in short sentences, punctuated by sobs; he knew some of it already but let her talk as she repeated all the horrors of her ordeal.

"Being captured and having to watch Grieve die horribly was the start," she said. "Then, the man I wounded was shot by the other thug."

Horis praised her for her bravery. "I felt anger," she said, "not bravery, how dare that man come in and try to hurt me?" She touched the scar on her face from the pistol butt. Horis took her hand away and kissed the puckered skin. She moved her face and their lips met again. After a long kiss she continued, "I wondered at the savagery of it. What had we done, save steal a rock and have some knowledge? And when I saw you from my prison in the mobile, but was unable to speak or get to you, I felt true despair. Then I recall a room and the smell of flowers. I must have slept because the next thing I recall was waking in that cold cell, not knowing where I was. Terrance seemed to take joy from my discomfort; it was only after he had received a call from his senior that my situation improved."

Horis tried to imagine the helplessness that Grace would have felt, knowing she was so far from help. "Your plight was all because of me," he said. "I'm truly sorry to have put you through such an ordeal."

She held him tight. "The one thing that kept me alive and sane was the knowledge that it was for you," she whispered. "I knew you would come and rescue me and I knew that I would have to keep you safe by being strong and revealing nothing that could help them destroy you."

They kissed again, against the ship's rail, whilst up in the wheel-space Hector gazed down on them. He envied their happiness, and again marvelled at the power of emotion to overcome the worst trials.

Grace told of her time after Terrance had relented somewhat and she had been given work to do. "Once I was working in the kitchens and had a little more freedom, then I felt better. At least I had a purpose, something to take my mind away from my situation.

It was when I became the steward to the flyers that I met Ralf. He showed me the truth, that he was just as much a prisoner as I was, in a better cage it was true but nonetheless still a captive."

She told him again of her despair as time passed and she began to wonder if rescue would ever come, and how Ralf's plan for her to escape had shaken her from her torpor. "It was wrong of me to give up hope," she said, wracked by more sobbing. "Can you forgive me?"

Horis held her against him. "There is nothing to forgive, I wish I could have rescued you sooner," he said. "We had to make plans and it was important to get things right."

"I had planned to follow Ralf's lead," she said, "make use of the items and information he had procured for me. But then Sapper came on his reconnaissance and that threw my plans awry. Once I knew that you were on the way, it was easier to think of the whole thing as a holiday with work. Even so, I had to be careful not to change my mood too much and arouse suspicion. As the day approached I became impatient for my release. But by then I was content, for I knew that I would be free."

"My poor love," replied Horis, "you have suffered so much and all because of a chance meeting with me, I feel guilt at your treatment and would do anything to make it right."

"Ahh, but you were not responsible for that," was her answer. "That was all Terrance's doing. We met and I chose to be with you and if I had known the future, I still would have accepted it." She looked into his eyes and he saw the truth of her words.

"In any event," she continued, "you gathered a band of helpers and risked all in coming to my rescue, I will never forget that. I knew the first time we met back in Aserol that we were meant to be and that whatever happened we would be together. You have proved yourself to me and if I had the chance, I hope that I would do the same for you."

The sea air and conversation did her good and helped her to exorcise the demons in her mind. They were blissfully happy together, yet that evening, as they embraced outside his cabin on the deck, with the moons shining in a starry sky and the air warm, Grace declined his tentative suggestion that they spend the night together.

Horis wondered at the reason, perhaps it was a result of her captivity. "Why not, my love?" he asked. He was perplexed; she had been the enthusiastic instigator when first they had met. Were they not now bound by more than the fate which had initially thrown them together?

She quickly sought to reassure him. "You silly man," she said. "It's too public and not for any other reason. Aboard ship, everyone knows what everyone else is doing. My uncle is Captain here and will doubtless tell my parents of my actions. I could not bear it if the first news they heard of me were about what they would see as my sinful behaviour. And they would think badly of you, which is not what I want. I love them both dearly but they have a different way of looking at things. They would say that we were not yet wed."

Horis could see the logic but was unimpressed, he had been separated from her for long enough. "But everyone will assume that is what we are doing anyway," he argued.

"Hector would not approve, and he is the law here," she countered. "Don't fret; we will be wed just as soon as it is safe for us to return to Norlandia."

She slipped from his arms. "Goodnight," she whispered as she went to her cabin. Horis stood deflated as he heard the door lock behind her. He went to his own cabin but could not sleep.

Grace must have reconsidered her position; for Horis was woken later that night by the sound of her sneaking into his cabin. However, her reluctance to be discovered made her retreat before dawn's light.

They spent the next several days in happy companionship, talking all day and snatching moments in the night whilst they rounded the Cape and turned to run westwards, past Aserol to Omnipa.

Then Horis had an idea, he went to see Hector to explain it. As he sat in the captain's cabin he thought that the seat felt warm, it must have been the sun shining on it through the window. Even though it was late in winter, the further they had ventured from Northcastle the more the weather had improved.

"Well, young man, what can I do for you?" asked the captain, attired in his full uniform, his braid gleaming. He had a serious expression and Horis stammered out his request and then collapsed into silence. He thought that his speech had not gone as well as when he had practised in front of his shaving glass.

Hector nodded thoughtfully after he had said his piece, the delay in his response did nothing to calm Horis's stomach, which seemed to have taken on the form of a basket of serpents.

"I wondered how long it would take you to work that out," he said, the serious face cracked into a grin and there was a twinkle in his eye. "To be honest, I thought that the *Swiftsure* had been invaded by rats, with all the nocturnal scuttling that I have heard." Horis had the grace to blush while Hector found his discomfort amusing, after all, had he not been young once?

"Do not worry," he said. "I might not approve of your actions but I can understand them. Grace is safe from my criticism, and I will say nothing of it to my sister, should we speak. Grace is old enough to decide for herself how to spend her life."

There was a pause before Hector spoke again; he appeared to be weighing his choices.

"Very well," he said at length. "We have a few days to spare in our schedule before we are due to dock in Omnipa. I intend to drop anchor in a sheltered bay I know and perform some maintenance works once we have passed Aserol. We could do it then."

As Horis departed, Hector allowed himself a private grin, Grace had come to him with the same idea, and had departed not five minutes before Horis had arrived; 'great minds', he mused.

Terrance

Chapter 7

Terrance meanwhile was keeping himself hidden away in Northcastle; he had decided that Cavendish would be far too busy plotting to achieve his new role in government to bother with him. He had not heard any more of him since his admonishment on the parade ground, for Cavendish had left straight after that for the Ryde south.

Terrance knew that he had lost favour and was hoping that Cavendish had calmed down and forgotten his threats. In any case, he had the mine and the rocks. He was sure that he would be needed. He called Grantham at the mine and Lucy in the Ministry, he was missing her but it was a small price to pay. His wife and children he ignored.

The mine, which was the source of his wealth, was producing coal from two of its three seams and the rocks were being harvested from the third. Mrs Grantham reported that a second shipment was ready for transportation and Terrance told her to book space on a vessel when she could. She also reported that Obley, the manager, had been attacked in the town and was in hospital. Terrance told her that he could assume his job, she had been doing it anyway, this was his chance to reward her by making it public.

She also reported that the substance that the rocks were embedded in was also proving to be of interest, it seemed to be a sort of liquid coal. She said that it burnt well but that it needed to be warmed before it would combust. Terrance asked for samples to be sent north with the next shipment of rocks, he would see what the scientists made of it. If it was plentiful it might provide another source of income for him. Grantham also told him that the town had recovered from the shock of the deaths of the miners and now that its anger had been taken out on Obley, life was returning to normal.

The rocks that had arrived on the *Bold Cutter* were now safe in the camp and were under examination. And the flying machines were being refined and improved daily. Everything was settled in Terrance's world.

He stayed in the camp for a couple of days, listening to reports of the search for Grace and her accomplices, apart from a contact to the south and a group of soldiers who had gone missing there had been nothing. The search had found no trace; the new vehicle was damaged but in its demise had given the scientists an idea for a better version, using endless ridged belts for traction instead of the wheels. Even his flyers had been unable to locate any signs of a party of intruders.

He faced the facts, Grace must have been in the steam lorry; perhaps the majority of the group had been in there with her? The town had been searched, somehow they had all disappeared.

He interviewed all the flyers and the heads of the searchers, there had been no definite sightings. Flyers had spotted a group that appeared to have fallen over the cliffs, it was thought that maybe they were the intruders, except that a patrol of six men had also been lost, after reporting a breach in the fence and sending for reinforcements. The survivors were quite clear, they had seen nothing. They had been sent back for fencing and artisans, although one thought that he had heard firing, there were flyers about and he was not sure. When they had returned there was no sign of their fellows, but a section of fence had been removed and the ground was disturbed. Terrance was unsure of their story; there was always the possibility that they were hiding something.

Ralf the flyer was the last person he called in to see him; it had been he who had flown over the cliffs and seen the party on the beach. He had also been patrolling in the south after the escape.

"What do you know about the men on the beach?" Terrance asked him.

Ralf stood to attention in his full uniform, his cap under his arm. He had decided to tell as much of the truth as he could, omitting only the parts that would condemn him. "I flew searching missions as ordered, sir, after the Drogan attack," he said. "I saw nothing, save a broken fence on the south border of the camp, by the cliff edge. I reported this when I landed to refuel and was told to fly over again, as a patrol had gone missing; the one which had reported contact with some unidentified men. This time I ventured further and saw the bodies of several men on the beach."

"Can we not get to them?" asked Terrance.

"I could perhaps land on the beach, sir," said Ralf, "as long as the tide was out and there were no rocks, a boat could approach but there is no other way."

It was the only lead that he had; the whole place had been searched, as had the town and its surrounds and no sign had been found of Horis, Grace or anyone else whose presence could not be accounted for. The dead soldiers were the only thing out of place. He needed to get down to the beach and find if they had red caps.

But then he wondered, what if the patrol at the fence had mistakenly fired on their own men in the heat of the moment? The returning men might have realised this and dumped the bodies to hide the mistake. And besides, there was every chance that the tides or Drogans would have removed the evidence by the time he got a boat to the spot. And if it were found that the men were mistakenly killed, that would not help his cause. He would have to prove it and the soldiers would stick together against a civilian. It might take days, no doubt there would be torture involved, in the end it would only stir up animosity, and for what?

Terrance realised that he was unlikely to find his answers now;

he had not pursued the *Swiftsure*, the harbour office had told him that the vessel was headed to the Eastlands and was therefore out of his reach. To be ready for their return, he decided to send the details of Horis Strongman accompanied by a woman called Grace to the customs officers in all Norlandian ports. He could stress that they should be detained if they were found on any arriving vessels.

The dead men on the beach were a diversion, to waste his time. It mattered not if they were from the garrison or were intruders, it would be best to draw a line and start again with the ship.

"That will not be necessary," he decided. "They will tell us no tales, you may go."

As Ralf shut the door behind him, Terrance sighed, it was time to return to his other duties, the mine in Aserol, the rocks, and all of his Ministry work.

In an attempt to catch up he placed a call to Lucy in Metropol City, she was not at her desk but he left a message for her to call him on her return. Then he walked across to the laboratories.

He was sat in discussion with the scientists; they had been examining the rocks and had already made some useful progress, including a way of using them in the new flying machines, when Lucy called him from the Ministry. He had to leave them at an interesting point and hurry back to his office to receive the call.

To his annoyance, instead of matters of import, Lucy was full of the latest news from the corridors of power; she gushed that Cavendish had formed a new government with his allies, people like Barnard, who Terrance remembered from the Gavan Club.

"Isn't it wonderful, sir?" she said. "A new start and he is your friend as well, he will remember your help in the past I'm sure. You will be destined for great things."

Terrance said little to Lucy, the least she knew of happenings in Northcastle the better. He hoped that power would distract Cavendish from carrying out his threats. After all, Terrance reasoned, he may have been partly responsible for the deaths of the previous administration, but Cavendish should be in his debt, he would not be where he now was without it.

The days passed quickly, when the speaker trilled at five in the afternoon on the third day he assumed it would be Lucy or Mrs Grantham.

"Hello, Terrance speaking," he said.

"First Minister Cavendish here," the voice was stern and Terrance felt his stomach lurch. He knew that Cavendish had secured his position at the top of the government, had kissed the royal hand and was now running the country. Surely, he thought, Lucy was right, Cavendish should be grateful that Terrance had made it possible; perhaps he was calling to announce a reward?

"Yes, sir," he answered.

Cavendish was cheerful. "How goes the work with the rocks?" he asked and the two conversed for several minutes on the subject.

Then the mood changed. "Tell me then, what of progress in the hunt for your ex-captive?" he said in a colder tone.

"I have to admit that Grace has escaped," he said. "I now think it most likely that she is on the *Swiftsure* and on the way to the Eastlands."

"I see, so she has evaded you after all, no doubt you know that the Master of that vessel is her uncle."

Terrance did not. "I had my suspicions," he said, which was not an outright lie but ambiguous enough.

Cavendish was not convinced, his tone betrayed him. "Really," he mused.

"Oh yes," continued Terrance, "I've found that the vessel will be returning to Norlandia soon, it operates on a regular route. I learned that when I was arranging shipment of the rocks."

"It matters not, they can have their freedom in the East, no doubt they will settle there, out of the way, for they cannot harm anyone now." Cavendish was magnanimous; he had attained supreme power and was secure in it.

Terrance waited for what seemed like an age. Surely now must come the good news?

"You carry on there then, Terrance, your work is valuable to the state," the call ended, and Terrance was left holding a buzzing speaker handset, wondering if he also had escaped retribution. He noted that his hand was shaking.

Looking at the timepiece on the wall, he saw that it was time to finish up for the day and prepare for dinner, he felt relieved that he had spoken to Cavendish and that things seemed normal.

Next morning, Terrance called the mine in Aserol and asked to be connected to Mrs Grantham. The reply stunned him. "Morken Mine, Aserol," the secretary said. "I'm sorry, sir, there is no-one of that name here." Terrance felt faint. His wishful thinking had not been right; Cavendish must have been biding his time.

Next, he called Lucy at the Ministry, she was unwilling to talk. "My service has been terminated," she sobbed. "I have to clear my desk by lunchtime; what am I to do, sir?"

Even the scientists in their laboratory were engaged in 'secure testing' that day and would not converse. He suddenly understood why Cavendish had wanted him to remain in Northcastle. He had been out of the way, unable to muster the support of his friends.

Cavendish must have been working behind the scenes to remove him from any position of influence. Keeping him in Northcastle had meant that he had not even known what was happening to him, and the secrecy of the camp meant that no-one was able to warn him. He would have to act now; if he were to retain any of his possessions.

He called his bank in the city and instructed them to draw cash from his accounts and place it in his strongbox. And to hold the deeds for the mine, despite any instructions to the contrary they might receive, until he could arrive. The manager assured him that he would do so.

He had to return to Metropol City in haste if he was to salvage anything. He threw a few clothes in a case and departed on the next Ryde southwards. All through the journey Terrance was deep in thought, he had money stored in safekeeping, most seniors did and so he felt secure.

Inside he was angry that he had been made a fool of by a man he considered his inferior; Horis Strongman had neither breeding nor a good education. Admittedly he was tenacious and had proved to be capable but in Terrance's eyes the lack of family was all important. And to be outsmarted by him was inexcusable. He would have his revenge, on him and the girl and every last man who had helped him. In his imagination he caught them all and made them suffer. Then Cavendish would see the error of his ways and restore the mine to him.

The Ryde stopped in Honiford to change drivers and take on coal. Terrance alighted from his carriage and asked to use the speaker in the stationmaster's office.

There was one call he had to make, and it was the one that he had been dreading. If his membership of the Gavan Club had been terminated then his life was over. There were problems with the speaker line and he was attempting to place the call when the Rail guard entered the office. "Sir, we are boarding to resume our journey," the man said. "You must return."

Terrance reluctantly boarded the Ryde; that news would have to wait.

Horis and Grace

Chapter 8

"I pronounce you man and wife, you may kiss!"

Grace grasped Horis, throwing her arms around him. They kissed whilst the crew of the *Swiftsure* cheered and shouted. The watchman blew a long blast on the ship's horn.

The ship was anchored in a small bay, close under wooded cliffs; the sound of the blast disturbed many brightly coloured avian's which flew overhead in a flash of colour. The waters were so clear that they could see many piscora and corals in the deeps. They had passed Aserol the night before, bound for Omnipa, the westernmost port in Norlandia and were stopped so that the crew could perform some works on the cargo gear before arrival.

The derricks had been raised and the wires and blocks greased. Canvas awnings were strung between them; a table had been rigged in its shade on the hatch-top and a rough podium was at one end. Here Hector presided over the ceremonies of matrimony and Horis and Grace exchanged their vows.

They had no marriage rings as such, but the artificer, Hamman, had provided two small brass objects from his store which would suffice for the time. He had polished them until they gleamed.

Grace eyed hers. "It shines well enough for a ring," she said. "Under the circumstances it means more to me than any golden marriage ring could."

"I will obtain a proper ring for you as soon as I can," said Horis. "But it was not on my list of priorities at the start of this adventure."

"You silly man," replied Grace, taking his hand. "It matters not to me. I have you and that is the important thing, this is just a symbol for others to see, I know it inside me."

"Congratulations to you both," said Hector as he closed his hymnal. "I have never performed a marriage before, although I am so authorised by my rank."

"Thank you, Uncle," said Grace. "I'm glad I remembered that fact."

Horis was about to say that he was under the impression that it had been his idea when he caught the look on Grace's face and realised that she had thought the same as he, and acted on it that much quicker. He was glad that they would not have to wait until they returned to Norlandia. Omnipa could not be relied on for safety and it might be that they never returned.

"Now that is done we must have the celebration feast," said Hector. "Cookie has been slaving to give you a meal to remember and it would not do to keep him waiting."

They ate and drank for what seemed like hours. There were many courses, piscorae and fowl, and a porker roasting on a spit, all washed down with much toasting of the couple. The ship's company had been given the afternoon off and joined in with the celebrations. Grace was sad that her family could not be with her on this happy day but would explain when she had the chance. Hector had told her that Omnipa had no speakers for the public's usage; she supposed that she could write a letter. It would arrive in Aserol in a few days, as long as the mail wagon was not ambushed by brigands.

But the thought worried her; what would they think? She was the only daughter; her mother had been set on a new gown and her father on leading her down to her husband in front of all of the family. Would they think it a marriage of necessity, whereas in truth it was one of true love?

"Speech, speech!" one of the crew called out, during a brief lull between courses.

"Yes, go on, Horis, give us a speech," said Hector. Horis had had just enough ale and wine to feel invincible. He rose to his feet, the sudden motion making his head spin. He clutched at the table for support and cleared his throat.

"Gentlemen, my wife and I," he began, any more words were drowned out; there was uproar, clapping and thumping of feet that made the table shake.

"Silence," bellowed Hector in a voice that startled the birds again and the crew hushed at their captain's command. "Continue," he said to Horis.

"Thank you, Captain," replied Horis formally, "for performing the ceremony and making me so very happy."

"And me," shouted Grace.

"I had the notion that ships' captains could marry people out of the sight of land," continued Horis, "I'm glad to say that I was right."

"No, it was my idea," said Grace, clearly unwilling to allow Horis to take all the glory. "I approached Uncle Hector before you did."

Horis looked shocked. "I thought it my idea," he said.

"Well it was not," she replied.

"You were both set on the idea and in that there was no swaying you," Hector broke in. "Let's not have an argument else I might have to conduct a separation ceremony."

There was more laughter at that. "Horis, you will be used to Grace's forthrightness in no time," he added. "She will keep you in check, that's for certain."

Horis looked bemused by the comment. "I can think of worse ways to live, sir, than with Grace by my side, whichever of us decides things. Now that we are safe it feels right."

Hector nodded but he was not so sure. Horis had told him the whole tale and he had his doubts that they would be left in peace. He kept the thought to himself. "Now that you are man and wife you can move all your things down to the owner's cabin," he said.

"It would be more fitting and old man Vespa will not be aboard for a while. Let us continue with the feasting," he said, raising his glass.

The owner's cabin was sumptuous, fitted with a large bed and a separate washroom in the corner. Horis and Grace had stayed till the party turned into a round of toasting. Then, to much ribald commenting, they had departed. They went first to their separate cabins and retrieved their possessions, Horis having very few and Grace many more. "I have always kept some things here," she said. "It is much simpler than carrying a bag every time I wish to see Uncle."

The bed had been made up and Horis eyed it nervously. "I understand what you mean," he said as Grace emerged from the washroom and lay upon it. "Everyone knows what we will be doing."

She smiled. "Then come over here, husband; if they know, we may as well carry on."

"So, what will you do for a honeymoon?" Hector asked them the next morning, after a later than usual fast-breaker. They were still anchored and the crew were all performing their tasks with the wretched look of those who had overindulged. Only the captain seemed unaffected. "After our next port we are bound for Tarpitt in the Western Isles for cofé beans and cacao, returning to as yet unnamed port in Norlandia. We will be near two lunars before we see Norlandia again."

"That will suit us, Uncle," said Grace. "It will be time for people to forget us and we can perhaps start a life on our return, if not in Aserol then in Ventis."

"We have discussed it fully," said Horis. "If I can get to the bank in Omnipa when we arrive I can close my accounts and realise all my wealth, as you suggested. That is, as long as the fuss about us has not reached the place. But I imagine we will learn that when we arrive."

Hector nodded. "If there is no-one on shore to seize you when we berth then you may be safe," he agreed.

"We will then have capital for a new life together," added Grace. "I will do the same, although I have little enough savings, it is a joint enterprise now so we will share it all."

Hector thought for a moment. "It is a good plan," he rumbled at last. "If we finish our work we will be there the day after tomorrow. Tell me, do you intend to send a letter to your parents, Grace?"

The look on her face showed that she had considered it but was fearful of the consequence. "If you think it wise, perhaps I should," she said.

"I think that you should," said Hector. "If you explain all the circumstances then I'm sure that they will understand, you can always renew your vows in a proper way in the future. They will be glad that Horis is committed to you, given the arrangements they will assume you have been living under whilst on board. Write to them and give the letters to me, not to read but I can post them via the agent; it will disguise the sender and location from anyone attempting to find you. They will go to Aserol in the agent's bag and will be securely stamped and delivered from there. That way there will be no clue as to their origin."

"I would like to send news to Maloney," added Horis. "I need to thank him for all his help; I scarce got the chance to say all that I wanted on the quayside in Northcastle."

Sure enough, early in the morning two days later, the *Swiftsure* arrived in Omnipa and was secured alongside a frail wooden jetty. Horis and Grace were oblivious to the arrival; indeed they had hardly been seen since their nuptials and had only ventured forth when hunger had forced them. But they had found the time to write letters.

Grace wrote to her parents giving details of all that had happened since the day she had met Horis, her imprisonment and rescue and her marriage. She asked for their forgiveness and understanding in the haste and lack of a proper celebration in Aserol with all the family present but hoped that they would understand. She made sure to emphasise Horis's innocence in her original predicament, and made much of his successful efforts to save her. She also singled out Maloney for praise, knowing that both Caln and Divid approved of the man. She read it to Horis and he blushed. "I'm not that much of a hero," he said. "But thank you, I have also written a page to your father," he handed it over for her to read.

His letter to Caln was little more than a plea that he would accept the betrothal without the formality of permission. He assured Caln Fallowfield that he was in love with his daughter and that he would do all he could to fulfil his part of the marriage contract, as if he had been asking in person.

"Do you think he will accept me?" he asked.

"I care not," replied Grace. "Although he is my father and I love him dearly, you are not marrying him. He may choose to think what he will, I would rather have his blessing but if not, well that would not make me give you up."

Grace added a postscript, in which she told her father of her concern that Terrance would seek some sort of revenge for their escape. She appealed to them to keep her whereabouts a secret, and to ask Divid to ensure that he did the same.

"I will write the same to Divid as well," she said, "to make sure that the message gets through."

Horis wrote to Maloney, he thanked him for all he had done and wished him well, he was not much of a letter writer but felt the need to keep in contact with the one who had helped him so much.

The envelopes were sealed and placed in the posting box by the captain's cabin; the agent would take them when next he boarded.

"Aha!" exclaimed Hector with a leer and a wink when the two walked into the saloon, hand in hand. "I had wondered if you would make an appearance today."

Horis blushed as he took his seat. Grace had been right; the trouble with such a closed community was that everyone knew or at least could guess what you were up to. Grace was unperturbed.

"We are off to the bank after this, Uncle," she said as they were served soup.

"Good luck," he replied. "We will not sail for several days, cargo operations are slow here, and then there will be the coal barge, and that will not even arrive until all else is completed, to keep from contaminating the cargo with dust."

They ate luncheon and left the ship, walking up the jetty and then along a lane into the town. Hector was right; there seemed no urgency in loading their cargo, a mixture of cut timber and boxes of machinery. The port itself was small and had no Local to supply power. Hence there were no steam cranes. Nor had it any mobiles, all goods were brought on equine-drawn wagons. There was an absence of watchtowers, which was strange as the area was known as a producer of fine ovine meat and wool. Indeed, a large part of the cargo for Tarpitt would be bales of fleece. They were stacked in the sheds ready for the ship's gear to swing them aboard.

The port was a mile or so to walk from the centre of town and the road led between fields of grains and others containing beasts, mainly ovines but a few prime bovines were also visible. As they passed a farm gate, set in a tall wall, Horis stopped in surprise. "Look, Grace," he whispered, "a Drogan is sitting in that field."

They backed away from the opening and peered cautiously around the wall. The beast was sitting still and as they watched a man approached it. Horis held his breath; the Drogan was notoriously bad-tempered, surely he would be savaged by the jaws or the claws?

The man put a whistle to his lips and blew, Horis could hear nothing but the beast reacted, it flapped its wings and retreated. The man blew again and the Drogan took flight. Satisfied, the man approached the gate; ovines could be seen behind him, coming out from under cover to nibble at the grass.

"Good day to you both," said the farmer, in the slow voice of the provincial. "No need to hide there. Claude won't hurt you."

His assurance surprised the pair.

"You have named it?" said Grace. "Are you not afeared of it?"

The man laughed and held out the whistle that he had blown, it was attached to a cord around his neck. "Not with this beauty, I can train the beast now; it will come to my call, will leave my ovines alone and will serve only me. Once it had met my family it protected them from a strange Drogan as well." He waved his arms about. "This is its territory and no other Drogan comes near."

"This is all accomplished with that whistle?" Horis was still dubious; he wondered if the whole thing was not a show for impressionable travellers, although how it was done eluded him, but then so did the work of magickers.

"Yes," said the farmer. "I got the whistle from a vagabond, a man from the Western Isles; he told me that they all use them in that foreign place. He stayed awhile and in payment for food and a roof he showed me the way of the whistle. When he told me that he had to leave, I asked him to name his price for it and I paid it gladly."

"Well I never," said Horis. "Is it a simple thing to do then? In the city and the places I have been before now, the Drogan is vermin, to be hunted and killed."

Grace was amazed as well. She hated the Drogans for in Aserol they were known to have taken babes and killed many people; after all, there were watchtowers and balloons manned with armed soldiers to dissuade them.

"Here in the country we understand things that you city folk do not," the farmer continued. "The Drogans merely want to exist as we do. They understand not that they shouldn't take the things we value, our babes or our ovines are all the same to them, they see them only as food. And man destroys the Drogans' nests and lands, they are like any beast, they fight back."

Horis repeated a thing he had heard said of the Drogans. "They are dangerous, they fight back if attacked," he said. "I had heard that said and never understood the meaning; until now."

"Every farmer worth his crops has to understand and live with all the parts of nature," said the man. "Good day to you." He closed the gate and walked off down the lane, towards the sea.

"Well there's a turn-up," said Horis, as they resumed their walk, "and no mistake, what would people in Aserol or the city think?"

The road led them to a dusty street, lined on each side with wooden buildings. There were shops and dwellings mixed in together and a few people walking about. Everyone was dressed in drab working clothes, the men in overalls and the women in pinafores or aprons over their gowns. With little difficulty, Horis found the bank and they went inside.

The room was as quiet as a church, the only sound the scratching of quills on ledgers. There were a line of suited men at high desks, working by candlelight and a desk manned by a corpulent individual whose collar was so tight that folds of flesh cascaded over it like breaking waves.

"What can we do for you?" he wheezed; sweat dripping from his nose onto the white blotter in front of him. The sign on his desk said 'Balthasar Lewkenor, Manager'.

"I wish to close my account and take my money," said Horis. Beside him, Grace smiled at the man.

"If you please," she added, nudging Horis. "Manners," she whispered.

The man looked shocked. "Take your money!" he said in a high-pitched voice, quite at odds with his size. "Take your money," he repeated. He clearly thought that Grace was in charge of the situation and that Horis was acting under her influence. The scratching of the clerks stopped abruptly, as if a switch had been thrown.

"That's correct, sir, here is my passbook." Horis stood firm and looked the manager in the eye. He handed over the document and the man opened it with pudgy fingers. His lips moved soundlessly as he scanned the pages.

He put the book down and folded his arms. Fixing Horis with a pitying gaze he shrugged his shoulders. "You realise that you should not take all your wealth on a whim, or because a lady wishes it."

Horis was in awe of bank managers, they were a respected part of the community and their advice carried weight. Perhaps he was right.

Grace spoke before he could be persuaded. "We do," she said. "But we are now wed and need the money to set up our lives." She showed him the brass ring on her finger, smiling sweetly. "Perhaps you could mark my passbook as well?"

"Ahh," replied the bank manager, unabashed at her suggestions. "I wondered at your connection, my congratulations to you, in that case it will not be a problem, please wait for a moment." He took the books and stood from his seat, waddling over to one of the desks, where he held a whispered conversation with the clerk.

This was the moment of truth, Horis hoped that news of his actions in the north had not reached the bank; he knew of the reach of Terrance and officialdom in general and was concerned that access to his money may have been somehow stopped. The manager and the clerk were searching in a pile of papers, probably the lists of undesirable customers received by mail. There were no speakers in this place so the news would be old. It appeared that Hector had been right in his assessment that this was a good place to do business.

Satisfied, the manager returned. "I have marked both your passbooks to authorise the withdrawal, take them to the cashier and they will be honoured. And once again, my congratulations and best wishes for a happy life together."

When Horis and Grace left the bank to return to the *Swiftsure*, Horis's inside jacket pocket bulged with paper money and he felt finally free of worry over the ability of Terrance to harm him and Grace.

"Let us get this money safely on board," Grace said. "Then we can plan our future."

"I like this place," said Horis. "It is slow-paced and friendly; let us see what sort of dwellings might be for sale here."

They were passing a row of establishments selling old fashioned clothing and equipment for farmers and builders. Goods were piled outside the buildings, all sorts of implements that Horis imagined farmers using, but like most city dwellers he had no idea what most of them were for. If he were to be a farmer he would have to learn, or be taught, and quickly. Another glass frontage displayed drawings and descriptions of plots of land for sale and Horis was surprised and encouraged to see how inexpensive they were.

"Look, Grace," he said. "We could buy a plot and farm here. We would see Hector when he came in with the ship and pass messages to Divid or Maloney."

"That sounds like hard work," laughed Grace. "I'm not sure if you are cut out to be a farmer. And could you build us a home?"

"We could grow apple trees, for cydir," said Horis. "That takes little effort, or perhaps we might keep a few ovines to fatten for market. And who knows, perhaps we will find a plot with a dwelling already made."

They passed the field again; there was no sign of the Drogan or the farmer. The ovines grazed placidly.

The thought of settling in Omnipa stayed with Grace after they had returned on board the *Swiftsure*. She saw the attraction of a farmer's life and the solitude was appealing enough but all the time she wondered what Terrance might do to spoil her happiness. They had their money but that did not mean that they were safe from his attentions. She worried that they both might have to spend the rest of their lives looking over their shoulders.

Terrance

Chapter 9

As the Ryde slowed and entered the vast, glass-roofed terminus in Metropol City, Terrance had regained some of his calm. He had a plan and a purpose.

He had spent the journey from Northcastle seething at his treatment at the hands of Cavendish; he guessed that once the mine had been taken from him his membership of the Gavan Club would follow. Now that he had had time to think he had reasoned that all his troubles had been caused by Horis Strongman, a person who he considered to be his inferior, both in rank and standing. It did not help that he had been aided by Grace and Maloney, more lower-class people whom he had met by chance. He rued the day that he had decided to send Horis to Aserol; he had been wrong to think of him as suitable to take the blame for events. That day was when all his misfortune had begun.

He had left Northcastle in haste, with only the clothes he stood in and little money. No matter, he still had a Ministry pass for transportation and would shortly be at his home where he could bathe and relax. His wife and children would welcome him back, he could make up some story about a change in career, they could move to some remote part of the country and life would continue. He might not have the mine but he had money, and the house in the capital was worth a good sum. He had the deeds to the mine in his strongbox; if he could find a sympathetic justice he might yet regain ownership of what was rightfully his.

Or, he thought, he could cut his losses and spend his time hunting down the architects of his misfortune. This option was in his head as the most appealing when he showed his pass and moved into the terminus in search of a mobile. He saw that the concourse was filled with patriotic posters and they all featured the head of Cavendish. That annoyed him, as if the face were gloating at his misfortune. When last he had gone north, the face pictured had been that of his predecessor. Terrance had a sudden vision of his headless torso on the ground in Northcastle, a Drogan standing over it in angry ownership. It had not taken long for Cavendish to consolidate his grip on power.

He was still planning his revenge as he crossed to the steam-mobiles, there was a short queue but he was in no mood to wait. He pushed his way to the front, ignoring the complaints. He waved his Ministry pass and the grumbling subsided, that was the way to treat the lower orders, he thought, as he boarded the mobile and instructed the driver to proceed to his house.

The street was filled with large mansions, all behind walls and stout gates. Terrance's was not the largest by any means but it was comfortable and well appointed. His wife was forever insisting that they move to a larger dwelling, more in keeping with his function but he was happy here. Now she would have her way, his new role would require adjustment but the thrill of arranging a move would keep her sweet for a time. At least he had Lucy to distract him while she planned the move, providing that she had been spared by Cavendish.

He saw that the gates were closed as he signed the driver's sheet. The wretch could try and claim the cost back from the Ministry, and the best of luck with that!

As the machine departed he crossed the street. His man Billy would be in the gatehouse dozing, he merely needed to rattle the gates to be let in. At the end of the drive the lights of home beckoned, just a few moments more, a glass of spirit and a warm bath would be his.

He rattled and was surprised to see a stranger step from the hut.

"Who are you then?" the man asked, shining a bright gas lamp in Terrance's face. "What's your business here?"

Terrance shielded his eyes from the glare. "I could ask you the same, where's Billy? This is my house."

I don't think so," replied the man. "You must have the wrong house, maybe too much wine."

Impertinent fool, thought Terrance. He knew it was the correct house; after all, he had lived here for most of his adult life. "Let me in, Isabella will be expecting me."

"No Isabella here, Colonel Arbuth is a bachelor and dines alone tonight."

Now Terrance was confused. "How long has he been living in my house?" he demanded.

"None of your business; now get lost before I call the Watch." The man was becoming surly.

"Very well then," said Terrance, standing his ground. "Call the Watch; I have papers to prove my ownership." As he said it he realised that they were at the Ministry, no matter, the Watch would see him right.

He waited in the gloom as the man went back inside the hut. A few minutes later he emerged. "The Watch are summoned," he announced triumphantly. "It'll be a cell for you tonight."

Terrance was about to argue when the door of the house opened and a large man, in uniform, came down the step. He had a ceremonial sword at his belt and a gas pistol in a leather holster. His medals gleamed in the gaslight.

"What's amiss, Henry?" he called. "Is that another ruffian after something?"

"No, sir, he claims to live here," shouted Henry.

Terrance joined in, "I do live here, with my wife and family."

Arbuth had reached the gate; close up he looked to be in the prime of life. He regarded Terrance's travel-soiled clothes and general demeanour. "I rather think not," he finally said. "But you are welcome to come in and look before the Watch gets here. Open up, Henry."

"Do you think it wise, sir?" said Henry.

"Oh I think I can manage one scruffy man in a suit," was the light reply, his hand on the sword.

He led Terrance across the gravelled path and up the steps. Terrance walked into his house, the rooms were the same but the furniture was different. "Bella," he called. "Children... Father's home."

The cries echoed but were not answered. Terrance noted that even the familiar smells of home were missing, replaced by a masculine odour of polished leather. He felt dizzy; his vision swam with the shock of it. He grasped at a table for support but only succeeded in pulling it over as he fell. Glass ornaments shattered.

"You see," said Arbuth. "I am alone here, this is my house, and you are obviously mistaken."

Terrance tried to recover his senses and rise, the room spun. Arbuth caught him and lifted him up. As their heads touched he whispered in his ear, "Cavendish sends his regards."

The comment stung Terrance and awoke him; in a flash he understood. Pulling away he ran for the gate and into the road. His life was ruined, as he knew that others had been. Cavendish had done to him what he had done to so many before. Terrance remembered that he had been amused to see men fall, never thinking that it could happen to him. And it was all Horis Strongman's fault. Horis and that bitch Grace, aided by fortune and the soldiers.

He knew then that it would be pointless to make any more protests. The Watch would have their orders and all avenues would be closed to him. The Ministry was out of bounds and Lucy would not be able to help him. She may have already been disposed of by Cavendish's version of his man Eavis. As for his family, it was unlikely that they were dead, they had probably been told some tale and spirited away, they could be anywhere.

In a daze he wandered the gas-lit streets, he needed to think, he should go to his apartment, no-one save Lucy knew that it was his. He would feel better after a bath and a meal, there was little else he could do at this hour. He needed sleep, in the morning he could retrieve his money and papers from the bank.

Terrance had been careful to set himself up for a possible fall from favour. All seniors did it; such was the atmosphere of fear and mistrust in official circles. Terrance had made good alliances, or so he thought but had still had the sense to insure his future. He had money and other things well hidden in various locations, a dwelling he had used for trysts and now a use for them all. He was going to get his revenge. He thought little of his wife and family; if they were not dead they would be far from him and would want nothing to do with him anyway.

No, his objective now would be to make people pay, it might do him no good in regaining Cavendish's favour but it would make him feel better. He had to retrieve what he could and get to Aserol. Now he went to the apartment that he kept near the Ministry, taking a circular route and watching for anyone following him. Satisfied that there was no-one interested in his movements he entered the apartment building and rode the lift to his floor.

To his surprise, Lucy was there when he opened the door. She flew into his embrace. "Oh sir," she said. "What has happened?" She stepped back and regarded him, dressed as he was in a dirty suit; his tie askew. Her face bore signs of tears, many tears. There was the smell of stew coming from the kitchen. "I have been evicted from my lodgings," she said. "Here was the only place I could go." Behind her in the hall was a single suitcase.

"I'm ruined, Lucy," he said in a whisper. "Cavendish has taken my house; my family are gone. I must go to the bank on the morrow and retrieve my deeds for the mine and my money while I still can."

Lucy thought for a moment, the dismissal from her employment had come as a shock and she had wondered at the reason. Learning that Cavendish was behind events was no surprise. Everyone knew how things worked, she was connected to Terrance. If he was to be removed, then she had to suffer as well. It made her realise that Terrance would only be a hindrance to her regaining control of her destiny. She needed to get away from Metropol City and reinvent herself. Still, she had kept her life, which was not always the case and she could use him for a while till she could get away.

She wrapped herself around him again. "Let me help you relax," she cooed. "You need a bath and clean clothes; there is plenty of food for two and a bottle of wine from the store. At least we have each other. Later we can plan our revenge."

After a soak and dressed in clean clothes, Terrance felt much better, he sat with Lucy and ate a meal which, although not to the standard he was used, was enough to satisfy him. Lucy's talents did not extend to fine cooking, although she had done her best. And the wine was a help.

"What will we do?" she asked him later when they lay together. The use of 'we' amused Terrance, he was sure that she would be gone once she had what she could get. Oh well, they were both in the same boat, they could use each other for comfort. He did not enlighten her as to his plans for Horis; he knew that she was fond of the man. Instead he suggested a possible future for them, together in some unspecified location, which seemed to lull her.

Next day, after Lucy had cooked him fast-breaker, Terrance set out to retrieve his money and papers from his deposit box at the bank. He tried to use a mobile, the driver waved him away. "I heard that your Ministry pass is no good," he said. "You can pay me upfront or you can walk."

Terrance used the omnibus, with what he considered the common rabble, to get to the bank. When he arrived he found that his friend, the manager, was absent. In his place was a man unknown to him. When he signed into the vault register, he saw that his name appeared on the previous day's page, written in a strange hand. With a sinking heart, he retrieved his strongbox from the vault. He was not surprised to find that it had been emptied, all that was inside was a note 'You're finished', it said.

It was all gone then, his title to the mine, his cash and his notebook. The deeds to the mine were here as security against his borrowings, the house had been his wife's but he had seen that had gone last night, now all he had was in the apartment. There was some good news though; the papers for his loans had also vanished.

Then it occurred to him that even now, Lucy might be relieving him of what little he had left. His suspicious mind wondered if her arrival might not have been contrived, perhaps she had been offered some reward, like her life, to turn against him. Perhaps she had Watchmen awaiting his return.

No, he thought, you are seeing shadows everywhere; Lucy was too open and honest to have been playing him. She could not pretend ecstasy, as she had done last night, if she was a traitor out to rob or betray him at Cavendish's command.

He should have been downcast but he was still hopeful, there might be nothing here but this was just one cache. He had to put on a brave face, Cavendish's men might even now be watching and he did not want them to see him frown. He took the paper as if it were the thing he wanted, forcing a smile.

"Thank you," he said to the manager. "I'll not be wanting the box any more, kindly close my accounts and give me the balance in cash."

There was an embarrassed silence. "Well, man?" said Terrance. "Where is my cash?"

"There is none, sir," replied the manager. "There were monies due for the rental of the box. Charges and such. Once these were taken there was no balance."

"Very well," he said. "Thank you."

He was not too worried by the loss; he had more money safe at the apartment and a second bank account, in a different name and location, which his wife and everyone else were unaware of.

With his last remaining coins, he took another omnibus the

short distance to the bank where he kept copies of his papers. The manager here was the same as the one when he had opened the account and knew him as Mr Wasterman.

This place was secure and out of the reach of Cavendish, after the manager had given him char in his office and engaged in small talk he was escorted to the strongroom. To his relief, the ledger contained no record of his box being disturbed since the last time he had used it and he found it to be untouched. The box contained the cash he had left there and copies of all his papers. Satisfied that it was secure, he took cash from his account and the deeds to the apartment and returned there.

When he opened the door and called out Lucy's name, there was no answer, she was absent, and not only that, all the signs of her presence had been removed. Terrance made himself char and sat to think. Had Lucy abandoned him because she could see that her future was bleak in his company, or had she been found by Cavendish and removed from the scene? Despite his annoyance at not having her with him, he hoped the latter was not the case; if Cavendish or his men had found her she would be in a worse position than Grace had been at Northcastle, assuming that she was allowed to live.

The apartment was otherwise untouched; nothing was out of place and the cash had not been taken from its hiding place behind the fire. Terrance hoped that this meant Lucy had merely left him, but to be safe he would have to move on again. Now that he had funds, he had an idea as to his next move. He was sorry that she had gone but could understand her motive, he was a pariah and she would gain nothing from him. She had to be the master of her own fate, the same as he did.

Firstly, Terrance intended to visit the Gavan Club and confront Cavendish, he would tell him that he intended to kill Horis, Grace and Maloney, his hope was that this declaration would lead to his reinstatement. Then all he had to do was to find the three and do the deed. Now his plans were set he rested.

Next morning he journeyed to the street where the club was situated and loitered by the entrance.

He had to be circumspect; there was no reason for him to be on the street, no shops to browse and no bench to sit on. He found an alleyway from where he could stand in a shadow and watch the entrance. Time passed slowly, the street was quiet once the workers who lived here had departed. The occasional woman would depart, with a shopping basket or perambulator; the folk who lived here were not wealthy enough for servants and appeared to do most of their daily routines themselves. Gradually they returned from their errands and the street basked in the afternoon sunshine.

In the end, after waiting a day and a night and most of the second day, Terrance, by now nearly asleep on his feet, saw a carriage draw up outside the club and Cavendish descend. Quickly he ran across the road and grabbed him by his collar. Cavendish turned and saw his attacker, shaking himself loose they faced each other.

"Why?" asked Terrance. "Were it not for me, you would not be where you are."

"You are a fool and unworthy of my attention," replied Cavendish. "You brought it on yourself by your actions."

"I admit that some of my actions were wrong," replied Terrance. "But you have taken everything from me."

"You still have your life," was the curt reply. "If you wish to keep it I suggest you get out of my sight."

"I will deal with them all, just give me time," Terrance said in desperation, moving forward again, grabbing at Cavendish's lapels. The other man stepped back and pulled his coat aside to show the holstered pistol he wore. Terrance stopped his advance. "I will kill Grace and Horis and Maloney."

Cavendish laughed. "I doubt it, they have outsmarted you before and I have no doubt they will do it again, they are of no import now anyway, I am content to let them be."

"Give me a chance," pleaded Terrance, uncaring of his own safety he beat his fists on Cavendish's chest in frustration, the blows having no effect. Other people were attracted by the shouting, a crowd formed, encircling the pair. Cavendish waved them back. "I can deal with this beggar," he said.

"Please," wailed Terrance, in a last desperate attempt to make the man see reason.

Cavendish was impassive. "Never let me see your face again," he hissed. "If I even think you are near I will show you no mercy." He turned his back on Terrance, who was reduced to sobs, and strode into the club. The crowd melted away and Terrance was left standing on his own. An hour later, when the gas lamps were being lit, he was still standing there, staring at the entrance that once he had been proud to use. Finally, in the darkness, he trudged back to his lonely room, where he fell into a troubled sleep.

He dreamt of killing Horis in various ways, with a pistol and then with a knife, even by driving a mobile over him. He awoke with a fever, it must have been from standing out in the alley for so long in the cold, he drank some spirit and had some of the food that Lucy had left behind, dry bread and an old piece of pie, then he went back to sleep.

In his next delirium Grace was dispatched in many horrible ways, time after time he watched her die in front of him. Each time in his dream he attempted to ravish her, but each time she taunted him, "You are not the man Horis is," she said, over and over; even as he applied the killing stroke.

Finally, he faced Maloney, wrestled his false arm off and beat him with it. He woke again sweating and ravenous, his muscles ached and the bedclothes were a soggy tangle from his thrashing. He sat propped in a cool bath for the next twelve hours, frightened to sleep unless he had more of the nightmares, till at last the fever broke and he slept soundly, without dreams.

Later, Terrance sat alone in his apartment, eating the last crumbs from the pantry. He thought of Eavis; could he contact him and gain his help? He discounted the idea almost immediately. Eavis was unsuited to this kind of work, beatings were his speciality, he lacked the intelligence to locate a person in another town. If you took him a mile from the city he would be useless.

Then he remembered; there was an agency he had used to apprehend a man who had stolen from the mine. It was a long time ago; they were a company of investigators based in some town in the south. He could give the job to them, no doubt they would be expensive but Terrance did not wish to travel around the country until he had a better idea of where the three were. Let someone else do all the hard work. He searched his papers until he found the details. The company was located in the town of Bingham, south of Metropol City.

He should leave the city anyway, in all likelihood Cavendish would have people looking for him. He could make a base in Bingham; it was about halfway to Aserol. He thought of trying to find Lucy and take her with him. She would be a compensation for his troubles but in the end, he decided that the risk to himself in doing so was too great.

Two days later his preparations were completed. He had ventured to the speaker office and called the agency in Bingham, a torturous process in itself, and was expected. At the same time he had enquired about lodgings in the town, to be told that could be arranged by the agency on his arrival. To realise as much cash as possible, everything of value had been removed from the apartment, the furnishings were sold and taken away.

The notes and coins made an unwieldy pile, he would carry it all with him, he was not going to trust it to banks again. He had a sword concealed in his walking cane and a Ministry issue gas pistol for protection. Taking all his worldly possessions in two suitcases, he set off for Bingham. He was hopeful that this was the beginning of his journey to gain his revenge, with the final destination of redemption. In his mind, he thought that if he could show Cavendish that he had dealt with the three, he would surely welcome him back with open arms.

It was only a three hour Ryde to Bingham but the journey was delayed by a fallen tree on the line. Then they had to wait at Crowburgh for the Ryde from Ploughtown so it was late afternoon when Terrance finally stood in the street outside the offices of the Picton Agency in Bingham. The office was closed and shuttered.

Terrance had never been to this place before, he had passed through it on the way to Aserol when he had business at the mine and had always thought the place looked quaint and provincial. Now he decided that it was slow and backward. Offices shut at four in the after? And when they knew he was coming and in need of a place to stay. How was any business to be done? In any case, the building had seen better days; they were not the premises of a successful enterprise. In the city, there would be secretaries and a presence at least until six. And the window frames would not have peeling paint.

He needed to set about finding lodgings, but had only spied the one place, the hotel belonging to the Rail company. Rail hotels were known to be expensive, although he had money he knew not how long he might have to exist on it. He took a room for two nights only; the agency had promised him lodgings, no doubt they would be arranged on the morrow. It may have been expensive but the dinner was excellent and the bed comfortable. Filled with relief that he had escaped the city and was now anonymous, he slept like a babe.

Next morning, he returned to the office after nine. Terrance had remembered more about the agency, their chief investigator, the titular Mr Picton was an expert in all manner of nefarious pursuits.

He found the offices open and walked in; there was a girl at the desk, young and pretty, even in her provincial dress. "How may I help you, sir?" she asked.

"I am Mr Terrance, I was expected yesterday. I wish to engage Mr Picton in a business matter," he replied.

"Certainly, sir," she replied. "The Ryde was delayed was it not? He is with a client at present but if you will take char I will tell him you are here. Have you dealt with us before?"

"Mr Picton and I have had dealings before, but never in person."

"One moment then," she said and walked from the office.

Ten minutes later she returned with a char-tray. "Mr Picton bids you good day," she said as she served him. "He has almost completed his work."

Terrance drank his char, the girl went back to her writing and a few moments later a man appeared at the door. "Mr Terrance," he said. "Welcome to Bingham, I am Josiah Picton. It is a pleasure to finally meet you, come into my office."

They walked down a short corridor and entered Picton's office. The man himself was tall and thin, he moved with short jerky movements and his thin neck rose from his collar like a knobbled reed. His suit hung from his frame as if it belonged to another. Yet when they shook hands his grip was firm and his eyes close up, burned with life. There was stubble on his chin from an imperfect shave.

They sat in soft leather chairs. "How may I assist you?" asked Picton. "Before we start, I have heard on the rumour mill that you are in disgrace, and that the Waster Mining and Metals Company is no longer yours. I assume your visit today is in that connection. I should tell you that it is against my better judgement to see you, but you have paid me well in the past and I feel that I owe you something."

Terrance took a deep breath, he had hoped that the news had not travelled but then, this was Picton's line of work so was only to be expected. If Picton knew of his downfall there would not be another who would work for him. "It's all lies," he began.

Picton nodded, as if he had heard this tale many times.

"Cavendish has taken everything from me," he said.

Picton paled, "I cannot move against him," he said. "Not if I wish to remain alive."

Terrance reassured him, "Cavendish and I are not the issue. I have no more business with him. I wish to strike at those who have brought me to this place."

Picton looked relieved. "Then that is another matter," he said. "Tell me the names and what you wish."

"There are three but one is most important, his name is Horis Strongman." Picton made a note in a small leather bound book. "He was one of my juniors at the Ministry. And a woman called Grace, she was from Aserol but I know little more than that. Oh, her brother worked at the Waster mine, as was. I sent Strongman to Aserol on an errand at harvest time last year and I assume they met whilst he was there."

"'Tis little enough to go on, but no matter, I have found people with less information. And the third person you seek?"

"He is an ex-army man who goes by the name of Maloney. He is also from Aserol; the three together were my downfall." Picton wrote a few more notes and then looked up.

"What do you wish me to do once I locate them?" he asked delicately. This was the nub, for all Terrance's talk of killing the three, he would much rather have someone else do it, and this man seemed willing. Very well, let him, then he could hang if he was discovered.

"Kill them all, and horribly," said Terrance. "I wish them to suffer as I have suffered."

Picton looked at him. "But you are not dead," he said simply. "You are well fed and clothed, you have all your limbs and senses, it seems to me that what you want is more than your suffering." Terrance was about to break in, it was his money and he could choose, Picton did not understand, he was dead, dead to society and to him that was as much death as the extinguishing of life for anyone else.

"You are squeamish?" he said.

"Not at all," answered Picton. "I would kill them all with as little thought as I would squash a fly, no death is so... well, final that it does not equate to a lifetime of suffering. At least not the sort of suffering that you say will be yours."

Terrance could see what he meant, in a way, perhaps death was too good for them, all except one. He modified his request.

"Very well then, I understand your logic. For Strongman alone then. But not until he knows my name as the one responsible, it is important that his last thought is of the time he thought he could best me. The girl, well she need not die unless it is necessary, the loss of a limb or public dishonour should suffice. And Maloney should be taught a lesson, involving pain."

"You say he is an army man, it might prove risky. May I leave him until the end?"

"That is your affair, as long as it is all done I care not for the order, perhaps Strongman last, it may prolong his suffering if he can see what is coming."

Picton nodded. "Very well, I require a sum of money then, considering the risk to me and the fact that should it become known that I have helped you I will be finished; it should be enough to allow me to live out my days."

He mentioned a sum that made Terrance feel weak; he had not such an amount. His mind raced for a way to raise the money. If he could not, then he would have to do it himself. That might cost him more in the end; he had not the resources or knowledge of this man.

"I have not got that much cash on me," he said. "But I have an apartment in Metropol City, it is no use to me now, you may have the title to it and some of my cash."

He offered Picton half of the notes he had on his person. Picton took them and counted them. "Very well," he said. "Give me the title deeds to the apartment and we have a bargain."

"I will return with them on the morrow," Terrance promised. "When will you start work?"

"As soon as I have been to the City and viewed my new home," was the reply.

Terrance left Picton in his office and returned to the receptionist. "Picton has asked me to return with some paperwork on the morrow," he said. "I'm presently staying in the Rail hotel; you said that you could recommend a good lodging house?"

The girl thought for a moment. "There are several I direct clients to, sir," she said. "It is dependent on your budget but I would recommend Mrs Walsingham. Her husband is an invalid from the wars and she needs the money, she is a fine lady and housekeeper." She wrote on the back of a Picton Agency business card. "This is her address."

Terrance thanked her and proceeded to Mrs Walsingham's abode. It was a large house on the edge of Bingham, with a walled enclosure and some privacy. Similar in style to his old house in the city, which seemed almost like it had existed in another life to him now.

It was the sort of house that should have servants and many staff; he could imagine it echoing to the excited cries of children at play, like his house had been before all this started. The Walsinghams must have once had means. But the gardens were filled with bedraggled plants and as he got closer he saw that the house itself needed work, there were damaged roof tiles and damp patches on the walls.

Terrance guessed that it was Mrs Walsingham herself who answered the doorbell, by the fact that she was not in servants' dress. She was a lady of perhaps five and thirty years, dressed in an expensive gown, dyed in drab black. Even her hair was covered in a black laced net. Through her sorrowful gaze and slumped posture he could see that she was a beauty, she was tall and well curved, though modestly covered.

"My name is Bryan Terrance, madam. The Picton Agency sent me," he said, offering the card. "I was seeking lodgings and the girl there said you might have a room for rental."

The woman was subdued and said nothing, a deep male voice called out from inside. "Who's at the blasted door?"

"My sister has sent a prospective guest, Simeon," she answered. "Come in, sir, and I will show you what's available."

The house was unkempt, dusty cornicing and faded carpets. Terrance felt a sense of loneliness and despair in the air as he stood in the hallway. There was a noise behind him and a man emerged from a side room. He was seated on a clockwork chair, not unlike the trolley that Terrance had seen in the Gavan Club. With the difference that this one had no bottles, just a tray arranged with personal items.

"Who might you be?" said the occupant, a man as faded as the décor. He bore the regimental jacket of a soldier of rank, there were medals and braid enough to impress Terrance, but the man ended abruptly at the hip. His arms, however, were as large and muscled as many a leg.

"A prospective lodger, my love," said Mrs Walsingham tenderly, placing a hand on his shoulder. "Sent by my dear sister Viola."

Terrance offered his hand. "Bryan Terrance at your service, sir," he said formally. "I'm in Bingham on official business, pleased to make your acquaintance."

The man ignored the proffered hand. "We need none of your sister's charity," he said to his wife, "her and her attempts to interfere in our lives."

His gaze moved to Terrance. "What are you, another government man? They have already cost me dear."

The man was bitter and Terrance could understand that, he thought against saying more. Mrs Walsingham broke the uncomfortable silence. "We are in straightened times, sir," she said, in an apologetic tone. "My husband sacrificed much in the Western Isles and now we cannot afford to keep house in the style we did. We live on this floor, upstairs is not accessible and our reduced income does not allow funds for an elevator."

The man was getting red faced. "No need for our sob story, woman," he barked. "He seems inoffensive enough, not a fighting man. Just show him the room and take his cash."

She seemed close to tears as she showed him upstairs to a fine bedroom, with a self-contained washroom. It was well lit by the sun and moving to the large window, Terrance saw that it had a pleasant outlook over the wall to fields and orchards. In the distance, there were wooded hills.

"The let is monthly," said Mrs Walsingham. "There are two good meals per day included in the price," she added.

No price had been mentioned. Terrance was not concerned about the cost; it would be cheaper than the hotel, yet he hesitated. There were things about the prospect of lodging here that he did not like.

Beggars could not be choosers. "I'll take it," he said. "For a month at first, then as my business progresses I may require longer."

The woman looked relieved, there was clearly much on her mind. Terrance wondered, was it just her husband's disability, or could it be the lack of funds? Maybe it was a combination of those things or something else that he knew nothing about? After all, the war in the isles had ended and the survivors were arriving home. Walsingham might be injured but at least he was alive. And there were many things that the government were doing to aid veterans like him. Cash was available from the grateful state to those who had given so much. Artificial limbs were being developed in Northcastle and elsewhere, surely Walsingham could investigate the possibilities they offered. He would not even need to pay; willing volunteers were always wanted for testing.

Perhaps Walsingham was too proud or stubborn to accept charity, given the sacrifice of those who had fought tirelessly to provide such aid. His wife Isabella had been one of the more vocal supporters of the movement to honour the soldiers. She had worked to ensure that none wanted or were forgotten and he was proud of her for that.

The man's refusal of aid surely meant that he deserved his poverty. Although that was harsh on his wife, Terrance knew better than to interfere between them, he would just stay here until he heard from Picton and not a moment longer.

"I will move my belongings over from the hotel in the morning," he said.

That night, as he settled for bed, his thoughts were of Mrs Walsingham, there was something about her sad face that he could not get from his mind.

Next morning Terrance departed the hotel and together with his baggage returned to Picton's offices. He handed the deeds to his apartment to the girl, along with the keys. She produced a bundle of parchment sheets. "Kindly sign these documents, sir," she said. "Mr Picton will communicate with you when he has something to report. Otherwise, he requests that you do not visit these premises again. I assume that you are staying with my sister?"

Terrance was not worried; he knew this was how Picton worked. He felt safe from a trick. Picton was not clever enough to gull him; above all he had his instructions and payment. Terrance knew where he could be found and could still cause him trouble if he reneged.

"I am," he said, he did not bother reading the densely worded clauses. No doubt they were the usual things, indemnity from legal consequence and a usurious contract that meant Picton got paid whether results were achieved or not. He was hardly in a position to quibble. More importantly, he had remembered that, like Eavis, Picton enjoyed causing pain and suffering. He would enjoy this task. With a flourish, he signed.

"Then I have the number of the speaker there," the girl continued. "That will be the means of communication. Mr Picton will call you when he has something to report."

She turned back to the papers on her desk. It was clearly a dismissal.

Terrance returned to the Walsingham's house, he was met before he could knock by Mrs Walsingham, she put her finger to her lips as he was about to speak.

Quietly she let him in and beckoned him to follow her. They went upstairs, along the bare floored hallway to the bedroom he had seen the day before. "Here is the room then," she said, sitting on the large bed. "I trust that it will be satisfactory?"

"Thank you, yes," he replied; being careful not to get too close to her, her manner was making him feel uncomfortable.

"I asked for quiet as my husband is resting," she said. "It's Gloriana's day away, so the house is peaceful and I do not wish to disturb him. I have dressed his wounds and settled him for a nap."

"Do you not have a manservant for that sort of thing?" Terrance asked. In his world, the wounded had therapists and help for their daily lives.

She shook her head and again he saw sadness. "He will not have them," she said. "Although our doctor has told him that there would be no charge. It was hard enough to get him to take the chair. He considers his care to be women's work and as I am his woman it falls to me. We have Gloriana, but she only cooks and cleans downstairs in our apartments, we do not venture upstairs so you will not be disturbed."

"Madam!" rang out a voice in the quiet. "Madam, I need assistance."

Mrs Walsingham got up quickly and went to the door. She turned and smiled; her face seemed to come alive. "Make yourself at home," she said. "My husband needs me. I will attend to him. You must come down to the kitchen for char when you are settled."

Terrance unpacked his cases and laid out his shaving things in the washroom, he noted the quality of the porcelain and the abundance of brass fittings, in all it was a fine dwelling. He returned to the bedroom and sat on the bed, in the place Mrs Walsingham had vacated, and considered his position. Having stayed in hostelries all over the country, Terrance considered that the Walsinghams could make a good profit from the house. All that would be required was to run it as a business catering for travellers. It was perfect for his needs, and yet, he realised that he did not want to be here. It was clear that the marriage was strained and he could guess the reason why, the man was stubborn and she was clearly frustrated.

He left the bedroom and ventured back down the passageway.

Peering into the other rooms he discovered the master suite; it was splendidly appointed in rich cloth and wooden furniture but every surface was covered in thick dust. There was also a small room decorated as a nursery, with a painted crib and a servant's room adjoining. There were clothes and female articles in the bedroom, which must be Gloriana's abode.

He went down the stairs and entered the dining room. Mrs Walsingham saw him through the serving hatch. "Come into the kitchen," she said. "We have char and biscuits by the range, where it is warmer."

Walsingham was sat at the table in his chair. His wife was changing the spring box that powered it. The discharged one lay on the flags while she was struggling to attach the replacement to the frame. He bent to help her, Walsingham shooed him away. "You are our guest, sir," he said. "Paying it's true but that is not your work, my wife can manage."

It was not his place to argue so he sat. When Mrs Walsingham stood upright her sleeves were smeared with grease and one finger was bloodied from the job. He wondered again how she kept her patience with this brute.

She poured char and offered the accompaniments, together with a plate of biscuits.

"It's a fine house you have here," said Terrance in an effort to lighten the mood.

"It was my father's," said Walsingham. "After his demise he left it to me, I've tried to keep it in good repair but..." he waved his arms at his torso "...now it becomes more difficult."

"I will show you around after we have had our char," his wife said, Terrance could see that she was relieved that he had managed to speak a whole sentence without belittling her or complaining too much.

"If you feel that you must," her husband said, his tone sarcastic, "but endeavour to keep some of our privacy, I beg you."

She showed him around the house, starting with the ground

floor. "I must confess that I have peered into the upstairs rooms," said Terrance as they stood in the dining room, looking out onto an overgrown vegetable garden and orchard. "I thought that you might not appreciate showing me those places that you no longer use."

"That was thoughtful of you, sir," she replied. "We are hopeful that we can have an elevator installed if the projects that my husband is working on are fruitful. Then we may be able to reclaim our upstairs." Terrance diplomatically said nothing about the child's room he had seen; that may be another wound it would be unwise to open.

The ground floor was fitted for many more servants than Gloriana, and a large family to boot. There was a grand open lounge and a fine drawing room; the masculine library had been converted to a bedroom for the couple, it had the space to negotiate a chair all around the bed. There was another space that he was not shown.

"That was the drawing room," she explained. "Now it is a bathroom, but adapted and fitted with hoists and other mechanics so that I can tend to my husband, bathe and massage his body and dress him.

"We dreamed of many children running around the place," she confided in him as they descended into the cellars, there was a wine store, empty save for a few bottles and a barrel of ale. Across the passageway was a large cool room served by a stream; it was furnished with a stout door, lockable with a high bolt.

"We planned the place to be safe from inquisitive young minds," she explained as she pulled the bolt. "But then there was the war and…" she stopped and sobbed. "Now children will no longer be a part of my future," she said.

Terrance took her in his arms. "I'm sorry," he said. "I can see you love your husband."

She pulled away. "I'm a married woman; you forget yourself," she said breathlessly. But he had felt her mould herself into him, despite her protestations. She marched away from him, up the stairs, and for the rest of the day was aloof and kept her distance.

He wondered what Walsingham was doing to raise cash, his wife had mentioned several projects, every time he saw him he was staring moodily at something he alone could see, turned in on himself. His replies to conversation ranged from grunts to sarcastic barbs.

He waited for two more days, the atmosphere strained and the three of them speaking little to each other. Terrance had most conversation with the maid, she was a pleasant sort, not the person he would normally choose but he found her intelligent and with a good sense of humour. She was in the habit of rolling her eyes and tossing her head whenever Mr Walsingham behaved badly, which endeared her to him. When he was not talking to her, he spent time pacing up and down in his room or walking around and around the house.

The speaker trilled on the third morning while they were eating their fast-breaker.

"Who in Bal's name is that at this hour?" muttered Walsingham, his mouth filled with food, he was sat at table in his chair. He had sunk back into grumpy silence.

The maid, Gloriana, answered the speaker and there was a short conversation. "Beg pardon, sir, ma'am," she said, coming into the room and curtsying. "There is a gentleman caller who desires to speak with Mr Terrance."

Walsingham gave him a look. "How do folk know you are here?" he asked, jabbing at him with his fork.

"Now, dear," Mrs Walsingham interrupted. "It will be about Mr Terrance's business with Picton. Viola knows of his whereabouts; after all, she arranged the rental of the room."

"Excuse me," Terrance left the table and went to the speaker. He took the instrument from Gloriana and waited until she had departed and closed the door before speaking.

"The apartment is to my liking," Picton said. "I am in the city now, researching your employee, I do not think I shall have any difficulties with this task. Very well, we have a deal."

"What will you do now?" asked Terrance; at last things were moving in the right direction.

"I will travel to Aserol and report again when I have intelligence."

Terrance was relieved to hear it. Picton had indicated that his task would be easy, perhaps he would not have to be here for much longer.

"Must I stay in this place or can we arrange to speak at a certain time?" he asked. If he could arrange a schedule he could at least get out of the house.

"You do not need to sit by the speaker," said Picton. "I will only call in the evening between six and seven, if you do not answer, I will leave a message and a time for another call."

Terrance now had only to wait, to fill time he took longer walks around the town. If Picton failed in his quest, he still had the *Swiftsure* to pursue. He knew from his previous enquiries that the nearest port to Bingham on its normal wanderings was Ventis. While he waited for news, he could gather information on the best way to get to that backwater of the country, should the need arise.

Picton

Chapter 10

Picton was meticulous in his research, it was the reason he was so successful, and also why he had survived so long, he planned everything in detail. And the first thing he did was to inspect Terrance's apartment in the city. He wanted to make sure that, whatever else, he would not be worse off for taking the job.

The apartment was indeed to his liking, it so happened that among his clientele was one who was in need of such a place, he could make a tidy sum on that. He retained a lawyer and lodged the deeds with him, intending to complete the sale on his return from the south. Meanwhile, he could live in the place, saving on expenses. It was a pity that Terrance had removed all the furnishings but he found some blankets that had not been taken and could cope with a hard floor to sleep on for a few nights.

Whilst he was in the city, he took the opportunity to ask questions among his contacts about Terrance and the replies he got gave him food for thought. He also managed to question employees at the Ministry about Horis Strongman, he wanted the best idea of the fellow, he had outwitted senior men; there must be something about him.

To his surprise the ones he spoke to were not very complimentary in their opinions; 'lazy' said one and 'performs tasks to his own satisfaction' another. To Picton this meant that the other two persons he had allied himself with had been the brains of the operation, what was their motive? he wondered. Had Horis's arrival been fortuitous to their plans in some way, and might he just be their dupe?

He found that his information about Terrance had been correct. He was no longer an employee of the Ministry, indeed Picton could find few who were willing to acknowledge that he had ever been any sort of employee at all. Nearly all the people he spoke to were recent appointees. So Cavendish had purged the lot, he thought, well it's what he would do. In the basement with the dusty archives he found some who had longer memories. The ones who did admit to knowing him agreed that he had been removed on the orders of the First Minister.

Picton did not want to come to the attention of the First Minister in any way, he was glad to have it confirmed to him before going to the Gavan Club. He was an associate member, he had planned to make discreet enquiries there. To his relief that would no longer be necessary.

So Terrance was a pariah, Picton knew how that felt; why else would he be practising his dark arts in the provinces if he had not been forced to leave the city he loved?

After he had spent two days on his searches he decided that he had enough information on Strongman to move his operation to Aserol, there he could search for the others but before he travelled he went to the Rail-Ryde station and there perused a copy of the traveller's handbook.

Where would a man like Horis stay in Aserol? It would not be a grand hotel, nor would it be the cheapest. If he was on Ministry business and in receipt of expenses then it would be somewhere acceptable but not extortionate. It would have been booked by the Ministry, in all likelihood after reference to this very book. Picton found the following paragraph in the chapter on Aserol:

There are several hotels and guest houses where reasonable rates are charged for rooms and meals of good quality. Among the best are the Waterfront Hotel and the Aserol Grand, this last one is owned by the Rail-Ryde company. For those on a more modest budget the Provincial is adequate.

Picton now had a place to start his search; he already had the names, now he also had a choice of places. Hopefully, one of these hotels would have a record of Strongman's stay and that would probably lead to the other names. He could travel as soon as he was packed. He did not need to stop in Bingham; he had everything he needed with him.

Once in the town he could see how matters progressed. If he could not find a record of Strongman in the hotels it would probably be easier to find an ex-army man than a woman called Grace who had an unnamed brother who worked in the mine. That was his plan then, firstly he would seek Strongman, failing that, Maloney; the name should be easy enough to find.

He made his call, then bought a ticket and boarded the morning Ryde south. As it passed Bingham he wondered how Terrance was finding the Walsinghams' welcome. He remembered them well from before the war. They had been such a happy couple and famous in Bingham for their dinner parties, there had been dancing and happiness in the house. It was so sad to see it now.

The Voyage to Tarpitt

Chapter 11

The *Swiftsure* headed south-west from Omnipa, past the massive granite and sandstone cliffs at the very edge of Norlandia. They passed the naval base at Last Cape and saluted the patrolling vessel with flags and whistle. To Horis's relief, they merely dipped their flag in return and did not ask them to stop. Ahead was nothing, just a line where the sky met the sea.

"Now we are off," said Hector, altering the vessel's course slightly, "to the Western Isles for cofé beans and adventure."

"How long will it take us to arrive?" asked Horis, he was learning of the vastness of the world, keeping watch astern as Norlandia disappeared behind them.

"It will be a voyage of ten days," Hector announced. "Here, Horis, take a look at my sea-chart." Horis left his vantage point, where the last peaks of his homeland were now no more than a grey line on the horizon and went to the chart table.

There was a map with no land on it, save a thin triangular point, coloured yellow, on one edge of the chart, and a collection of large dots in the corner on the opposite side. The blank area between them was covered with a jumble of numbers and letters in hairline writing.

A thick pencil line connected the two places.

"What are those numbers?" he asked, aware that every time he spoke it was a question.

"They are the depth of water and the nature of the bottom,"

said Grace, who had come to stand beside him. "The navy surveys the sea, they throw a weight over the side and measure the length of rope it draws before it touches bottom."

Horis understood. "But how can they tell the nature of the seabed?"

"They put a piece of sticky wax in the bottom of the weight, it brings up a sample. If there is nothing on it, why then it must be bare rock."

Horis saw the simple genius in the idea; it made him view the chart with renewed interest. "I suppose that the pencil line is our intended route," he said.

Hector clapped him on the back. "You have it, Horis. We will make a navigator of you yet, if you are interested." Horis thought that he might be, as long as it was not too complicated.

"Perhaps," he said.

Grace smiled at him. "I can teach you the rudiments, Horis," she said, and not for the first time he wondered if there was any limit to her talents.

"He needs to be free to learn without you telling him he's wrong," Hector said. "Your eye on his mathematics will only make him nervous, and it would be silly to fall out over a thing as trivial as declination."

"Are those the Western Isles?" Horis changed the subject, pointing to the dots on the map, or perhaps he should think chart if he were going to do things properly? The pencil line went between two of them before reaching the edge of the sheet.

"No," said Hector. "They are the Drogan Islands, the home of the beasts, they were the focus of our glorious navy's efforts before the war started."

"The navy set out to destroy the beasts' nests," added Grace, "but the Islanders went to war to stop the killing, they regard the Drogans differently to us."

Horis thought back to the farmer in Omnipa. "Perhaps not as differently as all of us," he said. "Do you remember the farmer?"

Hector looked up. "Did he have the whistle?" he asked.

"How do you know of that?" said Grace.

"It's common knowledge among educated travellers," he replied. "All those who are prepared to see beyond the ability to kill. The Drogan is a noble beast, a relic from a bygone age, when they most likely ruled the planet."

"So they can be trained?"

"Most definitely, and if you show them kindness they respond by becoming loyal, not unlike a canine would. I have heard tell that once trained they regard your home as their territory and will protect it, and you, to the death."

"One of them would stop Terrance in his tracks," mused Horis.

Grace shuddered at the thought; she too had seen some of the destruction in Northcastle. "I would rather that we never saw Terrance again than wish that fate upon him, even though I hate him for what he did."

"Do you have some guide, or information about the Isles?" asked Horis. "I only know of them what the government says; that they are full of evil people who control the cofé and cacao and make us pay in honour as well as coin for them. And they war on anyone at the drop of a hat."

Hector smiled. "I will let you have a look at the sailing directions," he said. "It is a book of unbiased information, for seafarers of all nations, the bare facts about the place without agenda."

He looked in a cupboard for a moment and handed Horis a thick blue covered tome, one of many. "You will find all you need in these pages," he said. "Return it to its place when you are done."

Horis took the book to their cabin and spent the next few hours absorbed in its contents. It was laid out in sections, detailing every aspect of the Isles, from the nature of the country and its customs to the salient points of navigating its coasts and harbours. In short, it was a school book, but quite unlike any school book, he had ever read. This one was much more interesting and devoid of any judgement on its subject matter. There were pages of drawings of the shape of the coast, with titles such as 'The view of Cape Bolghom from the South-West', or 'The watering holes at Flekhurst Pass.' They made it all sound exotic and interesting even when the drawing only showed a hill and a few trees.

Almost immediately, he found out things that he didn't know, most notably that the situation was not as simple as the government would have the citizens believe. The Isles were not one country, they were a collection of states, and Norlandia, initially at first, had only been fighting the outer Islanders. The Isles were ruled by a combination of kings and priests, backed by an army and a force called the Dhalbies, a regiment that sounded like the worst kind of religious fanatic to Horis. According to the book, their ranks were drawn from the faithful and they served for life.

That was fascinating but there was more to come, the dwellers on the inner islands, where a lot of the cofé and cacao grew, had developed a civilisation equal to that of Norlandia. They had coal and gas in abundance but did not use steam as Norlandians did, preferring to use water power, in their hilly land this was cheaper and more effective. They used running water to drive machinery, wind clockworks (indeed the book stated that their clockworks were superior to Norlandians!), and perform many other tasks. There was a high point in every town where a head of water was kept in a small pipe; this provided the pressure to supply water everywhere below the level of this pipe with no need for pumps. They had Rail-Rydes driven by steam and coal gas was used to power the engines of their mobiles, which were few and mainly for the transport of produce.

Horis recognised the words of Mr Hammerman, his teacher, but with praise instead of criticism, there was no bias towards Norlandia as being better, merely the fact that it was different. Slavery was alluded to, in use throughout the Isles in place of equines. Human slaves also did much of the work that had been automated in Norlandia and had replaced so many Norlandian jobs. Yet for all that, the peoples were described as happy.

He recalled that fact from his schooling at the hands of Mr Hammerman, "The Islanders use slaves to perform a lot of their menial tasks," the teacher had explained to the class. "They have conquered territories far to the south and use these captives mercilessly."

The book went on to describe Tarpitt as a bustling centre of trade from all over the world, and friendly to all. There was a warning that traders were unscrupulous and that haggling was essential to obtain bargains, unlike in Norlandia where the price was the price.

The picture painted was so enticing that Horis could scarcely wait for their arrival. He would have to read the whole row of books, what else could he learn about his world from their pages?

He told Grace and was shocked to hear that she had been to Tarpitt before. "Many years ago," she said. "Before the last wars; I was only small but it made an impression on me, it was all so exciting."

"You never mentioned it," he said. "There is so much about you that I do not know."

She took him in her arms. "I'm sure there is, now we have all the time to discover everything," she began, her words stifled by his kiss.

"What can I do to pass the days?" said Horis the next morning, he was stood in the wheel-space with Hector, watching the vessel's progress, no land was in sight, the sky was scattered with small clouds. "'Tis all very well but there is a limit to how much sleeping and eating and strolling the decks that a person can do. And I worry that the crew will see me as a burden or a wastrel."

"Well," replied Hector, "if you are interested, you could learn the rudiments of a sailor's life, you could learn to steer the ship, navigate by the sun, keep a watch or join the crew in their other duties."

"I can steer the ship," said Grace. "I am qualified at the helm. With my uncle's permission I could instruct you."

Horis was impressed; Grace, his Grace, could control the direction of the *Swiftsure*, he glanced over to the wheel, a large wooden and brass thing, it was currently unattended, the clockwork was controlling their course.

"I think that I should like to steer," he said. "Then perhaps learn a little of the ways of vessels."

"That will be a good start," the captain said. "Come up in the evening, after you have eaten. Mr Reedsmith will be on watch and can assist you."

That evening, Grace and Horis went to the wheel-space. Ahead of them, the sun was dipping into the sea, one moon shone brightly in the cloudless sky and a few stars fought the last rays of the sun to shine in the east. The mate, Newton Reedsmith, was in charge of the ship and was expecting them. With his permission Horis began his instruction in the art of steering.

Timidly he approached the large wood and brass wheel; it was nearly as tall as he, mounted on its stand, with pipes leading away from the back of the pedestal through the deck. "What are those?" asked Horis. Beside him Grace was poised to speak.

"They carry fluid, pumped by your turning the wheel," explained Reedsmith, before Grace could speak and show that she knew the mechanics of the telemotor system.

"The fluid alters the state of gears in the space over the rudder; they are sympathetic to another, larger set on the rudder itself. Imbalance in the two controls the action of a large pump. It is this which moves the rudder to the position set by the wheel."

Horis nodded, although he did not really understand. Did it matter anyway? he wondered, as long as it worked.

"Here is the compass, Horis." Grace pointed to a circular card, set with numbers. It was fixed on the pedestal, ahead of the wheel but level with his eyes. "You have to merely bring the number on the card, that is the course required, into line with the mark, watch."

Grace nodded to Reedsmith, who disconnected the clockwork. "The ship's course is now under my control," Grace said, gripping the wheel, her legs spread and balanced. "We are steering two-three-zero," she added.

Horis looked at the card; that was the number under the mark. There was a click. "That is us deviating in our course; we are swinging to starboard. Look at the number."

Horis looked, the mark was now nearer to two-four-zero. Grace gripped the spoke at the top of the wheel, rotated it to the left then she suddenly bobbed down on bended knees, the wheel spun in her hands. When her hand passed its lowest point she straightened. The movement was almost balletic in its ease.

"That is one turn of the wheel to port," she said. "Done quickly it will be enough to stop the vessel's swing."

Slowly the card stopped rotating. Grace turned the wheel the other way as the numbers started to decrease. "You have to centre the wheel before the swing becomes too much in the opposite direction," she said. "Else you will be weaving a crooked line to the Isles."

"As well as using twice as much coal as you need," added Reedsmith, who had been watching.

"Your turn," said Grace, stepping back. The compass was steady on two-three-zero. It was so much to remember, thought Horis as he gripped the spokes of polished wood, worn by the hands of every person who had steered the ship before him.

He watched the number, it stayed still. He looked up at the view, there was a click. In a panic he looked down, the number had changed, now it was moving towards two-two-zero. Which way was that, which way should he turn the wheel? He grabbed at the top spoke, like he had seen Grace do and bent his knees. Pain shot through his wrist and he yelped. The wheel had not moved, how had she made it look so simple?

"The other way," Grace said, between giggles. "You need to turn the wheel to the right, move it a quarter of a turn before you bend your knees."

An hour later, Grace had to admit defeat; Horis could not keep the *Swiftsure* moving in a straight line. "Why can I not grasp the basic idea of it?" he said.

Unknown to him, Hector had been watching over the stern of the ship. Their wake resembled the wanderings of some myopic ovine seeking good pasture. The engineer had called him to say that the steering engine was running hot, could Hector please check that the clockwork was functioning correctly.

"Perhaps we will start you on something a little less taxing," Hector suggested, as the clockwork steering was restarted. The vessel's motion settled. "The engineer is not happy."

"I'm sorry if I have upset the engineer," said Horis, it seemed to him like he was not cut out to be a sailor, or at least not a helmsman.

"Don't fret." Grace put her arm around his shoulders. "The engineer cannot steer, and I was the same when I started, we all have to learn."

"I think that perhaps I should learn of some other duties, apart from steering," said Horis and after consulting Hector he went in the morning to offer his services to the crew Boatswain. The man, called Henry, was pleased to have a willing extra worker and found him jobs to do, working with the deck crew on the never-ending maintenance of the vessel. The metalwork and equipment was under constant attack from the elements. According to him, the wind and the salt spray conspired to rust the *Swiftsure*'s plates and dry the lubricant on its wires, these things were a personal enemy to Henry and he oversaw the crew as they battled them.

Every day thereafter, Horis went to work with the crew on deck. On the fifth day they were greasing things; Horis was coming to the conclusion that most of a sailor's life was spent either in washing, painting or greasing. That was when they were not chipping oxide from the paintwork, after washing and before painting it.

The two sailors that Horis was working with, Winthrop and Sam, were opposites. Winthrop was an old, grizzled veteran of many years at sea. Sam was little more than a boy with barely more sea-time than Horis had himself. He was the butt of the crew's jests; they would send him to the stores for a thing called a long stand, which seemed to involve him being absent for most of the day, or to fetch a pail of steam from the engine space, to the engineer's amusement. He bore these trials with a bemused acceptance. "'Tis what all first trippers go through," Winthrop said with a grin.

Winthrop was a font of knowledge regarding the Isles. "I was there on the old *King Lucien*," he said, mentioning the name of a famed warship, "back in the days when Norlandia had a proper navy. We went ashore with all sorts of gear to destroy the Drogans and their nests."

Horis knew what had happened next, the whole of Norlandia knew.

"You found that the Islanders were waiting," Horis said. "They had tamed the Drogans and meant to protect them. You were under attack from the ground and the air, from man and beast."

Winthrop nodded and Sam's eyes grew wide as he recalled the tales he had heard when he was a small child. "Were you there, Mr Winthrop?" he said in a hushed, reverent tone. "When the navy retreated?"

"I don't want to recall," replied the old sailor. "The only time I'd ever gone backwards but there were too many of them for us. We had thought the Isles uninhabited, at least by humans."

"But spies and traitors had told the Islanders that you were coming, and they got there first," completed Sam, with the official story from all the schoolbooks.

Winthrop nodded again, his eyes glazed as he saw the past. "At the time, we were told it was a manoeuvre, a tactic to draw the enemy out but we knew better. It was a rout, a matter of shame. They were like madmen, the blasted Daubees were little men but fierce, they kept coming at us like waves on a beach. You could stick 'em and they never noticed."

Horis too remembered. He remembered the *King Lucien* arriving in Metropol City in disgrace, a beaten force. The ship had docked in darkness, hoping to be unnoticed but the dock was still crowded by a booing throng of citizens. He recalled its crew and officers, vilified in the streets. And the result had been another long and drawn out war with the Western Isles over the Islands and the rights of the Drogans. Norlandian pride had demanded it, after they had removed the leaders who had underestimated things and the suspected spies of the enemy.

"And now there is peace," said Sam, in youthful optimism.

"Pah!" said Winthrop. "There will never be peace, only a strategic pause to re-arm until some other grievance is found to stir things up again."

"Tell me of the Isles," said Horis, desperate to change the subject from warmongering and politics. He had had his fill of conversations like this in the Ministry. "After all, we are not at war now and we will not be landing on these Isles."

"They are wooded," they said in unison. "The great trees bear the nests of the Drogans, huge affairs of tangled branches."

"Others live on the ground," said Winthrop, "in the shelter of rocks and gorges. There will be men living there as well; they seem to have gained the beasts' trust."

Sam shook his head. "I've only seen Drogans in the distance," he said, sounding disappointed. "What about you, Mr Horis sir, have you seen them close up?"

"I have," said Horis, "in Aserol and in the camp at Northcastle. And I saw the strangest thing in Omnipa." He was about to elaborate but Winthrop spoke over him.

"Never mind Northcastle, I don't know what you were doing there, it's secret, that place. You don't want to be telling Sam of Northcastle, he might be a spy."

Sam went red, he puffed out his chest. "I'm not a spy," he said. "I'm a loyal Norlandian, I am."

Winthrop laughed. "I know you are, lad," he said. "But then, least you know, the least you can reveal when you've had a few ales in some tavern. There are those about who will torture you to see if you know more. Or kill you because they think you know more. Best forget you ever heard of the place."

Sam went pale, his patriotic bluster vanished and he looked about him, as if to see who was lurking.

"The beasts will fly out and investigate us as we pass," Winthrop said. "We will have to keep inside and hang flags to dissuade them, make foul smelling smoke to keep them away."

"Will you tell us later of your adventures with Drogans?" asked Sam as they went in for luncheon.

"Perhaps another time," Horis answered, Winthrop's words had reminded him that Grace had been imprisoned for little more than her association with him. A lad shouting about a secret military camp could suffer the same or worse.

The days passed one into the other as they journeyed across the ocean, Horis lost weight and became fitter than he had ever been, he also acquired a darker hue to this face and arms, from his daily exposure to a stronger sun than he was used to. When he removed his clothes to wash in the evening a patchwork of light and dark was revealed on his torso and legs, which Grace found most amusing. She sheltered under a canvas awning from the sun and her skin was still as white as finest porcelain plate. He spent the evenings reading the books about the Isles and the other lands of the world; perhaps one day he would visit them all. Who could tell? Less than a year ago he had seldom been out of the city.

Then suddenly the voyage was nearly over, they were less than a day's journey from the Islands.

Hector announced the precautions at fast-break.

"We will navigate the Lucien passage through the Drogan Isles tomorrow," he said and there were groans.

"Why go this way, Captain?" enquired the engineer, his tone sarcasm itself. "Is it due to the wanderings of our new helmsman?"

The rest of the officers said nothing. "That is in poor taste, Cuthbert," said Hector. "The man is doing his best to learn our ways, and as you know, the Drogan Islands block all routes to the west, we have to pass between them at some point. This one is merely the most convenient."

The engineer looked around for support for his attempt at humour, finding none he turned to Horis. "My apologies," he said. "I meant no offence."

Horis smiled. "Accepted, I admit that I cannot steer but I'm willing to learn, tell me, how long did it take you to master the art?" The words were said in a questioning tone; inside, Horis was annoyed at the aspersion. He was doing his best to fit in and help with the work of the vessel.

"I have never tried," the engineer replied, his face reddening. Horis wondered if he had gone too far and would now receive admonishment.

"Then perhaps you should," cut in Hector and coming to his rescue, "before you form an opinion. Now then, to business, we will hang flags and prepare the smoke barrels as usual, set them tonight and then we will stay inside."

After the meal, Henry took Horis aside. "Take no notice of Cuthbert, he can be sarcastic but he has a good heart. His boy was lost on the Islands and when we are close to them he remembers. I would be glad of your help today; will you help me set the flags and the smoke barrels?"

Horis was pleased to be included but saddened to hear of the engineer's loss, there were so many who had been touched by the wars, he was fortunate to have been left unscathed, reckoned too short to fight; all he had done was man a balloon in defence of the city.

"Of course I will help," he answered. "I will change into my overalls."

He returned to the cabin clutching a mug of char for Grace, who had been sleeping when he had left for fast-break. She was awoken by the door opening and looked at him through sleep filled eyes. "There you are," she said. "I woke briefly and you were gone, I must have fallen asleep again and I dreamt you had been taken from me by Terrance. Hold me for a moment."

Horis lay down beside her and took her in his arms. "I am here," he said. "It's naught but a dream, I promise that I will never allow us to be parted again."

An hour later, Horis, who was not afeared of heights, found himself atop one of the Samson posts, reeving halyards through metal blocks attached to a heavy ring of steel. The boatswain had explained that the flags, long strips of black fabric edged with tassels of white and yellow, kept Drogans away from the vessel. That, combined with the smoke made by burning a mixture of herbs would hopefully keep the beasts at bay. Still, they would have to remain inside until the Islands were passed.

Horis was starting to wonder which method was really the best, the Norlandian way of persecution and killing, or the ways of the Islanders, acceptance and befriending. He had seen the results of both, destruction at Northcastle and in Aserol, and the man with the whistle in Omnipa, at one with the Drogan. His reading made him wonder at his countrymen, he had been brought up to believe that Norlandia was special, that it was better and more civilised than other lands. Yet, in all his reading, it was the only land where he could find talk of Drogans being regarded as pests.

Nowhere else had watchtowers or nets to protect the populace, nor were Drogans slaughtered. Other races seemed to have developed the art of living together with the beasts in harmony. Why, he wondered, could not we do that, if we are so superior?

The next morning, as soon as the sky was light, the boatswain ventured out of the safety of the ship's accommodation and lit the barrels. Soon the smell of sweet herbs filled the ship; how this could distress Drogans was a mystery. Horis and Grace went to the wheel-space after eating and watched as the islands grew bigger.

First, the tops of the heavily wooded mountains appeared. Then the islands themselves grew from the ocean. After so long with no sight of land they seemed to spoil the perfection of the horizon with their bulk and Horis, to his surprise, found himself longing for the emptiness of the ocean.

They were headed for the gap between two imposing islands, and the restricted space meant that there were several vessels forced into proximity, Hector took the chance to gain information from those heading in the other direction, shouting across with the aid of a device shaped like an oversized cook's funnel. He alternately bellowed and listened through its small end. His words were magnified by a system of levers and a rubber diaphragm mounted in the device, which he called an ampli-fone. His words boomed across the void between the vessels, yet the effect of Hector's shouting was local to the direction of the device, Horis was stood next to him and was not deafened by the noise. And it was very effective; he could hear the replies clearly.

"So, there is a good supply of cofé and cacao for loading," Hector said after one such conversation. "Captain Mulgren is just out from Tarpitt and reports favourable conditions in the harbour, there is plenty of wharfage clear for us to secure alongside, so we will not be forced to wait at anchor for a berth."

Finally they were so close to the islands that wide white beaches could be seen. Many Drogans were visible, both aloft and in the nests which Winthrop had described. As one, a group of twenty or so flew towards the *Swiftsure* in arrow-head formation, only diverting away when they caught a smell of the smoke. They circled the ship, squawking loudly and investigated it by turning their heads this way and that. Horis was pressed against the window, feeling secure when a particularly inquisitive one braved the smell and swooped in for a closer look. His talons hooked into the railings at the front of the wheel-space and they bent and wobbled alarmingly as he sat, folding his leathery wings. His nose rapped against the glass, not an inch from Horis's face. Horis jumped back and fell over his feet, but as he fell he saw intelligence in the beast's eye. That and a questioning expression; even though he had always considered that beasts in general could not show emotion, there was no aggression in that gaze.

Among the others in the wheel-space there was consternation, Reedsmith, who had the watch, turned to the ship's horn and blew a long blast. Hector picked up the ruler from the chart table and waved it at the beast like a sword, both these actions had little effect.

Horis stood and, emboldened by the glass that separated him, moved close to the Drogan's head. It was much larger than he had realised from the others he had viewed and its scaled neck sparkled in the sunlight as it moved its head about.

"Horis, what are you doing?" asked Grace; she had come into the wheel-space at the sound of the horn. "Keep away, it will break the glass and bite you."

"I don't think so," he answered. "I sense that it just wants to investigate."

The Drogan suddenly flew away and joined its fellows in the sky above the ship. Horis looked out at the Isles, they were past them now, ahead of them was a sheet of water blue and clear. More islands sprouted from the sea, ahead a larger one was becoming visible

"We are in the seas of the Western Isles now," said Hector. "I can bring out the next chart; Tarpitt will soon be in sight."

"Tomorrow we will dock and can explore," said Grace with excitement. Horis felt like it was the end of something, his world had consisted of a few square yards of metal and the person he loved the most. Now he would be part of the world again, he did not relish it as Grace did.

Aserol

Chapter 12

Sayrah Faith was unused to flattery. So that when the stranger leant over the reception desk in the Provincial Hotel and complimented her on her appearance; she was unsure just how to reply. Flustered, she put her hand to the side of her head, patting her tightly wound hair.

"Oh sir, you should not," she answered breathlessly, unaware that her normally well-hidden feminine instincts had made her react in the same way as the girls she considered 'flighty'. The cheap novels she read so avidly described such situations as this, but she had never been part of one herself. She found that she quite liked the sensation it produced. It was just as the novels had described it.

"How may I help you?" she asked, attempting to strike the sort of pose that 'heroines' did. In her bone corset and tight gown and with her stomach sucked in she found the posture uncomfortable. Still, she reasoned, it might be worth holding it for a while longer.

"I'm looking for a room," the man replied. Sayrah was on safer ground here. She pulled the pencil from behind her ear and automatically licked the point. Then she thought that perhaps she should not have done, as the man's eyes widened. Flustered again she opened the ledger and ran her finger down the page.

"We have a single available," she began but the man shook his head.

"Oh no, a double room for me," he said. "I may be on my own but I do prefer comfort, a single bed leaves me no room to spread myself, don't you agree?"

He was tall and thin, with a heavy moustache and side whiskers yet had an air of mystery and excitement about him. Sayrah was unworldly; in her mind she could hear her mother's voice. 'Double beds are only for marriage and the worst kind of adventures,' she had used to say. Sayrah had never been a party to these 'adventures' and although she was aware of their nature had never been in a position to experience them. In her life thus far, men had treated her at best with indifference, it was because of her plainness and larger body she was sure, but this man had a twinkle in his eye and a kind face. Perhaps he was what the novels referred to as 'the one'.

"I couldn't say," she blurted, then realised that wasn't the right answer for a worldly wise woman to give. She blushed but the man never noticed.

"Now, my dear," the man continued, "where might I get a good meal tonight with pleasant ambience? I know," he added, "perhaps you could accompany me, I wish to know all about Aserol and I'm sure we might have an enjoyable time."

Maloney was sat in the porter's office, close to the desk, reading a news-sheet, his ears pricked up at the conversation. Sayrah was unable to hear the insincerity in the stranger's voice and he did not like to think of her being gulled by a stranger. And there was another possibility; this may be an attempt to elicit information about Horis and Grace.

Since he had returned to work, Maloney had been alert, waiting for such a moment, he had no doubt that Terrance would seek Horis and Grace out for revenge and he wondered if this was just the start of things. Sayrah was an easy target for an unscrupulous agent, after all. He merely needed to flatter her and she would be his. Maloney put down his sheet and crossed to the door, to better hear what else transpired.

"There is an excellent eatery on the sea promenade," Sayrah said, she had never tried it but had longed to. As she walked alone some nights she had looked through the windows at the couples inside and wished herself there, in happy communion with 'the one'. Pride would not allow her to go alone, perhaps tonight might be her chance to sample its fare. "It is called the Icthyus."

"After the piscorae," said the man. "Very well, I will call by speaker and arrange a table, is eight of the clock suitable for you?"

"Why yes," said Sayrah. "I will be delighted to accept."

"Good," said the man. "Where is your speaker booth? I will set the wheels in motion."

Maloney's office was between the desk and the speaker room; he busied himself as the man passed then went to the other wall and listened carefully. He could hear the man on the speaker as he called the operator. But instead of asking for the eatery, he heard him ask for a number in Bingham. That was a town halfway to Metropol City. That alone served to warn him that his suspicions might be well founded.

The connection was made. "I am in Aserol," he said, "with good news. Already I have a possible source of information about one of the persons you wish me to find."

There was a space while the other party replied, Maloney could not hear the words but guessed that the man was speaking to Terrance, or perhaps some representative of the government.

The man suddenly laughed.

"Some old spinster at the hotel where I suspect the three met. I think that the two were employees and your man was the guest. I've turned on my considerable charm and I have the lady eating from my hand. I will try to get more information from her tonight."

There was silence as the other person spoke. The man laughed again. "If I must, if there is no other way," he said. "But I would rather not; hopefully she will tell me before I have to do that."

Again there was the silence. "Very well," the man said. "I will report to you again at this time tomorrow, assuming that I survive the night." Maloney heard the click as the call ended, then the noises as a second call was quickly made and a table at the eatery was booked.

Maloney stretched and straightened, peering through his door he saw the man speaking to Sayrah; no doubt he was confirming their meeting.

The bell rang. "Porter," called Sayrah, "there are bags to take up."

Maloney quickly removed his arm and pulled on a greasy cap, it was not a perfect disguise but it would have to do. Using the other arm and his hook he carried the stranger's luggage to his room; the cases were of good quality and showed the name tag 'Picton' and an address in Bingham. Maloney kept his face down throughout the operation and spoke only in grunts. Picton clearly considered him incapable of intelligent conversation and did not engage him.

Maloney did not linger in the room, he dropped the bags and left, without a tip, returning to the foyer, where he sought out Sayrah. She was flushed and excited, distracted by the attentions of the man. This would be difficult, the pair did not have a friendship; what Maloney was about to suggest would shatter any illusions that the man Picton had placed Sayrah under.

"Sayrah," Maloney began, "I need to talk to you about that gentleman."

"Oh him," she replied, "isn't he just the kindest, most perfect find," she gushed, smoothing her gown. "We've only met and he's taking me out for supper at the Icthyus."

Maloney sighed, as he had feared this would be hard work. And it was not in his nature to be cruel.

"Listen," he said. "That man is up to no good, I overheard him on the speaker, I'm sure he means to use you to help in some dubious plan."

Sayrah tossed her head. "Mr Maloney," she spoke sternly, "hard as it may be to believe that a male might find me attractive, I'd thank you not to spoil my happiness. What nonsense you talk sometimes. It must be from your service in the military, seeing conspiracy everywhere."

Maloney pressed on. "Sayrah, this is serious. If I am right, that man seeks to do harm to Grace and to others, I seek not to spoil your enjoyment. But consider this; if, when you are dining, he seems more interested in the whereabouts of Grace than he is in you, question his motives and tell him nothing."

Sayrah tossed her head again. "Mr Maloney," she said quivering with indignation, "you might think little of me but I have been asked to supper by a gentleman. I will talk of what I wish. I'm sure he will be more interested in me than in Grace; she was an ungrateful wretch, she waltzed off and left a good job here without so much as a note."

Maloney wisely left it at that, he would have to trust that he was wrong. But meanwhile he could investigate the name Picton and his life in Bingham. He returned to his office and sat, thinking how best to proceed.

Chapter 13

Sayrah rushed to her lodgings at the end of her shift, she bathed and washed her hair, and squeezed herself into a corseted gown, slightly too small for her but that was the fault of the seamstress, she had obviously measured her incorrectly. Humming contentedly to herself, she considered the characters in the novels she had read and how they would act in this situation.

She might be swept off her feet tonight, she thought, and who could know what may await her at the end of the evening. She tidied her rooms carefully, if it were not too forward they may return here, she would never go to his hotel room. There was a chance that folk like Maloney, who didn't understand, could see her sneaking to a guest's room and laugh behind their hands. Or hand in his case, she thought wickedly. How dare he, a rough soldier, presume to lecture her on proper conduct.

She walked to the Icthyus, the night was balmy and her gown was made of thick fabric, she could feel herself perspiring as she neared the entrance. She was having second thoughts about her choice of attire. There was little room in it for the consumption of much food and it was her intention to try some of the delicacies that the place was famed for. She was contemplating a return to her rooms and a change of clothes when Picton saw her and waved.

"Good eve, you look stunning in that gown," he said, lifting her hand and brushing the back of it with his moustached lip. It tickled her and she suppressed the urge to tear it away.

"Thank you, sir," she said, "that suit does you credit."

Picton cringed inside, already he had received glances from people, at least he was disguised by the false whiskers he had purchased in the city, and in any event, he had never been to this provincial town before. And he resolved never to return, once his work here was done.

"Come, my dear, let us inside and eat, I for one am eager to try the fare." He held the door for her and they entered.

In the Icthyus the atmosphere was refined, a pianoforte played softly and there was muted conversation, muffled by the clink of plates and cutlery. The large glazed windows looked out over the sea; both moons were in the sky and casting long silver shadows on the waves. The lights of a few fisher boats could be seen sparkling in the distance.

Sayrah saw the great and the good of Aserol, eating and talking; it was not her world and she attracted several glances from the other customers. She wondered if they thought her one of their kind or knew who she was.

They were seated at a table by the window, near a wood fire which flavoured the room with a wonderful scent. The cooking area was open and she could see the chefs rushing around preparing food. Sayrah and Picton perused the menu, many of the descriptions were in what seemed like a foreign tongue to her; as she puzzled, Picton came to her aid.

"They are written for gourmands," he explained, "in the style of the city, where pretension is seen as a mark of status." With his help she chose courses and enjoyed a fine repast, piscorae and meats cooked in ways that she had never tried before. In her eagerness and with his encouragement she consumed far too much food and wine than was ladylike.

Before dessert, she excused herself in what she thought was a demure fashion, but her voice was shrill and loud. Other conversations stopped as she got unsteadily to her feet and wove her way to the facilities.

Picton held his head in his hands, the night was a disaster and for the first time he cursed Terrance and his 'job'. He was getting nowhere in his quest. They had talked; he had told her that he was a financier of business enterprises, recently arrived from Metropol City in search of new ventures.

He suggested to her that he knew most of the government, at least those which she had heard of, and had an amusing tale about all of them. She clearly did not realise that they were either fabricated or drawn from the news-sheets and laughed loudly or shouted out 'Oh I say' at regular intervals.

He had then turned the conversation to her, he seemed eager to learn about the hotel and the staff, first in a general way, then more specifically, gently leading her towards Grace. The wine had helped; it had loosened her tongue a little. But not enough to gain the information he needed. Very well, he decided to press on as she returned and took her seat. The final course made its appearance, a fruit flan with local heavy cream. This was her weakness and she fell on it rapaciously. He had declined, pleading that there was no room in him. He asked her if she minded him smoking.

When she indicated that he may, Picton drew a large cygarr from a leather case in his pocket and lit it from the candle on the table. Replete from a fine meal he gazed at Sayrah, who had given up on the dessert and now sat, puffing slightly as her bone corset struggled.

"Do you enjoy the aroma of nicoweed?" he asked.

"It minds me of my father," she replied, "the smell of him on a weeks-end after high luncheon, do continue."

Picton nodded and blew smoke from his mouth in rings that ascended to the ceiling. Sayrah clapped. "Why, he could do the same." Again several of the other diners stopped their meals and stared at the pair.

Picton shuddered, how much longer would he have to bear this one before he could get to the meat of his mission. Bloody Terrance, he thought, not for the first time; let him come and seduce this creature to find out for himself.

Picton understood that he was a pariah in business circles; too many failed missions and upset patrons had destroyed his reputation.

In common with Terrance he was *non grata*; he had nowhere to turn; save to those at the lower end of the scale who required help. The agency was failing and his money was almost gone. His plan had been to relieve Terrance of his money as quickly as possible, do as little as he could get away with and disappear. To this end he had wined and dined Sayrah, now it was time for payment from her. He would gain the information and then leave. If he did not, then he would leave anyway. He leant forward, holding her hand over the table. She blushed.

"So, my dear, we have had a pleasant meal have we not? The tales of times at this hotel are fascinating. Pray tell me, how long have you worked at that hotel, or are you its owner?"

She laughed what she imagined was a feminine tinkle, it was not and again Picton flinched as they became the subject of scrutiny. He preferred to be anonymous, with luck they were getting to the nub.

"I am not the owner; no, sir," she replied. "I am in charge of the staff though, and a worse bunch you could not imagine, 'tis a pity that the hotel is not a branch of the military, then I could run a tighter ship!"

"Do they misbehave?" he said. "Avoid work, run off without notice perhaps?"

"Yes, some do, we had one girl recently…" she was about to mention Grace when Maloney's words came into her head, he was a silly old fool sometimes but he had a nose for trouble, no-one could deny. She paused, testing his response.

"What is it?" She felt Picton's hand tremble slightly as he spoke. "Did you have one girl run away, all of a sudden?"

"Why do you need to know?" she asked, innocently.

"No reason," he said, but a little too quickly. Perhaps Maloney was right; was there some motive in his asking?

"I'm tired," she announced. "Perhaps I should be off to my bed, it will be a long day tomorrow. Thank you for a pleasant evening."

"Wait," Picton said, a little too loudly. "You cannot leave now, we have so much to discuss. You were telling me of this girl."

Through the wine, Sayrah tried to think of what she had already divulged but her mind was too full of different thoughts, the correct thing to do next and the impression she gave chief among them.

"Why all this interest in others?" she said. "Are you not with me tonight?"

Picton noticed her change of mood and cursed himself, in his haste he had gone too far, too fast and now she was wary of him. He had learned nothing yet that he could pass on to Terrance.

He tried to mollify her. "You're right, my dear," he said, pouring her more wine. "I apologise. I'm inquisitive 'tis true and yet I should be paying you more attention than any other, it's just that I love gossip."

Ahh, thought Sayrah, it made sense to her fuddled mind now, the man loved to hear all the details, she could understand that; it was a weakness of hers as well. Maloney was a fool. She took another draught of wine, it was strong and she struggled not to cough. And he had called her 'dear', surely that was a good sign; it certainly was in the novels. Her head was spinning with the wine, fresh air may help

"Well," she said, "I should not be so rude; perhaps we could take a walk along the promenade?"

That would be a relief to Picton; he would be out of sight of the pitying gazes. "What a good idea," he said, tipping the last of the wine into her glass. "Drink up and we shall stroll in the moonslight."

The bill was considerable, at least as much as it would have cost in the city and Picton handed the notes over grudgingly. "Have a pleasant evening," the cashier said, with a barely disguised sneer as they left and joined the people walking along the promenade.

Arm in arm they ambled along the walkway, above the gently murmuring waves. Sayrah held Picton's arm tightly, her world was rotating gently and she needed the support to stop from falling.

She giggled, she could get used to this sort of treatment.

"So," said Picton. "Pray continue your tale, the girl who left, what was her name?"

Yes, what was the wretch's name? thought Sayrah; she could not remember it, her mind would not obey her desire to recall the information, she had curled hair and a slim waist, Sayrah was jealous of that, but her name... Then she recalled a fact, the girl's brother had got her the job, she could see him, tall and handsome he was.

"Her name escapes me," she said, her words slurred and faint. Picton had to lean in closer to her, a manoeuvre that she interpreted in the wrong way. Then it came to her, "Divid her brother was called, Divid Fallowfield. He drove an Exo at the mine, his parents lived in..." Her mind went blank again and she stumbled, nearly dragging him down. "Oh dear," she giggled again. "The wine has gone straight to my head."

At last, Picton had something to work on; he had a name and a place, and something to tell Terrance, surely now he could rid himself of this hag who clung to his arm like some sort of leech. He could get back to the hotel, he needed a long bath. But even though he wanted to be alone, he could not bring himself to leave her in the street, drunk and at the mercy of people like him. He should escort her to her dwelling, one last thing to do and then he would be free.

"Here, let me escort you to your home," he said. "A rest will restore you."

Sayrah led him towards her lodgings, at the door she fumbled for the key; should she invite him in? In the novels they did, but then 'things' happened.

Yet these 'things' were always described as enjoyable and thus far her evening had not been as enjoyable as she imagined it could have been. The door opened and they both fell into the room, laughing. Picton was desperate to extricate himself but had no chance. Sayrah was bigger than he and even in her condition possessed enough strength to hold him still. Her foot kicked the door shut, to Picton it sounded like the door of a prison cell, trapping him.

"Kiss me," she said, surprised at her boldness. "Like they do in the novels."

Picton complied and found to his surprise that he rapidly forgot his hesitation and began to participate enthusiastically. He was not completely sober himself and it was obvious to him that Sayrah had no experience in the activities that she was discovering. He felt it was his duty to instruct her, after all a night of passion was on offer and after what he had suffered for Terrance, he would be a fool to refuse it.

They grappled wordlessly for a while; Sayrah found that her mother was wrong, these 'things' were pleasurable and not the chore that she had been led to believe.

They woke with dawn's chorus, gulls cawing and the calls of the milk-sellers. Sayrah had a pounding head; she sat up in the bed and saw Picton laid next to her. She flushed as she remembered the events of the night, how she had awoken him twice for more lovemaking and how she had never considered that she could feel so much pleasure.

Today was her rest day from the hotel, perhaps he could be coaxed to perform again?

"Good morning, lover," she said. "Are you rested?"

Picton felt like he had fallen down a mountain side, he ached all over. "Good morn," he said weakly. "Have you any char?" He remembered the night's exploits, he had matched her enthusiasm but now felt remorse, she was a sad creature and he had taken advantage. And then he recalled his purpose, he had some intelligence to report to Terrance. He would have to see if he could add to it before the evening.

Sayrah got up and went to make char. "I have a day of leisure," she shouted from the small kitchen. "Will you spend it with me here?"

Picton saw his chance to get away. "Ah lady, pardon but I have some work that I must do today, I wish it were not so but there we are."

He waited for an answer but none came. "I can return after I have finished," he added, still there was no answer. He got up and walked to the kitchen.

Sayrah was stood by the stove, sobbing quietly. "You are leaving?" she said. "Like my mother warned me, men will take and leave, she used to say. I hoped after last night that she was wrong, that we would be wed and all would be well."

Picton knew then it was time to leave, and in a way so as to ease her mind, and keep her from making a fuss. "My love," he stated then wished he had not begun that way.

She grabbed him. "Oh I knew it," she said. "You will return to me, I knew it."

While she made char he washed and dressed; his mind in a whirl. She talked of marriage, let her think that then, his compassion was fading as he realised that her sheltered life and lack of experience had led her to that conclusion, life here in the provinces was certainly different.

"I will return later," he promised, kissing her, as he made to leave. He intended to return to the hotel and retrieve his bags, then move into another establishment while he continued his task. He would be safe enough during the day; surely she would not follow him. If all went well he could be away before she had noticed that he was gone.

Picton had the whereabouts of Divid, and with that he could find his home. After he had moved his bags into another hotel and taken a bath and a sleep he would go there and find the man. One way or another he could be persuaded to divulge his sister's location. Then he could finish things up and tell Terrance at the appointed time.

Picton returned to the Provincial Hotel, a man was on duty at the desk. Picton thought that he looked like the porter who had taken his bags when he arrived, except that this one had both arms.

"Good morn, sir," the man said. "How can I help?"

"I have to leave," said the man. "Work you know; kindly prepare my account whilst I fetch my bags."

So Sayrah had divulged something after all. Maloney was annoyed that she had not listened. He knew that she would not be coming into the hotel till the next morn and he needed to know what she had said.

Picton returned about ten minutes later, with his own luggage. He must be in a rush, thought Maloney, if he was prepared to carry his own bags. He paid his account and practically ran from the building; there was no way that Maloney had time to see where he went. He would have to find out from Sayrah later.

Sayrah had spent the day in a daze, after all this time and she had a lover, who would have thought it. She wanted to shout it from the streets, especially to all those who had said she would be forever a spinster. She had quite forgotten about Maloney and his warnings. When the door rattled to a knock she assumed it was Picton returned. "Coming, my lover," she called, then when she opened the door and saw Maloney she was crushed.

"Good after, Sayrah," said Maloney, he had a grim face. "I need to speak to you."

"What is it?" she said. "I'm waiting for my lover to come home."

Chapter 14

An hour later, Maloney followed Picton through the streets. Sayrah had been defiant, she told Maloney that Picton had sworn his love, that they were to be wed and how wrong he had been. His requests for what she had told Picton were only partially answered. "I may have told him of Divid," was all she would say at first.

He persisted. "Divid or Grace may come to harm because of your loose lips," he said. "I warned you. If he does then Caln shall hear of it and you can explain yourself to him and to Permilia."

Sayrah was petrified but determined not to show it. "It's naught to do with you," she added indignantly, "what I chose to discuss with my paramour in the privacy of our bed."

She glared at him, why must he spoil her happiness.

In answer he threw down the things he had found in the street outside the hotel, the false whiskers nestled together on her table like a sleeping feline.

Maloney had left her crying, sat in her lonely room. He felt no guilt, he had tried to warn her but she had taken no notice. He went first to Divid's house; Bess had not had visitors that day. "Divid is at work in the yard," she told him. "He will not finish until the wagons are loaded, then he may have an ale or two in the *Rest* with his friends before coming home."

He was on his way to the Fallowfield's residence when he spied Picton approaching him from the direction of the town. He shrank back into the shadows as Picton turned at the junction of the street and walked ahead of him.

Picton appeared to be in a good mood, he hummed a popular

song and there was a spring in his step. It must be true love, mused Maloney, that or he had found out what he wanted. Sayrah had certainly thought it love, but then she had a strange view of the world, based on the cheap novels that she was wont to read.

Maloney kept back, a gas lamp behind at least but Picton never hesitated. He went straight to Grace's parents' door and knocked loudly. Caln Fallowfield opened the door. He was tall and his broad shoulders and narrow hips bore witness to his employment at the mine. Picton was dwarfed by his frame in the doorway. They spoke for some time, there was much waving of arms, then Picton departed and the door slammed shut.

Maloney was in a quandary; he decided to follow Picton and return to question Caln later. Was Picton just after Divid's location? Maloney already knew that. If he went to Divid's house, Bess might need protection if he were not yet returned from the day's work.

Picton ignored the road that led to Divid's house; instead he went straight to the railyard, up the hill towards the Rail terminus. At the entrance he waited in the shadows until the gateman was distracted by some traffic.

He crept into the yard and disappeared into the shadows. Coal was arriving from the mine on the belt, as it did all through the night. Bright gas lights, mounted high on metal frames gave pools of light but also dark places to hide.

Maloney strode into the office. "A man has just sneaked into the yard, Archie," he said to the gateman, an old soldier like himself.

"Mr Maloney, I'm very busy with these mobiles," replied the man, shaking his head. "What can he do, fill his pockets with coals?"

"He is after Divid Fallowfield," Maloney replied. "I think he means to do him harm."

Archie's back straightened and he became a soldier again. "Right," he said to the group of drivers waiting for papers. "You lot can wait; I have business in the yard."

The yard was lit in patches, the lights on the Exo-men and their generators moved around as they performed their tasks. Maloney and Archie had no trouble locating the man. Picton, believing himself secure now that he was inside the gate, was so intent on his task that he never looked behind him. As he passed a bright patch of ground, light gleamed on the blade in his hand.

"You're right," said Archie. "That's a knife there. Divid is over by the wagons, we can get there quicker this way."

They lost sight of Picton as they rounded one of the heaps of coal, but found him again on the other side, he was now between them and a group of Exo-men, all shovelling coal with gigantic metal tools, moving easily to the commands of their manipulators. Steam blew across the yard in small, warm clouds, obscuring the view. Picton went to one of the drivers and asked him a question. He was clearly directed across the yard and set off again, keeping out of the way of the Exo-men and their hoses.

"I'll follow him," said Archie. "You see what he was told." Maloney went to the driver and waved him to a stop.

"What do you want?" the man asked. "'Tis busier here than the omnibus halt when the ale houses close."

"Pardon me," said Maloney. "The man before me is up to no good. He seeks Divid to do him harm."

"How do you know Divid?" he asked; he shone his light in Maloney's face. "I know you now," he said, "you are the one-armed man from the hotel. I told him that Divid was over at the stockpiles." He called down the speaker to his manipulator. "Kenson, we must away to the stockpiles; sharpish."

The man, held aloft in his harness, moved his arms and legs and the hoses stretched as the Exo dropped its shovel and moved off. The man let in the gearing for the mobile as the hoses tightened and it followed. "Jump on," he shouted at Maloney, who swung aboard.

They moved through the yard, past many other Exo-men and Maloney wondered at how the manipulators kept their hoses from tangling. They rounded the corner of the sheds and found themselves among the stockpiles, great heaps of coal awaiting transport. There were deep shadows, any one of which might hide Picton. Maloney had used the journey to acquaint the driver, whose name was Lesworth, with more of the tale.

"That is awful," said Lesworth. "Dear Grace Fallowfield cannot return to Aserol because of this man Terrance and his thirst for revenge? If you can call him a man; being as how he has bravely sent another to do his dirty work. It does you credit that you are trying to stop him."

"I owe it to her," said Maloney. "We have had adventures but Terrance seems unwilling to give up. I cannot understand it for he has surely lost. His mentor Cavendish has swept him aside following the turmoil at Northcastle; there is no power base for him to operate from."

"What turmoil?" asked Lesworth. "We have heard nothing of turmoil, but we have heard of this Cavendish. Apparently, he is now our leader."

"There have been goings-on, let's say no more than that, just the usual wheedling and corruption of our rulers."

"Maybe then," replied the man, "this Terrance has naught to lose. There are none more dangerous, you know." Maloney realised that in his simple provincial way, this Exo driver had distilled the essence of it. And this man Picton would carry out his orders, whatever they were.

"Lesworth," called the manipulator, high above him. "I can see Divid's rig. It is stilled."

Kenson shone his Exo-man's lamp onto the rig; there was a struggle in progress, between two men on the bed of the mobile. A third man hung helplessly in his manipulator harness. He needed his driver to release him and he was otherwise engaged.

Maloney jumped from the rig and ran across the ground. "Halt," he called and the distraction was enough to stop the fight. The two separated, although one of them seemed the worse for wear and moved slowly.

Picton moved towards Maloney. The blade in his hand was now

dull in the light of the lamp. Maloney realised it was dripping blood. "Divid," he called.

The man in the harness answered. "I am here, Mr Maloney, this brute had cut my driver and turned off my steam, I cannot move myself or my Exo."

"I am wounded," called out the other man, now lying on the rig. "I'm bleeding bad." His voice faltered and Kenson leapt from the mobile and went to him whilst Maloney faced Picton.

"When I have finished," Picton said, "I will know where Grace is."

"Divid knows not," said Maloney. "No matter what you may do, he cannot tell."

"Ah," said Picton, "who said about asking him. Terrance has explained it all, he believes that the woman and the traitor left on some ship. It stands to reason they will be in contact; when she hears of her dear brother's death she will come. And I will be waiting."

"You fool," said Maloney. "Will you kill us all then? Because you'll have to now."

"You must be the soldier, Maloney," said Picton. "Your name is also on Terrance's list. I will attend to you now, you were to have been the last and only to suffer a beating but I can see that you are keen to die."

Picton swung the knife at Maloney, who danced away, his boots crunching on the loose coals.

"Maloney," called out Lesworth, from the rig, "Monte here is dead by the hand of this man. I will release Divid."

Kenson shouted at that, "You have killed Monte, he was my cousin," he flailed in his harness and his Exo moved quickly. Picton froze as the mechanical man, pistons wheezing, bent over him and picked him up, wrapping its articulated arms about his waist. He struggled but the grip of the metal arms was strong. They moved together and Picton squealed.

"Stop! Kenson!" said Lesworth.

"I will squeeze the life from him, and throw him onto the pile," replied the other.

"Wait," said Maloney, "we need to know what he knows. Let him tell us before you have your revenge."

Lesworth must have released Divid from his harness; he joined Maloney whilst Lesworth moved to regain the controls of his generator.

Picton was screaming, "Watchmen, I am attacked! Watchmen, come to my aid!"

"They will not save the likes of you," said Maloney. "You have killed one man and that will gain you the noose. Now tell us; where is your paymaster? Where is Terrance?"

Picton was in a panic. "He is in Bingham," he screamed, beating at the arms of the Exo. "It's hurting me, let me down."

Another joined them, it was one of the drivers who had been left at the gate. "Archie came to us bleeding from a knife wound," he said. "We have tended him, 'tis not serious but we called the Watch at his command. They will be here presently."

"Keep him secure." Maloney shouted up at Kenson, "The Watch is summoned."

"Very well," said Kenson. He moved his arms and the Exo lifted Picton up into the night. Picton wriggled and somehow got free of the grip. He screamed as he fell, his arms and legs whirled as he landed on the side of a stockpile, tumbling over and over, bringing coals down with him. In a lifeless tangle of broken bones he slid to a halt at Maloney's feet. Divid ran over to him.

"He is dead," he said after a moment, "his neck is broken."

There were bright lights as the Watch arrived; the drivers had directed their wagon to the scene. Two Watchmen jumped out, one ran to the body of Picton while the other approached the group.

"Now then," said this Watchman, a sergeant, shining his gas lamp around him. "What might be happening here, we received calls for aid."

Lesworth spoke up. "There was a man here, he threatened Monte and drew a knife on him. Look."

The Watchmen went over to his mate, who had seen one corpse and was moving to the second. They were both close together in death, one in workers overalls with blood stains covering the torso and one in a dark suit. "This man," said Lesworth, pointing to the suited body, "was the attacker."

The Watchmen bent and looked at the body; he turned it over, bones grated. "I see no wounds," he muttered. "How is he dead?"

"I grabbed him with my Exo," said Kenson, "to stop him harming any others. I lifted him from the ground to hold him for you but he wriggled clear and fell."

"Is that the truth of it? And who is this?" came the stern voice of the sergeant, looking at Maloney. Like Picton he was not dressed for work in a railyard.

"I am Maloney. I was following the fellow, he seemed to be up to no good, he has been skulking around at Divid Fallowfield's father's dwelling, asking questions."

"Divid Fallowfield?" said the second Watchman. "We know of him, we have attended to the results of his brawling many a time, is he involved here as well?"

"I am," said Divid, stepping forward. "But I was in a harness and not part of the fracas this time."

"Well, we shall have to ask you all to come with us," ordered the sergeant. "We need to sort this out at our station." Just then the loading master came over.

"Why has the loading stopped," he shouted. "We have a Ryde of wagons to fill." He stopped talking when he saw the Watchmen and the corpses. "What's amiss?" he spluttered. "Archie is injured in the office, he says he was stabbed. And why is Monte lying there?"

"Murder," said one of the Watchmen, "most suspicious in the execution thereof. You'll have to shut up shop until we sort this lot out."

Horis and Grace in Tarpitt

Chapter 15

The *Swiftsure* was secured alongside the stout stone jetty in the port of Tarpitt, discharging its cargo of timber and wool. When that had finished, the holds would be cleaned by the crew before loading commenced. There would be cofé and cacao beans and other delicacies to take back to Norlandia. Trade disrupted by the recent wars had resumed, to everyone's relief, for the Norlandians had fallen in love with both beans, once they had been roasted, ground down and infused.

Horis and Grace intended to go ashore as soon as they could to view the sights. Initially Horis had been hesitant. "We have only just finished fighting these people," he said to Hector. "Maloney tells me of their savagery."

Hector reassured him. "You will be safe enough here, Horis. The folk in Tarpitt are a pragmatic bunch, they see traders from all over the world, and to be honest, they fought the hillsmen themselves not so long ago. They may be kin, but there is little love lost between them. In a way they were pleased when us Norlandians did the job for them."

That was an interesting idea, thought Horis, and certainly different to the propaganda of the government, which had all the population of the Isles baying for Norlandian blood. He had not realised that initially they had only fought some of the Islanders; he thought them all one nation. As he walked up the road from the port to the town, the smell of sandalwood and spices on the air,

Grace on his arm, he realised that the saying was correct. Travel broadened the mind. That and the books he had read on the *Swiftsure* had changed his opinion on many things.

It was the first time for Horis to be on land that was not Norlandia, he had travelled further than Norlandians who were not in the military would do in their entire lives.

Almost at once he was struck by the foreignness of the place. The book had said it was so but it could never hope to tell it all. It was a hot day and the sun shone from a cloudless blue sky. Brightly clad traders, men and women dressed in patterned robes rather than gowns and suiting thronged the marketplace. They were darker skinned than the people of Norlandia and in contrast, many of the men were clean-shaven. And Hector was right, there was nothing but friendliness; to be sure, the traders were out to make money from them, but that was the same as everywhere. The majority of those they passed smiled and greeted them. There was not even a hint of malice based on their obvious Norlandian dress or speech.

And the book was right about other things. Horis knew from his reading that Tarpitt had no piped steam system; even so, the lack of Locals and coal dust was a surprise. There were only a handful of mobiles on the streets but again no smoke came from these vehicles. Of course, thought Horis, these were the gas powered ones from the book. But where was their technology, the machines that were everywhere in Norlandia? He saw water running down the streets and guessed that the pipes that provided this were hidden as were the steam pipes at home.

The old Horis would have thought that despite their obvious contentment this lack of technology showed their backwardness, the new Horis understood their different approach to civilisation and remembered that they were very efficient in prosecuting war. Then he saw a man in chains tending a profusion of flowers in the market square. His first slave! The sight brought him up short, the man was smiling as he worked. Why, he even waved his hand, clanking as he did so. "Good day to you, welcome to Tarpitt," he called out

Horis and Grace stood out by the conservative clothes they wore and as they got closer to the marketplace they were thronged by a mass of pedlars and children. All of them seemed eager to relieve them of their cash. They tried to ignore the press as they wandered through the market, past great piles of spice and stalls selling an array of foodstuffs, all of it looking strange to them. And everywhere, the noise of mobiles and Locals was replaced by chatter and the wailing of humanity.

There were more slaves, drawing carriages with curtained cabins containing passengers. There were equine-drawn wagons and barrows of goods pulled by sweating slaves, overseen by richly dressed men; and there were groups of soldiers, lounging on corners, armed with fearsome blades. Horis and Grace held hands tightly, in case the press of humanity might separate them.

Peering into a shop window at the range of golden jewellery inside, Horis saw a selection of rings, intricately patterned with jewels set in them. Remembering his promise he said to Grace, "Look at these fine rings, my love. Would you find a proper adornment among them to prove our marriage?" Grace also peered, they were pretty and unlike anything she had seen in Aserol. One of those would mark her out as different and she liked them. While they were looking, they were accosted by the merchant. He was short and greasy, dressed in soiled robes but his Norlandian speech was clear and understandable.

"How might I help you, honoured visitors?" he said, washing his hands with invisible soap.

"I seek a ring for the lady, we are wed and she deserves the best one," said Horis.

"Come inside," he said. "Will you have a cup of tea?" He frowned. "Ah excuse me, you would call it char I believe. We can drink and talk of your purchase."

There were no chairs in the shop. Horis and Grace sat cross-legged on a rich carpet whilst the merchant's family prepared their tea. Why, wondered Horis, did it have a different name here? After all, it came from the Spice-lands and they called it char there.

Whatever the name, when it arrived it was the same drink, stronger than they were used to but still delicious, served without milk but with a spoon of spiced honey, which was another exotic touch.

The merchant produced a tray of rings and Grace tried several of them on, a heavy thing with fancy carving on the band and a large clear jewel set on it took her fancy. "This one is perfect, Horis," she exclaimed.

The merchant beamed. "That is my finest creation," he said with pride. "It can be yours for a small price." He then quoted a figure that almost made Horis choke on his char, he could not think of it as tea, what sort of a word was that? Tea was only a letter.

"Why for that I should want a ring for myself as well," he said, and haggling commenced. The merchant was adept at keeping his price high but Horis, assisted by Grace, won him over, or at least that was the impression he gave. At one point Horis threw up his arms and made to rise. "I cannot reason with you," he said. "I will go to another merchant."

At that the merchant cried out, "You are a hard man," and promptly reduced his price by a large amount. After another round of haggling, a second ring, the mate to the first but more masculine in appearance was produced and joined into the bargaining. As time passed they arrived at a price that Horis considered reasonable. Then the merchant produced his finale. He pulled from his pocket a whistle, made of ornate brass and silver and passed it across. "What do you think of that?" he asked.

Horis and Grace exchanged glances. "Is this a Drogan whistle?" asked Horis. He was thinking of the farmer in Omnipa and his own need, should he decide to pursue the farming life.

The merchant bobbed his head. "Indeed, I can see that you are a man of learning, most of your countrymen see the beast only as a menace, but with one of these they can be tamed, like any canine."

And that was that. Horis had to have the whole package. He agreed on a price for all three items, which pleased both parties. As they left the shop, the rings were on their fingers and the whistle nestled in his pocket, next to the rock that he still carried, in its leather pouch. As he touched it, he realised that all his adventures had hinged on that blasted rock. If he had never gone to Aserol, never grabbed at it as it had floated past his astonished face, he would not be here now. Then he thought, 'but I would not have Grace. And I would never exchange her for the rock.'

They wandered through the marketplace, the smell of cofé and spice filled the air, it was just so foreign to them. There were performers like in Aserol, jugglers, fire-eaters and magickers and also exhibitors of exotic beasts, caged in metal and wood. Grace saw a stall selling fabrics and purchased so much that Horis joked, "You could start your own business with that much cloth."

"If we are to remain on board, I need to make some new gowns," she explained as the goods were wrapped and haggling commenced. After much negotiating, Horis was delighted to find that the price paid was a fraction of the Norlandian price.

Now laden with packages, they were set on returning to the *Swiftsure* but took a wrong turning. They moved away from the market and found themselves in a quieter part of the town. "I do not remember this place," said Horis. "We should go back to the square and start again."

They were debating that when Grace pointed to the position of the sun and suggested a direction to get back on their route. It all sounded a bit far-fetched to Horis but he went with her.

They turned a corner and there was a Drogan in a vast metal cage. The beast sat quietly as people passed it without a glance. Its owner, dressed in the greasy robes that seemed to be the norm for merchants, recognised them as strangers and beckoned them over for a look.

"We should engage the man in conversation," Grace suggested.

"We can see if he owns a whistle like the one you have just bought. Maybe he will use it on the beast."

They approached the cage and the Drogan looked up at them with what appeared to be a bored gaze. They could see that it was injured; a line of scarred and deformed scales rippled across one side of its head, its eye on that side was half closed and the ear flap was missing. It was strange to see the normally fearsome Drogan sitting so still, with no apparent urge to eat anyone, or rage at its enclosure. Horis wondered if it were drugged, or perhaps a stuffed animal with some clockwork making it appear real. Perhaps it was a ruse for tourists to wonder at.

"Welcome, strangers," said the man. "I am honoured. What do you think of my pet?"

"A marvellous creature, how did you capture the beast?" asked Grace.

"With this!" The man reached under his robe at the neck and with a flourish pulled out a whistle. Hanging on a leather thong it was the image of the one that Horis had seen in Omnipa and the one that the jeweller had just sold him.

"How does it work?" he said.

"It is simple," the man replied, his eyes narrowing. "The whistle produces a noise beyond our hearing, but the beast recognises it; watch."

He put the whistle to his lips and blew, Horis strained to hear; the beast did not. It flapped its wings and rose up on its legs, making squawking noises. It was definitely a real Drogan then; he remembered the beast in Omnipa and the farmer's words. This must be the same thing.

"It is trained to perform tasks, depending on the note," the man explained.

Horis had been over the events in Omnipa several times in his mind, the farmer said that he had been taught the technique but Horis had since seen a flaw in the notion.

"How can one tell which note is produced?" he asked. "If none but the Drogan can hear it?"

The man laughed, showing several gold teeth. "Well, my Norlandian friend, that is a good question. If the beast bites your head off, your last thought will be that you blew the wrong command!"

Horis looked shocked; the man could not be serious. "He is teasing you," Grace said. "No doubt the method is a secret; you will have to pay for instruction."

The Islander nodded wisely. "The lady has the answer, it is a skill passed down, and there are subtle ways of making the noise audible. I can let you into the secret, for a price."

Horis was intrigued. "Let me think on it," he said and the man nodded, recognising his prey. He had him hooked, let him stew. He blew again and the Drogan settled back into his watching pose.

"We have seen this before, in Omnipa," Horis told him and the man nodded wisely.

"Yes, there are those even in your country that can do this."

Grace sensed that Horis was about to spend all his, no *their* money and wanted to discuss it further with him before he did so. She looked around. "Tell me, sir," she said, "we are lost, which is the way back to the port?"

"It is down there," the man pointed at a narrow lane. "That will take you back to the market, then you merely turn right and follow the road."

"Thank you; come, Horis," she said. His face fell, he did not want to go, he wanted to learn. Grace took his hand and moved him away.

"I may return," he told the man as they departed.

"I will be here," he replied.

They walked back towards the ship, discussing what they had seen.

"Before you rush off and give him our money," she said, "consider whether he is a rogue or not."

"Very well," replied Horis. "But how do you think it was done?"

He knew he could be gullible and found it hard to believe what he had seen. But twice? Was it really some sort of trick? Surely Grace could see how unlikely that was.

Grace thought for a moment. "In Omnipa it seemed so natural, like man and beast in harmony, yet here it felt more contrived. Almost like a means to snare the traveller."

"Surely it cannot be both," Horis replied. "I cannot see how the farmer in Omnipa could trust the Drogan not to eat him unless the whistle works. And it must be a well-kept secret if we have never heard of it in Aserol or Metropol City."

"Not so," she said. "After all, Hector knows; the ways of the country are not known in the cities, the two worlds seldom mix, and tales like that would be dismissed without question."

"Perhaps we should think on it then," said Horis. "We have time before we leave."

Once safely back on the *Swiftsure*, Horis showed the ring to Hector. "Wonderful," he said. "I hope you haggled for a good price."

"Of course," said Grace. "We found a mate to this one for Horis. We spent an hour drinking their version of char and wearing the price downwards. In the end I think it safe to say that a bargain was had."

"They are fearsome negotiators, but fair, and now I'm afraid that there are some serious matters to tell you of," Hector said. "My agent has brought me the latest news-sheet from Norlandia with the mails and it makes interesting reading." He passed the printed paper across and Horis nearly dropped it. 'Minister accused of espionage' read the bold headline, together with an artist's drawing of Terrance. Grace took the sheet from his hands.

"That is the man who imprisoned me," she said.

"He was my superior, at the Ministry," added Horis.

"It says," Hector observed, "that in the words of First Minister Cavendish, this man Terrance is responsible for the deaths at Northcastle and the accident at Waster mine, he is the agent of a foreign power and is to be detained on sight. His mine and all his monies are forfeit to the state."

Well, how the mighty have fallen, mused Horis. "He tried to blame me for the events at the mine; I was to be dead and unable to defend my actions."

"Maloney and I saved you," Grace said. "I hit one of your assailants with the chamber pot, in your bedroom, do you remember?"

Horis did, and he remembered the night that had preceded it.

Hector shook his head. "I hesitate to ask," he began and Horis steeled himself for an inquisition on Grace's presence in his bedchamber. Instead the mariner said, with a straight face, "Was the pot primed?" He dissolved in laughter, no doubt imagining Grace defending her man, like some fury of legend.

Grace laughed also. "No, regrettably, it was a relic from the days before the washrooms were installed. As I worked in the hotel I knew it was there, and it made a satisfying noise when it broke."

"So Terrance is out of favour; then surely he is no threat to us," said Horis.

"On the contrary, he is more," said Hector. "If he sees you as the architect of his misfortune, and if he is at large then he must have escaped from the clutches of this Cavendish."

In their cabin after dinner, Horis and Grace discussed the news. "If only the speakers extended to Tarpitt," she said, "we could find out what was happening, Terrance may have been arrested by now."

"I'm sure that one day we will be able to converse all around the world," replied Horis, "and in the blink of an eye, but to return to the whistle, I have been thinking."

"What?"

"I know that we felt differently about the whistle in Omnipa," he said. "We saw it and believed it there. The result was the same, here and there. The whistle blew and the beast responded. It cannot be a trick here and truth there. It must be one or the other in both places. I will return to the man with the Drogan and learn the secrets of the whistle; I feel that it may be of use if I am to be a farmer."

Grace smiled. "I cannot fault your reasoning, if you think so, just be careful that he does not spin you some story to part you from too much of our money. I will not come with you, now that I have bought fabric I have sewing to keep me amused."

Next day, Horis found his way back to the cage, the beast was still present, it watched him and showed little interest. As he looked its head drooped and it appeared to fall asleep. Horis looked around and spied the Drogan-keeper at the same time as the man saw him.

"Good day, my Norlandian friend," he greeted him. "Are you alone today? Where is your beautiful companion?"

"She is my wife," said Horis, proprietorially. "I have left her aboard ship; I seek to learn the way to train a Drogan."

"Then you are in the right place, my friend. I am Hannith; come to my room and I will instruct you." He laughed, a dry chuckle, "after you have shown me your money."

Horis followed the man around the back of the cage, the Drogan was definitely asleep, it had tucked its head under one wing, not unlike any anatine you might glimpse in a village pond.

"Before I show you, I must see the colour of your money," Hannith said again as they stood outside a doorway, mentioning a sum that seemed reasonable for what was on offer, assuming it was genuine. However, he felt honour bound to haggle.

He offered half that sum, hoping that would not insult Hannith. But he merely smiled and made a counter offer. Eventually, a price was agreed and paid. Hannith tucked the notes into a pocket in his robe. "You negotiate like a civilised person," he complimented Horis. "So many of your countrymen pay the first sum suggested."

"It is our way," Horis replied truthfully. "We are not used to the idea that the first price is only a basis for argument."

Hannith's room was a simple place, just a bench and a desk. The doorway was covered by a screen of some coloured fabric, which

Hannith pulled shut. "No-one will disturb us," he said. "Once the screen is drawn, it is as if my door is locked."

"Not only that, you have the Drogan, who is better than a lock," said Horis.

"Exactly, he regards this place as his and my enemies likewise."

He bade Horis sit and rummaged around in a large cupboard. He placed an ornate wooden box, bound with brass straps on the desk in front of him. "This is what you will need," he said. "Everything is in here."

He folded down the front of the box, inside was some sort of clockwork device with parts of rubber on a brass cylinder, all connected with fine gears and levers. An arm extended from the final wheel; fitted with a nib it rested on a paper chart. The lid contained a book and a whistle. There was a drawer under the workings.

Horis felt in his pocket. "I have a whistle," he said. As he produced it the rock in its pouch escaped his pocket and floated up on its string. Hannith's eyes widened at the sight.

"Where did you get a Yanneh?" he asked, looking quickly to the window.

Horis tucked the rock back in his pocket, how had this man known of them? Were they common in this land? "I found it in my country," he said.

Hannith nodded. "Then they must exist everywhere," he said. "We have them but only the priests can possess them, on pain of death. They claim that the priesthood alone are permitted by the gods to have them. They form a part of many of our rituals and ceremonies. Not only that, they are used in our more secret devices."

His voice had dropped, now he was almost whispering, "My advice would be to keep the Yanneh to yourself, at least while you are in Tarpitt. And as for the whistle that you say you have, that is a fake, a lure to part innocent folk from their money, I will show you how I know that later."

Horis inspected the clockwork in the box. It was similar to the mechanism of the ampli-fone that Hector used to communicate with other ships, a rubber diaphragm with gearing attached to the pen on its arm. He looked for the funnel; it was cleverly collapsed in one end of the box, with a small brass catch to unfurl it.

"What is this machine?" he asked.

Hannith explained. "We call it the Fenesh." He considered for a moment. "I suppose you would say 'tamer' in your tongue. The whistle's note sets the pen moving." He pressed a switch and the paper moved, the pen drew a straight line. "Watch," he said and blew his whistle. Instantly the Drogan outside flapped its wings and the pen drew a curve on the moving paper.

"Now," said Hannith, "look in the book."

Horis took it from its slot in the box, the volume was bound in deep red leather, tooled with the image of a Drogan in gold and writing in the tongue of the Isles, which Horis could not read.

"I cannot understand the words," he said.

"It matters not," replied Hannith. "It is mostly pictures and the meaning will be clear. All else you need, how to wind the clockwork and change the paper roll, is easy enough to fathom."

Horis opened the book at a random page, there was the picture of a Drogan sitting obediently, underneath it was a drawing of a curve on the moving paper. Below that a picture of the whistle held in a hand, fingers placed on it in a pattern.

Horis understood immediately. "So you arrange your fingers on the whistle and blow to make the curve on the paper," he said.

Hannith nodded. "Yes indeed, and the beast will do as the picture shows. You can practise whenever you wish, as long as you are inside where no beast can hear."

It sounded improbable. "How can you be sure they will do what you wish?"

"A fair question. Let me get tea and I will give you a history lesson."

"Before you do, you said that my whistle was a fake, how can you know?"

"There are two reasons, firstly a real whistle would never be sold without the rest of the Fenesh. How would you know what sounds you were making; of course a foreigner would not be expected to grasp that."

Horis understood, any whistle was useless without the rest of the equipment. And there was no way of knowing if a whistle made any noise at all without the Fenesh. Then the farmer in Omnipa must have possessed one.

"You said two reasons?"

"First, take your whistle and blow it."

Horis did so, and when he looked properly he could see that there was nowhere to place his fingers, his whistle was different to the one in the picture. Putting it to his lips he blew, the pen never moved and outside the Drogan in its cage ignored his efforts.

"Now try the one in the Fenesh," Hannith said, as he rose and went through a curtain into the rest of his dwelling.

Horis did, and as he held the other instrument he saw that, as shown in the book, it had three finger holes on one side and another underneath. It was not unlike the piccolum he recalled from his days in the army band. His fingers sat over the holes naturally. He blew, he had no idea how he could copy the curve from the book; he could see that a lot of practise would be needed to do that. At least they had the voyage back to Norlandia for him to try and master the knack of it.

Hopefully he would be unheard over the ocean, until he had learnt the subtleties. Outside the Drogan took interest in his warbling and he could hear its feet click as it walked around the cage, then flew to perch on the bars. He looked at the curve; it was nothing like the illustration. In fact the curve continued to form. But he had stopped blowing. It must be the response of the beast. He pulled back the curtain. The Drogan had come to the bars nearest the cage and regarded him. Had he upset it? He ducked back inside and stopped the paper moving. He had no idea how much of it there was on the reel; the good thing was that he could compare the curve with the book at his leisure.

He inspected further, there were several rolls of paper for the drum in a drawer under the mechanism, along with a small bottle of ink for the pen and a winding key.

Hannith returned with tea and small cakes and they consumed them in silence. After a short time Hannith spoke, "You are not like others from Norlandia," he said. "They are noisy and never still, you have an inner peace."

Horis wondered then if this was just more sales patter, he wasn't sure how to respond.

"You said you would tell me some history," he said. "Does that require more of my money?"

The man looked pained. "You insult me," he said angrily. Outside the Drogan squawked. "You have upset Seph," he added. "As I said, the beast once tamed is loyal and will protect you and yours. They can tell by the tone of your voice when you are in danger or angry."

"I meant no offence," said Horis hurriedly, these Islanders may be different in some ways but they were like Norlandians in the speed at which they were upset by a chance remark.

"I take none," Hannith was smiling. "You Norlandians think that everything has a price, perhaps you are the same as all your countrymen after all."

Underneath it all then, Horis thought, they were both more alike than different in more ways than they might care to admit.

Hannith settled himself. "Come, I do not mean to take more of your money. I will tell you of the past, and how we of the Isles know that the Drogan will always obey the whistle; come closer and listen."

Chapter 16

Horis returned to the *Swiftsure* late in the evening, he was met at the head of the gangway by an anxious Grace. "Where have you been, husband?" she said in a stern tone. Horis had never been called husband by Grace but he remembered that his mother had called his father that when she was displeased. Usually when he returned late for his repast from the ale house.

He brandished the Fenesh. "I have not been to the ale house, I have been with Hannith and the time passed so quickly. But I have heard a fascinating tale and I think that I have struck lucky, look!"

Grace seemed less impressed with the Fenesh than he, but then she did not know the full story. Once he had told her, she would be mollified. Her voice was disparaging.

"What is in there? It looks like one of the boxes we saw in the marketplace to me. Have you been taken in by that rogue with the tame Drogan?"

Horis would not less his enthusiasm be damped by her. "This is the thing that will keep us safe from Terrance forever; I will tell you everything in the morning. Trust me, I have learnt so much."

"Come inside then, I must tell Hector that you have returned," she said, as they went to their cabin. "He was about to send the whole crew ashore to search for you, we feared you would be lying in an alley, robbed and beaten... or worse."

Horis hung his head, he could understand her distress. He had never known anyone who cared for his whereabouts, save his mother. To be honest, although he felt sorrow at her distress, her concern felt quite pleasant. "I cannot face Hector," he said. "I will go straight to the cabin."

A few moments later Grace joined him. "Hector is glad you are safe," she said. "Now show me what is in the box and tell me how much it cost."

"Not that much," said Horis and named the price. Grace said nothing; she stood by the end of the bed as he opened the Fenesh. She looked inside. "Well you certainly have something apart from an empty box for our money," she said acidly. "As a curio I suppose we could sell it for the same if it proves worthless to us."

"Come, my love, and I thought that you were in favour of my going back to see Hannith. I'm sorry if I worried you but I lost track of time. And this thing will enable us to do what the farmer in Omnipa did. All we have to do is learn the way of the Fenesh." Unconsciously he had repeated the words that Hannith had spoken with such reverence: 'The way of the Fenesh'. He had told Horis that at its most basic level it was the title of the book in the case. But there was so much more to it than that. Horis knew that if he told it right, the way Hannith had, then Grace would be as amazed as he had been.

Grace softened her heart, she had been anxious but he was safe, and he appeared to have acquired something of value, at least in his opinion. It was hard to be angry with Horis; he was so amenable and eager to please. She should sleep on it and let him explain when they awoke.

"Very well," she said, "we will continue this conversation in the morn." She had forgiven him but it would not do to let him know that straight away.

Chapter 17

At fast-break, Hector enquired after Horis's welfare. "I am safe," he said, "thank you for your concern and your efforts."

"I was not worried," the captain replied. "Although your wife was. Tarpitt is safer than Metropol City for the lone man at night, I told her so but still; she cares deeply for you. I would send the crew to search as much for her peace of mind as for your safety. I hope you achieved what you set out to do."

Horis nodded. "I believe I did. There is work for me to do but, well yes… except for one thing."

"Just one? What could it be?"

"I have a book written in the Islanders' tongue," Horis explained. "Are there any on the ship who can read it?"

Hector thought for a moment. "I would doubt it, but I have a book of words, for use in nautical matters, it may be some help, I will fetch it to you later."

Horis worked with the crew in the morning, shifting hatch-boards to allow loading of the bagged beans. The ship's gear hoisted great bundles of them aboard in nets, the local workers carried the bags into the corners of the hold and piled them up. As each deck in the hold filled it was covered and loading resumed.

After luncheon, eaten on the deck under a canvas sunshade, Horis went to their cabin. There was no work in the heat of the day. They would start again when the sun was lower in the sky.

Grace had the Fenesh open and was studying the contents, leafing through the book and fiddling with the clockwork. She looked up at him, her eyes shining.

"Are you fed?" she asked. "I'm sorry I doubted you last night, I was worried that harm had befallen you."

"I understand," he said. "But the story I was told was so fantastic that I had to hear it all, and when it was done, well it was quite dark. I realised that I was later than I had expected. You were worried and I apologise."

"Then we are friends again," she said. "And now I have had a chance to see what you have returned with, well I think you were right, this is a thing that I have never seen or heard of before, yet it appears to be what you suggested. If it works that is."

"We know that the whistle can be heard by the Drogans," Horis said. "We saw that in Omnipa and again here."

She nodded. "I surmise that this device shows us what the beast hears," she said. "I've been trying to make some of the noises, with the door closed in case one is loitering nearby."

Horis could imagine one in the cabin, called by Grace. "I tried at Hannith's house yesterday, but all I did was confuse the Drogan, it knew not what to do."

Grace laughed. "We will need to practise on the voyage back to Norlandia," she said. "But how can we be sure that any beast will follow the whistle?"

"That is exactly what I asked Hannith, and he explained it all to me. I will tell you the tale this evening."

"Tell me now."

"It is a long tale and needs to be told in one part, I will have to return to work before I have finished the telling of it."

And Grace had to be content with that.

"Let me tell it to you, as Hannith told it to me," Horis said and Grace snuggled up to him on the bed. He put his arm around her and began.

"In the past times, man and Drogan lived in an uneasy state in these Islands, each distrustful of the other. Man had tried to tame the beasts but had never succeeded, they would tire of trying and either the man would kill the beast or more often the beast would prevail. It all came down to understanding, the man could not understand the beast, he could only guess at what it was thinking and wonder what effect his actions would have.

"Then in the time of the Tomes kings, a man was born with a rare ability, by some chance he could hear the beasts talking to each other. And what he heard surprised him. The squawking they made was not their only form of communication, it was merely a quick means of conveying emotion, useful as a defensive warning or indicator of presence. This man, called Myganth, could hear a high pitched whistling noise from the beasts when two or more were gathered together."

Beside him Grace stirred. "That is fascinating, I never knew."

Horis continued. "Myganth spent a long time listening to the beasts; he travelled to the outer islands and lived among them. As he presented no threat to them they left him alone. Over time he learnt their language and began to talk with them. Once they could see his efforts were benign and understood his rudimentary language, they helped him to perfect his speech. Then they revealed many things to him. Things about their lives and desires, chiefly among them was the desire for peace."

"Yet they attack us in Norlandia," said Grace.

"Patience," said Horis. "I'm coming to that. Myganth journeyed to all the cities of the Isles, telling the leaders of his findings. But he was dismissed as a deluded fool by those in power. He told them of the Drogans' desire for peace and coexistence and they laughed at him. Still, he gathered followers by demonstration of his mastery of the language; Drogans appeared and did as they were bid when he called them."

"I can imagine the reaction of the rulers when they discovered that he was speaking the truth."

Horis nodded. "It was the same reaction as rulers everywhere, the government were aghast at this power, they feared Myganth and his Drogans; if he could control them, he could rule. They moved to arrest him but Myganth was alert to the possibility."

"What did he do?" asked Grace, although she knew what the answer would be, it was the same the world over, short-sighted rulers lashing out at that which they would not understand.

"Myganth took his followers and returned to the Isles, where he taught them to talk to the Drogans, using a whistle that he designed, his ear alone could tell if it were true."

"But there is a flaw in the story," said Grace. "How could they continue to do that after he died?"

"Well, that was the clever thing. The people Myganth had gathered were the brightest in the Isles, Myganth knew he would not live forever and he charged his followers to build a machine that could record his work and keep it until such time as the world was ready for it."

Grace looked at the box. "Then that is...?"

Horis nodded. "Yes, the Fenesh is the legacy of the work of Myganth, now all can learn how to do what he did. Anyone who desires it can learn to speak to Drogans and hear their response."

"Yet the world is not ready," she said.

"That is the sting in the tale," Horis said sadly. "Hannith told me that before Myganth died, he told the Drogans of his treatment at the hands of the leaders of the Isles. They were shocked but agreed to spread the word that men were not to be trusted unless they were prepared to converse. After his death, his followers spread around the Isles, teaching where they could. But they were persecuted by a jealous authority, fearing that one who could control the Drogan would wield more power than they. And they killed Drogans, creating more distrust between the species. In the end, the followers of Myganth were reduced to peddlers and wandering vagabonds, selling whistles where they could and trying to keep the work alive."

"What of the Drogans?" Grace said. "What must they think of us?"

"Hannith says that Seph, his Drogan, hears from his kin. The cage is a sham, for Seph's protection only; he is free to leave whenever he wants. The Fenesh works both ways, and can read the words of the Drogan as easily as those of the whistle."

Grace was wide-eyed and fascinated by now. "Of course, what do they say?"

"Hannith told me that Seph knows only a little of the Drogans of Norlandia, for the species seldom mix, but those of the Isles will not have peace now. They will listen and can tell that those who try and talk are pure in intention. They will serve in return for protection; any who persecute them, take their lands or do them harm will be destroyed."

"So this Hannith is one of the disciples of Myganth?"

"He is and he is wary of officialdom, but that is not the greatest part of it," Horis said. "Using the Fenesh, Hannith spoke to Seph, his Drogan, and the beast replied to me."

Grace was unsure. "So this is the proof then, are you sure?"

"I tell you, he blew the whistle and I saw the curve. Then he pointed the instrument at the Drogan and a curve was made. Hannith never touched the mechanism or his whistle. And I have the paper. I took it from the drum."

Grace could see by the passion in him that Horis was telling her the truth. "Very well then, and what did this beast say back? Good evening, I will not eat you, or did it sing a lullaby perhaps?"

"Grace, you are not being serious. Hannith asked it if it understood the whistle, it replied that it did. Then he asked it if it knew Myganth, and it said, only the memory."

"How do you know all this? It could have said anything."

Horis produced the paper from the Fenesh from his pocket. "Here," he said. "Look at that; now tell me that is not conversation."

The paper had a mass of curves, one after the other. "That is Hannith asking," said Horis pointing to a point on the curve, he reached for the book. "Here, this is the signal for understanding, this shape is for yes." He turned the pages. "Hannith marked them for me."

Grace snatched the book. "I can read some of the writing," she said. "A woman at the laundry in Aserol showed me some simple phrases."

She pored over the paper and the book for a moment as Horis waited, his fingers crossed behind his back. The only noise was of her flicking the pages.

Eventually she put the paper down and looked Horis straight in the eye. "Do you know what this means?" she said. She shook Horis by the arm. "Well do you?" She grabbed him and kissed him fiercely. "You, my husband, are a genius."

"Do you believe me now?" he asked as their lips parted.

"Believe you? Hannith has only told you the half and I cannot read every word, yet there is more than he said in the words of the Drogan on the paper."

"I was coming to the rest of the conversation," Horis said, "when I got my chance to speak. Do you need me to tell it or can you decipher the book by your own abilities?"

"We need a book of words for me to do it justice," she said. "There will be no need for any sarcasm."

"Then I shall return to the market tomorrow, and seek one out."

The next day, Horis excused himself from work and went back to the market, he wanted to see Hannith and get a translation of the book that was in the Fenesh. But when he came into the square, the cage was empty and Hannith's room by the side of it was occupied by a large woman. She was selling flatbreads that she was baking on a metal plate over a coal fire. "Where is Hannith?" Horis asked her but she merely shrugged and turned back to her baking.

Horis was sure he had the right place, how many squares could there be in this town with a cage in it? No, he was where he had been just two days before. "Hannith," he called out. "Hannith, where are you?"

Folk looked at him, and shook their heads; perhaps he should find some official and ask where Hannith had gone. He looked about him for a uniform. Everyone moved away as if he were contaminated with something. In the distance he heard the wailing of some sort of siren.

He was approached by a large bearded man, the only one who did not appear to regard him as poison. "Come with me," he said.

"No!" answered Horis, fearful of an attempt to rob him. "Hannith, help me!" he called again. The man, who was much larger, grabbed Horis and clamped his huge hand over his mouth, stopping him in mid-shout. The hand was rough and smelt of spices.

"Be quiet, for your own sake, Hannith sent me," the man said. "You are safer with me than if you stay here calling for him, the wrong people will hear you. That siren is their approach, come quickly."

Horis understood and followed the man, as he ducked behind the baker and entered the room he had sat in with Hannith. It was differently furnished now and the screen that Hannith had gone behind was now beaded. Horis went through it, the man beckoning him on. "Come quickly," he said again as they climbed a flight of twisting, narrow stairs.

Horis found himself on the upper floor of the building and paused for breath. He faced a window; it was unglazed but covered with a slatted screen. Horis peered through as a mobile arrived in the square, its wailing siren died away as it stopped by the doorway, now underneath where he stood. Several uniformed men got out and shouted at the baker in the tongue of the Isles.

They were all dressed in robes of yellow and they all appeared to be deformed. They had strangely shaped heads, more like blocks and were uniformly short. Yet their torsos and arms were normal, it must be their legs that were foreshortened, under the robes. They wore jewelled caps and carried wicked looking blades, short but wide. Their expressions were fixed, vacant and identical.

Horis understood none of the words they shouted at the woman but the meaning was unmistakable. The woman shouted back, waving her arms about. Horis was grabbed again and led through a maze of small passages, then across rooftops, past lines of washing, eventually through another door and down some stairs into a large room, guarded by two of the biggest men Horis had ever seen. The door slammed behind him.

The room was heavily carpeted and filled with low cushions. The windows were covered with more slatted shutters making it dark in the daylight. Incense burned in a brazier, its sickly smoke almost thick enough to be edible. Horis felt it in his eyes, in his throat and his lungs, it made him feel intoxicated.

He walked forward, there was a hooded man sitting on a cushion with his back to Horis, he was bent forward as if studying something. Horis got to within five paces and hesitated, unsure.

The man stood in a fluid movement and uncovered his head. It was not Hannith but a bald man with a huge black beard. He grinned, showing sparklingly white teeth and held out his arms. "Come, Norlandian, do not be afraid, sit and relax."

"Why am I here?" Horis asked, sitting on a soft cushion.

The man laughed and sat facing him. "Instead of where you are, think of where else you could have been. My man Radul saved you from the inside of a jail, one which your Norlandian friends would not have been able to extricate you from, for your very existence would have been denied. Do you know who those men were?"

Horis shook his head. "I do not, they looked unlike the soldiers that I saw in the streets. Were they what we call Watchmen?"

The man shook his head. "We have no Watchmen here, only soldiers and the Dhalbies."

"Dhalbies?" echoed Horis; the book had said they were the special guards of... something. What would they want with him? "What are Dhalbies?"

"They are the agents of the king and his priests, selected from those born with a certain deformity from all over the land. The affliction causes them all to look similar, they are taken from their mothers as soon as it manifests and trained to serve our rulers."

Horis recognised them from the book. He was perplexed. "But

what have I done?"

The man rolled his eyes. "Hannith has given you a Fenesh, yes?"

Horis shook his head. "Not given," he argued. "He sold it to me, I paid him, in Norlandian currency admittedly but I paid him and he took it. There was good faith on both parts; at least I believe that we parted as friends."

"Hannith is incarcerated," said the man. "By the Dhalbies, and his Drogan has flown away. I am Salmah and Hannith is my brother." He put out his hand and Horis shook it.

Horis realised that this was what Hannith had been talking about when he had said that those who could talk to Drogans were feared. "Was he taken because of me?"

"No, it is not your doing; it is because of what he could do, as I suspect he told you. Those who know the way of the Fenesh are hunted by the Dhalbies, the priests fear their power, as does our king. Your arrival was fortunate, some might say more than just luck. Now they will not find the Fenesh, you have it safe; you must carry the work on."

"What work?" Horis was confused, his voice rose in pitch, he started to gabble. "All I wish is to farm a few ovines in peace; I never meant to get involved with any work." The incense was having an effect on him, his head felt light.

Salmah smiled and placed his hand on Horis's arm. "I know, my Norlandian friend, but it seems like the fates have a different idea, why else would you return today?"

Horis was on surer ground here, he was not religious, the gods of Norlandia meant little to him and as for those of the Isles, they meant less. With difficulty he formed his words.

"I came to see Hannith," he said, then he stopped, why had he come to see Hannith? Ahh yes, "To help me to understand the book that was in the Fenesh, that's all I wish to understand."

"That is the right way; we all should seek understanding of life's mysteries. I sense that you will be a successful communicator and that many others will learn from you."

Horis realised at that moment that he was not alone with Salmah in the room, there was someone in the shadows, listening. He came forward into the light. A slight man, dark of skin, dressed in an open waistcoat and loose trousers.

"Here is what you seek," he said, in his hand was a slim volume, cased in the same red leather as the other book. "This is the same book," he said, "but in the language of your land, page by page."

"Thank you," said Horis, he took it and the man retreated into the corner.

"There is one more thing," Salmah said, his voice cold and serious. "There are few of us left here in the Isles, and every year the bond we have tried to keep between man and beast grows thinner. You must promise me that you will teach another to do what you will soon do, and pass the instruction on through the generations to come. So that the skill does not die out."

The room and the incense had Horis confused; he wanted nothing more than to sleep, although he knew it was not yet luncheon time. "Yes, I will," he said, speaking almost before he had realised that the words were formed in his mind.

"Good." Salmah held his hand again. "I know you will, now that you have said it. Seph is a good judge of a man and he told Hannith, who in turn told me, that you were a man of your word. Now Ardulh here will take you safely back to your vessel. Remember you must learn, then teach, and always say the name of Myganth when you first talk to a new Drogan, it will remind them that you can be trusted, with luck they will not eat you before you do."

Ardulh came out of the shadows again; he was clutching a robe in dark wool, which Horis allowed himself to be clothed in. The two pulled it on over his head and his clothes, keeping the book safe in a pocket. The robe stank of sweat and rancid oil. Horis remembered little after that, his journey a stumbling one of alleyways and shadows. He woke in his cabin, with Grace stood over him, it was late in the day and the sun was low in the west.

"Who was the man who brought you back this time?" she asked.

"Why did you return clothed in that smelly robe? I made him take it away with him. Have you been to some foreign ale house?"

Horis felt his head, the sensation was not unlike the one a visit to the ale house might produce but it was clearing rapidly. He sat up.

"No, there was incense where I was, the man and the Drogan had gone, arrested by the state, I was rescued from the Dhalbies."

"Wait!" shouted Grace. "What have you got yourself involved with, what were the king's agents...?" She shook her head in despair. "Oh never mind."

She wondered if the involvement of them was connected to Terrance and Northcastle. It was unlikely; his reach would not extend this far even if the government had sanctioned it. Besides, they would have come to the ship for their man. It must be to do with the Fenesh. Horis continued. "Then I met Hannith's brother and another man; they gave me this." He produced the volume and explained the rest of the tale.

"You poor man, you do have adventures; ever since we met you have been in one scrape or another." Grace looked at the book, comparing it to the other. "This will help us greatly, it is not a perfect translation of the other book but between the two of them we can master it."

Horis was relieved to hear it, after the trouble he had been put to.

"The man who left you here said that for your safety you should not venture ashore again," Grace told him.

"That will be no hardship, I've had enough of this place, I want now only to get back to Norlandia, with all its faults, and become a farmer."

"But you will learn the whistle?" Grace was concerned.

"Oh yes, I have said I would and I can see that it's important, at least to the men here."

"It will be important to the Drogans, if they are not to become extinct," Grace added.

Chapter 18

On their seventh day in Tarpitt, they woke to find that another Norlandian ship had arrived in the night. There was great excitement on board, the crew looked longingly at the *Pride of Scaledge*, she had recently been repainted and shone in the sun.

"Perhaps she has mail aboard," said one. "Or news-sheets," ventured another.

"That's Captain Blundy's ship," said Winthrop, who Horis was working with that morning, they were arranging hatch-tops again. Now the loading was in the top spaces of the holds, it meant that it was nearly completed. "He and our skipper are good friends; he'll be over soon for hospitality."

Sure enough, that afternoon the captain of the vessel, accompanied by his wife, came over to visit and Hector invited Grace to his cabin for char and conversation with the lady. Edwin Blundy and Hector were old friends, having met in most of the ports in the Isles and Norlandia, as well as in the exotic parts of the world over the years.

They talked of many things, affairs in Norlandia, the rise of Cavendish and the new political situation. Grace was glad of the female company, but in truth was not interested in such; she had had her fill with the machinations of the state, although her part in events was never mentioned. His wife seemed to be a quiet, unassuming thing, compared to her husband, a typical sea captain, full of opinion and loud in the expression of them.

"We sailed from Aserol," said Decima, the captain's wife, when Grace mentioned that she missed her home.

"Yes, and it seemed the same as ever," said Edwin. "A delightful place."

"But what of the excitement there?" Decima added and Grace looked up.

"Excitement?" she said.

"Why yes, there was some sort of commotion at the railyard, the night before we left, the talk was of it all that last day. I have a news-sheet somewhere." She searched in her bag. "Now where is it?"

Grace's stomach had lurched at the word excitement; she thought of Maloney's warning that she could never go home. Relief flooded her body when the yard was mentioned. All her family, Caln, Divid and the others worked in the mine. Decima found the sheet and passed it to Grace.

Grace scanned the sheet. "Here it is," she said. "There have been deaths at the coal yards, no names or details are given though one of the dead was a worker. The speculation is that the other man was engaged in some sort of espionage."

Even though she was sure that there could be no risk to her family, she was acutely aware that they had not spoken to her parents since before she had left for Metropol City with Horis.

She had not seen her brother since that night in the *Drogan*, in Aserol last harvest, and now it was a new year. They had missed so much that they normally did as a family, the celebrations for the return of Bal, and even her wedding.

"I hope my family are well," she said, fighting the tears. "It's been so long since we have exchanged news."

She stopped short, suddenly aware that even if this was nothing to do with her, one of her kin might die before she saw them again. "I need to speak to my brother," she said in a small voice, "to my mother and to all my kin; I need to know they are alright."

The cabin fell silent.

Hector sought to comfort her. "Of course you do, my dear. You should not fret overmuch, this is a meagre report, and anyway, your family would be safe. After all, Divid works at the mine and not in the yards. We will be sailing to Ventis in a day or so; you can send him a message from there."

"I had hoped that we were to go to Aserol first," said Grace. "I was expecting to be able to go ashore and see everyone if we went to Aserol, now it will be two weeks before I can find out if they are alright, and then only by speaker."

Hector smiled. "I'm sorry, my child, the call in Aserol was cancelled, the wars have altered the cofé scheduling, fewer beans were picked during the conflict, all the men were fighting. So we go straight to Ventis and thence to the capital."

Horis knocked on the door. "Pardon me, Captain," he said formally, seeing that Hector was entertaining, "but might I borrow my wife for a moment?"

"Come in, come in," said Hector. "Please meet Captain Blundy and his wife Decima. This is Horis, Grace's new husband and now family to me."

Captain Blundy muttered, "Delighted," and his wife blushed when Horis bowed and kissed her gloved hand, in the fashion of upper society. She had not expected that from the man in rough sailor's clothes.

"Family by the captain's good offices," he said. "He performed the ceremony on board."

"Horis was a minister in the government," said Hector, avoiding the addition of the word junior. "But he fancied a change of life, fell for Grace and the rest followed."

"A minister," said Blundy. "Then what do you think of Cavendish's appointment? It all seemed a little too convenient to me. Some sort of accident wiping out half of the administration. And what about the fall from grace of Terrance eh? The taking of his mine. It smacks of a coup."

"Hush, dear," said his wife. "All you see are conspiracies and coups. These things happen."

Horis knew not what to say, should he trust Blundy with the

truth or make up some tale. He looked at Hector, who shook his head, ever so slightly.

"Terrance, I know the name," he said. "But not the man, was he not in coal? I was in…"

Blundy looked him between the eyes. "Yes, you were in which ministry?"

"Ah, I'm sorry but I cannot tell you," he said. "Let's just say it was vital work."

He touched his nose and Blundy nodded. He was clearly curious but decorum prevented him from asking more. Horis got the impression that he considered him a spy, on some mission aboard the *Swiftsure*. That suited, to be honest, it deflected any further questions.

Grace saved him having to think up more elaborate answers. "Hector has heard, dear, we go to Ventis and not Aserol, after this place. I so wanted to see everyone at home."

"Oh," he said. "That is a shock; we will have to decide what to do now."

Blundy rose. "Well, I had better get back to my ship," he said. "Come, Decima, it was good to see you again, Hector, and you, Grace. My congratulations to you and Horis of course." He shook Horis by the hand. "Good luck in your mission," he said with a conspiratorial wink. They left and before they had gone down one deck Horis and Grace dissolved in laughter.

"He thought you were on a spying mission," she said, between giggles.

"That's a relief, in a way," said Horis. "I don't think going ashore in Aserol would have been a good idea until we had spoken to Maloney."

She turned to him. "How might we do that?" she paused. "Without going ashore?"

Hector laughed. "She has you there, Horis."

He was flustered. "I merely mean that it might be best if I were to contact Maloney first," suggested Horis. "He will know the

148

situation and what has occurred."

The next day, the last bags of beans were swung aboard and the *Swiftsure* had finished loading its cargo. The crew, Horis included, turned out to secure the vessel for the voyage back to Norlandia. Departure was set for later that evening and as the time approached Grace grew more excited. "We are going home," she said to Horis as he took a drink of water, stood by the hatch-top where he had been securing the canvas covers with wooden wedges. "Soon I will speak to Divid and learn what adventures they have been having in Aserol."

"They can scarce compare to ours," replied Horis, he was exhausted, his arms ached and he was drenched in sweat. "I have travelled, rescued you, become a sailor and husband and now look set to learn the language of the Drogan, surely there's not much more adventure left?"

Horis looked at the cargo shed, the man was still there. Ever since he had met with Salmah the man had been standing in the shadow of the shed. Horis was sure it was Ardulh, watching to see that he didn't come on shore, or perhaps he was making sure the authorities didn't arrive. The first few times he had caught the man's gaze Horis had waved, but he had never been acknowledged. He had not told Grace, lest she fret. Her mind was too full of the news from Aserol now to burden her with more worry. A few hours and they would be away, then it would matter not.

As darkness fell the engine was started and Hector manoeuvred the *Swiftsure* clear of the jetty, handling the vessel as easily as a child would spin a top. Horis watched as he let all the ropes loose save one, which he used as a lever to lift the bow clear of the wharf against the engine's power. Then this rope was let go and swinging clear of the wharf they passed into the ocean and set course for the Cape of Storms. Horis's last sight was of the man, now in the glare of a gas light, he waved to Horis as they departed. Clearly, his mission had been accomplished.

What Horis could not see was Seph, circling high overhead. His wings stretched into an effortless glide and he followed the *Swiftsure* through the night.

Chapter 19

In all the hours when he was not working, Horis tried to learn the use of the whistle. With practice his fingers started to become more flexible and do his bidding. He had the book to guide him and Grace to cajole him. She was also trying to master the knack, when he was not there, although after a day or so she admitted defeat. "I cannot get the pitch," she said. "It must be a masculine thing, although I hate to admit it. My lungs or some other part of me does not suit the whistle."

Horis was pleased, here was something that he could do which she could not, but he did not want to brag. "You can steer the ship and I cannot," he said. "I hardly dare say it, but for all we know the whistle is designed only for men to use, I did not think to ask."

She was mollified by that. "In that case, I will use all my efforts to help you master it," she said.

Horis had not really thought on how to approach this part of the process, he merely tried to blow and see what happened. The result was a long piece of paper with a pattern resembling a rough sea, but no progress on mastery. "You go off to your sailoring," said Grace on the third morning. "While you are away I will devise a plan to help us."

They were passing the Outer Isles, the crew were given jobs inside, cleaning and painting the enclosed spaces in the fore and after castles. Horis had been surprised to find that the flags and burning drums were not to be set. He asked Winthrop, who explained that their route back to Norlandia was different.

"We head to the Cape and not to Omnipa," he said. "Hence we use another passage between the Isles. This one is wider and there is less chance of the beasts taking an interest in us. We merely stay inside for safety."

One Drogan did land on the foredeck though, it was too far away to see clearly but Horis was sure it had a scar on one side of its face and a damaged ear. Hector blew the ship's horn and it flew away.

At lunchtime, Grace was triumphant. "I have it," she said. "A system that will make it easier for you to learn the commands. I have made a discovery as well. I will tell you when you have finished your work."

That evening, Grace produced several sheets of parchment, covered with neat writing. "We should treat this as when a child learns to read and write," she said.

Horis groaned; did they have to?

"Now, the first thing is to master each note," she continued. "Then you can learn the combinations and finally put it together."

Despite himself he saw that she was right. "Can you read the books?" he asked.

"Oh yes it's all very clear," she said. "Besides, I have an advantage, as I think I told you, when I worked in the laundry in Aserol there was an island woman; she taught me to speak and read a few words of her tongue. The book in the Fenesh, the volume you obtained and Hector's guide have also played their part."

"Do I need to learn the tongue of the Isles as well as the tongue of the whistle?" asked Horis. This suddenly seemed an insurmountable task, and they only had ten days more until they reached Ventis.

Grace saw his expression and laughed. "No, silly, all you need to do is learn the notes and the meaning of the combinations in our tongue."

"That is a relief, what was your discovery?" he asked, half afraid that it would mean more skills for him to master.

"The paper rolls for the clockwork," she said. "I feared that there would not be sufficient for your training, but I have seen the ship's stores and they are the same size as those that various things on board use, we have plenty for you to draw on."

With such little time, Grace was a strict taskmaster. Horis soon found that to add to the aches his body carried from the heavy work of seafaring, he could add stiff fingers and bleeding lips. The fingers he could put up with but the sore lips made kissing less of a joy.

He was determined to succeed and so spent every waking hour practising. First he learned the individual notes, repeating them time after time until the curve on the paper matched the drawing. Then Grace made him do the same again, only this time without sight of the result.

It took three late evenings and early mornings; at least no-one else on board was disturbed by the noise but Horis was glad that he had done it this way, for when he tried the combinations he found it much easier to master them.

All the time, Seph kept station, with his keen hearing he occasionally made out the notes that Horis made. As time passed he found them easier to decipher. He was pleased; fate had chosen a good subject. With his position in the sky he could see Norlandia long before those moving on the surface of the water. He spied the land east of Aserol in the dawn's light and left his station to head landward. His wings were tired, he had spent too long in the cage.

He had not visited Norlandia for many years but he was sure he would receive a warm welcome from his cousins in the north.

Finally, Horis had progressed to the words of command; he could warble so much more than just 'come' and 'stay'. To his surprise the language of the Drogan was complex but completely lacking in emotion, they had no words for fear, or love, or even hate.

At last, Grace looked up at Horis; she could see the paper while he could not. "That's it," she said with a pleased grin. "You have copied every phrase perfectly, if a Drogan cannot understand you, then it is a very backward beast."

Horis was elated; he could not wait to try his new skill out on a real Drogan.

"You will have to keep practising every day," Grace reminded him and his face fell. "Just to stop from losing the skill, now you have learnt it, but not as much, think of it as refreshing your memory, like any musician would."

Chapter 20

They made landfall in the night and Grace and Horis both stood in the wheel-space and watched the lights onshore as they approached the Cape of Storms and passed it by. Grace wondered at the safety of her family and what news they would find in Ventis. If Terrance was behind the events in Aserol even now he could be searching for them. Horis had told her that the man did not like the provinces so he doubted he would venture out in person. It was more likely that he would send someone to do his dirty deeds for him. In the city he had used the thugs Grace had seen at the hotel, and again when Greive had been slain. Even in his reduced position, she suspected that he would keep removed from the actual acts of violence he wished to perpetrate.

And Horis knew that Terrance, despite his bluster, was a coward at heart; he had thought himself such but had realised during the rescue of Grace and afterwards that he was not, even though Maloney had done most of the work he felt that he had acquitted himself well.

The next day when the sun rose the Cape was far astern and they were approaching Ventis, so much had happened since the last time he had been here. He thought sadly of Grieve, the foreman from the mine, he had escaped the killings at the mine and they had met him wandering here. He had joined their band but had been killed in Metropol City.

As was usual in Ventis they anchored outside the stone breakwater and the boats swarmed out. The customs boarded and there was an agonising wait for Horis and Grace as they completed formalities. Hector had warned them that, because of the official enmity between the countries, vessels arriving from Tarpitt were often searched, to ensure that subversives were not gaining entry. What if their names were on a list and they were detained?

Eventually the customs men departed with bulging bags of luxury items, satisfied as to everyone's provenance. They were minded to go ashore to send messages but Hector stopped them.

"Be warned," he said, "the customs have a list of undesirables and you are on it, Horis, as is Grace, yet I saw that Maloney was not."

"Then how did they not see our names on the manifest?" asked Horis, puzzled.

"Well it's quite simple," replied the captain. "When I filled it in I amended your names, as I did in the ship's official logbook. Grace Fallowfield and Horis Strongman have become Mr and Mrs Nabbaro. You are both crew members. Horis, you are a sailor and Grace is a stewardess. I hope that is satisfactory to you. As you have realised all your assets, Horis, I considered it prudent to obfuscate somewhat."

Horis was amazed at the foresight of Nabbaro, he had not thought of their return to Norlandia; that was one less thing to worry about.

"Then perhaps I should divest myself of my old identity documents," he said, "and somehow attempt to obtain new ones."

"I can give you a ship's pass," said Hector, "for your excursion ashore. If asked you can say your documents are aboard. There are those on our travels who would furnish you with excellent papers, but do you need them if the life of a farmer is for you, or even the life of a sailor?"

It was true, those in rural life had little need to prove themselves, just as long as they stayed clear of the big cities and dealt in cash they would be safe. A sailor's pass, even on land, was as good a proof as anything for most purposes in a place like Ventis.

They made their way ashore and to the speaker offices. Grace went inside to place a call to Divid whilst Horis went to gaze in the offices of the land agents. Now he had the idea of becoming a farmer he was developing the thought in his head.

Once again he saw that land was cheap, not quite as cheap as in Omnipa but still well within his means; he could tell Grace when she returned. Heartened, he went back to the speaker office.

Grace was outside, in some distress.

Horis took her in his arms. "What is the matter?" he asked.

"I have called," she said. "He was not in the mine, but works now in the yard. Where there was the attack we read of. I had to make another call, not knowing if he was safe. The staff have gone to find him. They will call the office back when they have located him, it may take a few minutes. To my relief he is well, the telephonist told me as much."

"Then that is good," he said. "Don't forget to ask him if he has seen Maloney," he said. "He may have left a message for us."

A woman came out of the office. "Grace Nabbaro," she said. "I have your call on the speaker."

Grace kissed Horis and went inside.

With nothing to do until she returned, and he had the feeling that would be a while, Horis wandered into the marketplace. There were displays of all sorts of fruits and produce and looking at the prices they were asking made Horis aware that farming as an enterprise would never make him rich. But judging by the look of the stallholders, while they might have had little cash, they were well fed and appeared prosperous enough, there was certainly none of them who looked undernourished.

It was obvious that they lived well; he could see that the goods they offered were of the finest quality and imagined that the slightly imperfect items would be for home consumption, being just as wholesome if unattractive. And he would have an advantage, with the cash to buy a farm outright, he might not have the need to use his sales to service a loan.

Horis found a stall where the farmer had set up a small cooking stove and was offering cooked ovine to passers-by; he got into the line of people queueing for a sample. The smell was divine; it had been a while since he had tasted a decent joint of ovine. There had been none aboard the *Swiftsure* for some reason; they had mostly fowl and bovine when meat was on the menu. The ovine seemed a trifle more expensive than the other butchery; maybe that was why Nabbaro never served it.

"Here you are," said the farmer offering him a piece of the cooked meat on a small wooden skewer.

Horis thanked him and bit into the ovine, it was delicious, as fine as any; there was a subtle tang to the flavour that he could not place.

"What do you think, sir," the farmer said. "You'll not find finer ovine hereabouts."

"The ovine is delicious, but why is it that your butchery is more expensive than that of the other stalls?"

The farmer smiled, recognising what he thought was a city dweller.

"The animals graze in my orchards and eat fallen apples all day in the summer and autumn," he said. "It gives the meat a finer flavour, people pay the premium happily."

That explained the tang, it was apple. Horis had not considered the idea of combining fruit and animals on a farm, the novelty value of the meat was something to consider, no doubt one could combine porkers with apples or plums for another unique flavour. This was an interesting idea and would certainly mark his produce out as something special. With a start he realised that he was already thinking like a farmer. Thanking the man he mused on the idea.

Grace came from the office, her head spun with the news she had received; where was Horis? She looked about and spied him in the marketplace, talking to some butcher. She marched over and grabbed his sleeve. "Come, Horis," she said. "I have news!"

The butcher grinned. "Caught you she has," he laughed. "No ale for you today!"

"Oh no," said Horis, "she will drink as much ale as I."

"That one's worth keeping then," he said. Horis showed him the ring on his finger.

"I know," he proudly replied.

"What is it?" Horis asked as they moved away from the stalls.

Grace was distressed. "The trouble at the yard," she said, "that we heard of. Mr Maloney was involved and the men who died, one was a worker called Monte and the other a stranger, Picton was his name. He confessed that he was after Divid."

"What!" Horis gasped, his good humour spoiled. "Was it Terrance's doing? Was he there or did he send someone else to do his bidding?"

"He was not in the yard, although he may have been somewhere in Aserol," she replied. "I knew not that Divid had been moved from the mine to the yard; I imagine he has upset someone in authority," she sighed. "Again!"

"Yet he was still found; that smacks of Terrance."

"Maloney says that the man was his agent," she said, talking quickly, the words a jumble. "I'm so glad that I knew not until today, I would have spent the whole voyage home in distress. This Picton was looking for me, for us, I don't know. He tricked Sayrah at the hotel, to give up intelligence. Apparently he plied her with flattery and wine. She told him of Divid, despite Maloney's pleas for her to keep her counsel. This man went to the yard and accosted Divid's workmates. Fortunately, Maloney had followed him; Divid was alerted and saved by the quick thinking of Maloney."

Horis remembered Sayrah, Sayrah Faith. He had named her 'Sour Face'. If she had been seduced, then the man was brave and must have been desperate for information.

"This man was sent by Terrance?"

"Maloney says so, but Divid knows little more of his thinking. Maloney says we are to keep away from Aserol for a while. Divid tells me that Maloney is leaving to track Terrance down. The man Picton said that Terrance was in Bingham before he was killed. I told him we would stay on the *Swiftsure* and speak again the next time that we could."

Terrance

Chapter 21

Terrance sat in Bingham, waiting for another call from Picton; he was sure that the fellow would solve his problems and looked forward to hearing news of the demise of his enemies. Yet the call never came. He had heard nothing since Picton had told him of his success in tracking Grace's brother and his plans to extract information. Terrance had been amused to hear that Picton had been seduced by the drunken woman. "It's not funny, I have had to change hotels and alter my disguise," said Picton. "I ache all over and I think my back is scratched raw. She believes that because of what we did, we will be wed."

"A fate worse than death?" said Terrance and they had laughed together.

"I will find this Divid at the yard and let you know what transpires," Picton said, ending the call.

He was becoming tired of being cooped up in the house with the Walsinghams, save for a few excursions into the town, and there was little enough there, he felt unable to go too far. Despite the fact that Picton had agreed to call in the evenings, he was still frightened that he would miss the call when it came.

He had tried to befriend Walsingham, taking an interest in his endeavours. These had turned out to be a book of memoires, of his life in the army and the wars that had cost him his legs. The words he had written were not perfect but conveyed the horror of war and the mental battles of a cripple in a powerful way. Terrance was moved to read them and more sympathetic to the man. However, he could see that the work would never be published, it was far too critical of the regime and its rulers to see the light of day in any respectable publishing house.

He hesitated to tell Walsingham that, it would take what little hope he had left. Instead, he encouraged his efforts and suggested things from his own knowledge of the government for inclusion. The result was the start of a grudging friendship and a share of Walsingham's store of spirit after dinner had been consumed.

Regrettably though, he was beginning to find himself more and more the subject of Mrs Walsingham's attention.

She would touch his arm or press herself into him as they passed, clumsily and apologetic at first then more brazenly as time went on. To begin with the contact was when they were alone, and then it progressed until she would do so in full view of her husband or the maid. Terrance did not respond at first, apart from an occasional 'excuse me' to avoid drawing the man's attention to his wife's behaviour. He was sure from the narrowed eyes and grimaces that Walsingham had noticed. The maid pretended not to notice, but he got the impression that she was not shocked; perhaps Mrs Walsingham behaved so with all her guests.

Inside he was torn, his plans were coming to fruition, the last thing he needed now was a complication. He may no longer be the subject of sarcastic remarks from Walsingham, how long would that last if she continued?

He was sure that an offer was being made but, as pleasant a diversion as it might have been, there was still a trained killer to be reckoned with. One who would not take kindly to such things, and to one whom he had come to feel some respect for.

After three days of hearing nothing, although he had been forbidden, he went to Picton's office in the morn. The girl was still there and she gave him a scowl when he walked up to her desk.

"Mr Picton told you not to come here again," she said. "He will call you."

"It has been three days," Terrance said. "He called regularly, every two nights, before then."

"Maybe things are at a delicate stage," she said. "He could be unable to call, you must be patient, now I'll repeat it again, do not come here another time."

Chastened, Terrance left, but he had a feeling in his stomach that things were not good. He passed a street vendor with his pile of the latest news held down by a stone.

"All the latest," the boy shouted. "Murder in Aserol, two slain."

Terrance bought a copy and returned to his room; Mrs Walsingham had taken to bringing him char in the afternoon, while her husband slept. He fancied that there was more to it than just the actions of a good host, he was spending more time in his room because she said that she never ventured upstairs, his idea had been to dissuade her from pursuit. She was attractive but there was a growing reticence on his part to succumb.

The presence of her husband, even though he was unable to climb the stairs, unsettled him. The man was a brave soldier and Terrance felt inadequate beside him, and he was coming to like him and felt torn. The logical thing to do would be to leave but until he had spoken to Picton he could not.

The few times that Mrs Walsingham had been alone with him in the dining room, it seemed that she was fighting herself, that she was desperate for him yet unwilling to take the fatal step. He had heard shouts in the night, and feminine sobs, all of that told him there was unhappiness between husband and wife. Yet he needed her to make the move, in his mind that would justify his actions, he would then merely be reacting, not instigating.

He was settled on the bed with the news, and had just started to read of the events in Aserol. Mrs Walsingham knocked on the door with a cry of, "Char for you, sir. Are you decent?"

Muttering, as he had just reached the part about the corpses in the coal yard, he shouted, "The door is open."

She entered and Terrance could see on her face that she had

made her decision. Today was the day to which she had been building over the last week. She wore a gown he had not seen before. It was not her usual black one, it had a brighter pattern, the skirt was split, showing her thighs, her corset was half unbuttoned and she had applied more rouge than usual, he fancied that it even adorned her knees. It seemed that she had made her decision.

"Mr Terrance," she began, sitting on a chair opposite him, the skirt falling open, "can you help me?"

She laid the char tray down and moved to sit next to him on the bed, removing the news-sheet from his grip.

"What can I do to help you, madam? Should you not be asking your husband for help?" he said.

She shuddered beside him. "He has come back from the war with more than his legs missing," she began. "His whole being is changed; he is no longer the man I married."

She put her hand on his thigh. "I have not felt a man's leg for so long," she said. "Forgive me but I can remember the feeling now."

"This is hardly decent," Terrance said, edging sideways. "You are married and so am I."

She started to sob. "But you have your body whole," she said. "I have only memories of a man. Can you not help me?"

"Your husband is downstairs," he said in desperation, tempted though he was. Walsingham was well within his rights to kill him if they were caught like this, and despite the sword and pistol he had close to him, and the use of his legs, he felt that he would be unable to fight a cripple.

"I have given him analgesia," she said. "He will sleep all afternoon, we are quite safe."

She moved her arm from his leg and Terrance relaxed, then tensed as she put it around his waist, pulling them together, as their lips met he tried one last time to dissuade her. "Mrs Walsingham," he said, "this is not right."

"I care not," she said. "I have sent Gloriana home for the day, and I am Hortense."

Their lips met and Terrance forgot about the lack of news from Picton at that point.

Later he awoke, Hortense was asleep beside him, as she sensed him move she too awoke and reached for him. "My husband… it's been such a long time," she muttered as their lips met.

Later still they both slept, the sun was setting as the door opened, Walsingham crawled through it, he must have heaved himself up the stairs and along the corridor with his arms alone, his shortened body looked strange with the empty trouser legs dragging behind the muscular torso. There was no mistaking the look on his face as he pulled himself up as far as he could and gazed across the bed at the sleeping pair, entwined as they were.

Walsingham gave an anguished cry, like a wounded beast which woke Terrance and Hortense. Terrance turned his head, the man's face was inches from his, the arms grasping. A knife was in one fist and Terrance wriggled desperately backwards across the bed, out of its range as it slashed at him. Hortense was shoved unceremoniously onto the floor by his actions but he evaded the swinging knife, the arm holding it was then tangled in the bedclothes as Hortense stood and threw the counterpane over her husband's form.

"I'll kill you both," shouted Walsingham, his voice muffled by the bedclothes. "Wife, you are naught but a whore!" He heard the knife clatter to the floor as Walsingham flailed his arms.

Terrance had also stood at this point and naked he ran to his suitcase. He pulled the gas pistol from its holster and swung it towards the thrashing form of Walsingham, who was untangling himself from the counterpane. He fired but as he did, Hortense threw herself at him, she was screaming, "No, No." He stumbled and the projectile thumped into the door frame. Terrance stood upright again and aimed the pistol for another shot. He had five more rounds loaded in the butt of the pistol and was unsure of what to do. Hortense had gone to her husband and pulled the last of the bedclothes from his torso. "My love, forgive me," she said to him. "I tried not to succumb but he made me."

Terrance's breath felt like it had been taken by her brazen untruth. "You seduced me," he shouted. "I pushed you away but you persisted."

Walsingham looked at his wife. "Liar!" he said. "I've seen the way you look at men since I returned, comparing them to your crippled spouse, I never meant to come back to you like this." He swung his arm at her, blood spurted as her nose was shattered. She screamed and slid sideways, away from him. Terrance stood, frozen with fear at the sudden violence. Walsingham, trained as he was, never hesitated. He picked up the knife again and advanced on Terrance.

Terrance could not believe that a legless man could move so quickly. Walsingham wriggled like an eel and drove himself forward on his massive arms. Terrance backed until he came to the wall. The man was six feet away. He paused and raised himself up on one elbow; he pointed the knife at Terrance's groin. "I will make you as I am," he shouted, then he dropped to the floor and resumed his forward motion. His arm reached out to grab Terrance, the other swung the knife. In blind panic Terrance fired his pistol at the man until the hammer fell on an empty chamber.

Walsingham was dead and there was blood everywhere, it coated the walls and pooled on the floor, there was a metallic odour. One of his bullets must have hit an artery in Walsingham's chest and as he convulsed in his death throes the blood had sprayed the room. There seemed to be such a large amount for a man with no legs.

Terrance staggered over to his bag and reloaded the pistol with trembling fingers. As he was bent to his task Hortense must have come to her senses and seen the charnel house that was the bedroom. Silently she got to her feet and crossed the room towards her husband's corpse.

Terrance completed his task and rose, he turned to see the knife in Hortense's hand flash towards him. "You have killed my man, you will..." she screamed, the sound cut short as Terrance, by now reduced to a mental wreck, fired his pistol again, just once.

Hortense looked down at the wound in her chest, her camisole staining red, her eyes glazed and blood bubbled from her lips as she tried to speak.

"Together again," she whispered as she fell and laid still.

Terrance slumped to the floor, sitting beside her corpse in a growing pool of warm blood but he scarcely noticed. What had he done? His mind was numbed, events had moved so quickly and now his situation had got so much more complex.

He knew the law; Walsingham would have been within his rights to kill him, and his wife, for their actions. He was now a murderer and could expect no mercy from a judge. It would be the noose for him. Especially, he realised, if Cavendish got to hear of things.

At least Hortense had dismissed the maid; she would not be back until the morning. Terrance got up and walked towards the washroom, his feet sticking in the congealing blood. He needed to dress, then he could commence hiding the evidence.

Terrance found bed sheets in a fancy cupboard; it looked to be foreign, with many shelves and spaces for linens behind ornate, carved doors. Walsingham must have brought it back from his travels with the army. He wrapped the bodies and with difficulty manhandled them to the cellar, where they were placed in a dark corner at the back of the cool room, together in death. He piled boxes and crates of produce around them, hoping to conceal them from an idle inspection. Walsingham's body was surprisingly heavy considering it was incomplete, while that of his wife was as light as a feather. Blood dripped onto the stairs as he half carried and half dragged the corpses down to their resting place. When he had them ensconced he closed and bolted the stout door. Hopefully it would hide the inevitable stench of death until he was long gone. He then took warm water and soap and proceeded to wash the room, first with a cloth on the walls and then with a mop on the wooden floorboards. He suspected that blood would have dripped between them but that was beyond his means to lift every one. Again, he was hopeful that he would be away before too long. Finally he cleaned the stairs and passageway, then took his clothes and the stained bedding and consigned it to the heating furnace. Drawing hot water, and with fresh lye and soap he bathed, scrubbing his body raw as he sought to remove the blood and its memory from his skin.

By the time he had finished his bath, it was the middle of the night and he realised that he was hungry. He found bread and cheese and made a meal, drawing a large stone jug of Walsingham's ale from the barrel in the cellar. Then he remembered the news-sheet, he had been reading of deaths in Aserol before Mrs Walsingham had come in and the nightmare had started. He went and fetched the sheet to read whilst he ate.

While he read, he considered the implications of the news. Picton was not mentioned as one of the victims, one was a miner, Montague Branchworth, the identity of the other was unknown but he was said to be a well-dressed gentleman. The sheet noted that his anonymity was an offence in itself, punishable by imprisonment. The article ended by saying that enquiries were 'continuing'. There was no mention of the name Maloney in the report. Terrance faced the facts; Picton had not been in touch since he had said he was on the way to Grace's parents' house. That meant there were really only two possibilities. Either Picton had completed his task and was even now on the way home, or most likely he was the unknown dead man in Aserol.

His flagon was empty, he refilled it from the jug, it was a tasty ale, and one that Walsingham in life had not seen fit to share with him. He was leaving the house anyway, the question was, where to go? He decided to sleep on it.

He slept remarkably well; maybe it was with the help of the ale and awoke to a bright morn, with the sound of Gloriana arrived and bustling in the kitchen.

Gloriana, he had been fortunate with her absence yesterday, she would have to be got rid of. She could not be allowed into the cool room. Quickly he dressed and went downstairs.

Gloriana was preparing their fast-breaker, porker sizzled on the range and char was brewing.

"Oh good morn, sir," she said when he entered the kitchen. "It's not usual for you to be up first, where is Madam? I must away and help her get Mr Walsingham into his clothes and chair for the day."

"They're not here," blurted out Terrance. "They had to go to see family yesterday, some emergency I think, they were all of a rush."

She frowned, suspicious. "No, sir, family you say, what in Bingham?"

"I know not," he answered. "Only that they asked me if I would be staying here for another two weeks or so, and if so could I mind the house."

She nodded, much to Terrance's relief, his lies had been believed. "I will ask Viola tomorrow, Mrs Walsingham will have told her sister where she was bound. Tomorrow is my rest day. I assume I am to continue in my duties in their absence, today is my day for cleaning the house and washing the bedding."

This was going badly, Terrance could hardly let her clean the house, she would surely spot something that he had missed. Not only that, she would find Walsingham's chair in their bedroom. He should have moved it out of sight. He had to think on his feet. If he kept her here that would be bad, if he sent her away she would seek out the sister and probably come back once she found that his story was false.

"There is no need to clean today," he said. "There is no-one here but me, all that can be left for another day."

"Then what am I to do?" she asked. "I cannot be here and not work."

Terrance had a thought. "I know," he said, "why not prepare food for me to last a few days. I will help you fetch and carry, I am waiting for a call on the speaker. You can then have more than a day of rest. Why, you need not return until after your next rest day. They may not be back before then. I will make but little mess for you to clean; a day will do it."

She brightened. "A whole week's holiday," she said in disbelief. "You would do that for me?"

"Yes of course," Terrance nodded vigorously. "Make me bread and pie for a week to seal the bargain. And maybe some sort of sweet concoction. It can be our secret, I will not tell if asked. Now, what do you need from the cool room and I will fetch it?"

When Gloriana departed in the late afternoon, Terrance was relieved. He had assuaged her curiosity, kept her in the kitchen all day and she, in turn, had provided enough food for his travels. He waited until she had gone through the gate and locked it behind her. He had decided what to do, he would go to Ventis, the *Swiftsure* would arrive there eventually. Picton, alive or dead, was no use to him now; he would have to finish this himself.

Viola arrived that evening for a visit. Gloriana had gone straight to her and asked where her sister had gone and of course she had known nothing. She had heard nothing from Picton, she needed to see Terrance to find out what was going on. Finding the gate locked up, she peered through, a light was on downstairs. Terrance must be in residence and had locked up for the night. All was well then; he was looking after the house. She went home, resolving to come back on her way to work in the morning.

Terrance spent one more night at the house; he decided that before he left, to cover his tracks he should make it appear that a violent burglary had taken place. Before he began, he located the strongbox in the master bedroom and smashed it open. There was a large quantity of money inside, together with diamonds and jewellery, these he took as payment for his troubles. He next spent several hours smashing furniture and covering the rooms with the contents of the cupboards. He broke for a meal and a rest, satisfied with his work. Just after luncheon, he packed up his things and departed for Ventis, leaving the front door and gate wide open as he went.

Horis and Grace

Chapter 22

And so the *Swiftsure* sailed on, after about half of the cargo was discharged in Ventis they sailed on to Metropol City.

As they approached the port, the crew were on the deck preparing the mooring ropes and the gangway when there was a noise from the air. They all stopped what they were doing to gaze at the source of the noise, as it flew sedately over them. It seemed such a solid thing to be aloft, it appeared to be flying in circles over the city and the sea.

"Look, Horis, a flying machine," shouted Grace. Horis, who had only had glimpses from the inside of the steam lorry of the flyers in Northcastle looked on with amazement as the thing flew over them, no doubt it was on its way to land in the great park. Horis left his place of work and went to stand with her.

This machine was so much different to the ones that Grace remembered, it was much larger for one thing, and it had two engines, one on each of its vast wings.

"I wonder who the flyer is?" she said as he arrived. "It may be Ralf and I would dearly like to see him again, to thank him for his kindness."

Horis no longer got out of breath from the climb up from the main deck to the wheel-space, and it no longer surprised him. If he could have gone back to his rooms, or his job in the Ministry, they would never have known him. He no longer had need of the clothes he had left behind; they would not fit him now anyway.

"I should also like to see him and tell him the same, yet we could never do that without revealing ourselves," said Horis. "It would not be safe, we must remain incognito."

"I know," she replied, sadness in her eyes.

"Hey, Horis," shouted Winthrop. "Come back here. You're supposed to be helping us tie the ship up."

Horis waved, kissed Grace and ran back to his station. They secured to the wharf and as they walked back aft, Horis saw a familiar face in the crowd of stevedores who waited to board. He practically flew into their cabin. "Grace, quick!" he shouted. "There is someone here to see us."

"Who can it be," she said but Horis had already gone. She followed him at a more sedate pace and found him clasped in an embrace at the head of the gangway, oblivious to the ribald calls of passing men.

The two moved apart, it was Keen who had come to greet them and Grace took a turn to embrace him as well. "What are you doing here, Mr Keen?" she said. "It is so good to know that you escaped from Northcastle and made it safe to the city."

"I have a message for you from Maloney," he said. "We were told by him to watch for you."

"We spoke to my brother in Aserol recently," Grace said. "He told us of trouble in the railyard and how he was nearly captured by the agent of that fiend Terrance."

"Ah but there is so much more to the tale," he said gravely. "I could tell you here but if you have time, how would you like to come with me to the barracks? Sapper and the others would be pleased to see you again and talk of old times."

Neither of them had to consider it for long. "We would be delighted," they said, almost together. Knowing that Terrance was most likely in Bingham it was safe enough to go with Keen to the barracks and see the soldiers who had been instrumental in their rescue. They settled Keen in the messroom with char and Horis went to dress in cleaner clothes. Grace told Nabbaro of their plans, he offered to send a crewman with them for their safety but she declined. "Thank you, Uncle," she said, "but if Mr Keen cannot keep us safe then we are safe nowhere."

The pair went to the barracks on a steam omnibus. Keen chattered about what the soldiers had been up to since they returned from the north. He would not talk about the events in Northcastle though. "I'll leave that until we are all gathered," was all he would say.

Even though it was not a holiday or festival Horis and Grace were surprised to see that the streets were lined with bunting. Metal barriers were also arranged to keep crowds back, although the streets were presently deserted.

"What's the reason for all the decoration?" asked Horis. "Is it to do with the flying machine we spied this morning as we docked?"

"It is," he confirmed. "A flyer has arrived from the north, First Minister Cavendish has brought him here to show the country and the world what he achieved when he was in charge in Northcastle."

Grace gasped. "But that was Terrance's doing. Goodness knows I have no love for the man but he was in control of the place where that machine was developed. And I should know! I wonder if Ralf will be the pilot?"

"That was the name," said Keen. "Ralf something, anyway he is to be feted in the city; he and Cavendish will parade together this very afternoon."

"We were talking of him when we saw the machine," said Grace. "I wish that I could see him again."

They reached the gate and Keen showed the guard his pass. The man recognised Horis by name. "You were the gentleman with Maloney a while ago, were you not?" he asked.

"I was," replied Horis. "I know he is not present, today we are guests of Mr Keen here."

"You are both most welcome," he said, raising the barrier.

Sapper was playing cards with his mates when he saw the pair. He rose and embraced Horis, then turned his attention to Grace. He held her till she gasped. "You look so much better than the last time I saw you," he said. She flushed at the truth of the compliment, in Northcastle she had been thin and undernourished, now she was in the full bloom of youth and good health.

"Well thank you, Sapper. I am recovered from my ordeal, thanks to you and your comrades. Where are they all? I would dearly like to see them again."

Keen went off to round up the rest of the men and soon they were all there, Sapper, Keen, Wilson and the rest.

"Where is Mr Meek?" asked Horis, noticing the man was not present.

"Sadly, we ran into trouble on our escape," Sapper said and proceeded to recount the tale of their battle at the fence. Horis went silent and Grace shed a tear to learn of the loss of Meek. Then they both gasped when Sapper described the intervention of the flyer. "When I heard the thing I thought we were all goners for sure," he said, and the others nodded.

"We had seen what it did to the Drogans and that was enough," added Wilson. "I was digging in that heather like a lupine." There were nods.

"It must have been Ralf." She explained how he had aided her whilst she was imprisoned. "He said he would help me, I hope that it would not have cost him."

"I think that it has not become known," said Sapper. "For he is the new favourite of the military. Let us get more char and we can hear your news."

"So where have you been, and what adventures have you had since we last met?" asked Sapper when the char had been fetched and they were all comfortable. "Unless I'm mistaken that is a fine betrothal ring that I see on your finger?"

Grace blushed. "Yes, Horis and I are wed and we have been on my uncle's ship whilst the fuss died down. We have voyaged to the west but beyond all else we desire to return to settle in Norlandia."

Sapper nodded. "The call of home is strong eh, it was always so when we were at war."

Horis then described his wedding, which drew a cheer, and his learning of the sailors' arts, to less approval, after all there was a rivalry between army and navy. Grace interrupted with snippets where Horis missed things out or told it wrong. But they never mentioned the Fenesh or the whistle.

"She has your measure," Sapper laughed.

"I would rather have her by my side with all her corrections than her be left in that place," he said. "I never had the chance to thank you properly and so I had to come here and say it today. Thank you one and all."

There was embarrassment and shuffling among the men. Wilson spoke for them. "We enjoyed it," he said. "It was just like old times, one last hurrah before the rigours of civilian life."

"What will you do now?"

"Who knows," the soldier said. "We need jobs and there are few, machines do much manual work and we are only educated in killing, there is not much call for that in legal employment. And there had been much upheaval lately, resulting from the events in the north."

There were mutterings of agreement from the men. "The government has changed because of it, you may have heard. Terrance is out of favour and Cavendish is running things now."

"We learnt of that, a turn-up and no mistake." Horis joined the conversation. "That was never part of our plan, we have seen parts of the news, in Tarpitt we saw a news-sheet."

"But that would be the lies of the foreigners," said Keen, and there was laughter.

"Even so," said Sapper, "the country is the worse for Cavendish, who lacks the subtlety of his predecessor."

"But the bigger news is that your friend Ralf is flying all over the land in his plane, as we must now call it," Daniel joined in the conversation. "There is talk of a bigger machine, one that will carry more people or goods. Did you see it today?"

"We saw a flying machine this morning as we crossed the bay," said Grace. "I have already wondered if I could see Ralf again."

"That would not be possible, he will be meeting with Cavendish and the government. You would not be allowed near him, unless...?"

"What is on your mind, Sapper?" said Horis; he recognised the look in the man's eye.

"We could maybe get a message to him," Sapper said. "If we can find where he will be staying during his time here."

"I will write something and leave it with you, have you paper?"

There was a flurry to provide it and Grace wrote a few short paragraphs.

"What has Maloney told you?" she asked as she sealed the note in an envelope. "I spoke to my brother in Aserol recently, he told me of the attack at the yard, by some accomplice of Terrance, but the man was killed."

"Well Maloney found out more after that," Sapper said. "The fellow tricked information from someone at the hotel, to locate you, his intention was unclear but I suspect that it involved luring you to Aserol."

This was what Divid had said. "The question is, where is Maloney now?"

"The last I heard, he was on his way to Bingham, on Terrance's trail, he cautions you to remain on the ship, or under the protection of false names should you decide to settle ashore."

Horis digested this information, the soldiers knew nothing more than Divid had told them, the message was the same. He held Grace's hand firmly, his duty was to keep her safe and at the moment that meant there was only the life of a sailor, or skulking under a false name to look forward to.

"What are your plans?" asked Sapper. "You mentioned living aboard ship, will you be forever a sailor?"

"Oh no," said Horis. "I've enjoyed it but I'm a confirmed landsman. I seek a small farm in the south, maybe Omnipa or

Ventis. I wish to grow a few apples and raise ovines, there was a man in Ventis told me all about it."

Grace smiled, she was in agreement, she had seen enough adventures and as long as she was with her man, she would be contented.

"But what of your safety?" asked Sapper. "Terrance has tried once to kill you, maybe he will try again if Cavendish doesn't get to him or you first."

"I think that Cavendish will leave us be," said Horis. "After all he has his desires and there would be little we could do to take them. Terrance is another thing though, he will see us as his nemesis, especially if he has been thwarted, as it appears that he was in Aserol."

"I imagine he will try again," said Sapper, "if he has naught to lose."

"I've always fancied the life of a farmer," said Daniel, his arm had mended from his wound at the battle of the fence, like all the soldiers he was awaiting discharge and a new life as a civilian. "I come from farming stock, I for one would be delighted to come and work for you on a farm."

"Well I may need farmhands 'tis true," said Horis with a laugh. "But could you really work for me?"

"You'd be a lot better to work for than Maloney," said Keen and there was more laughter.

"Well then, I will have to see, once I get myself organised." Horis was pleased, his plans were coming together; with men like Daniel by his side and possibly a trained Drogan as well, they would be safe.

It was after luncheon time. "I'd better see you safe back to the *Swiftsure,*" suggested Sapper. "Before the roads are closed off for the procession of the flyer. I'm afraid that I cannot offer you food, our mess is sparse and is not for civilians, I apologise for that."

"No matter," said Horis. "I'm full of char anyway, it has been wonderful to see you all again, save poor Meek, I shall feel guilt for that."

"You should not," Sapper told him. "He was doing what he loved and there is no finer way to go."

Sapper took them out through the gate; the difference from their arrival was immediately noticeable. The street was crowded with people of all sorts, working men, women with babes and children, the young and the old. They filled the pavements and spilled into the road, forcing mobiles to swerve and blast their horns.

And all the talk was of the flyer and the plane, those who had spied it were telling of it to those who had not and everywhere there were flags. The crowds sang patriotic songs as they moved towards the high road from the park into the centre of the city.

There was a good queue for the omnibus but they secured seats on the second one which came and headed towards the docks. But it had only got halfway there when it was forced to stop by a Watchman. He was stood at a junction, in front of a metal barrier, almost lost in the swirl of people. He climbed onto the omnibus and called for attention.

"Citizens! The roadway is closed," he said, "for the glorious flyer's procession."

"Then we shall have to walk," said Sapper and the three disembarked into the throng.

"Keep close to me," said Sapper. "If we are separated we will never find each other in this crowd."

They fought their way down the street towards the docks, as they did they could hear a band approaching. Over the heads of those squashed up against the barriers they could see that a parade was passing on the roadway. Grace stopped, and dragged Horis with her, seeing a small gap at the front. "Come in here," she shouted, above the noise. "We may see Ralf." Sapper was twenty feet in front of her when he realised that he was alone. Where had they got to?

Turning, he looked for them, finding them impossible to spot in the throng, which was all now stopped and gazing at the road. The procession was passing, a line of mobiles and lorries decked with bunting rumbled past, with bands standing on their load beds. The crowd cheered and waved their flags. As he scanned the crowd he spotted Grace leaning over the barrier, she was gazing down the road. The roar increased as the flyer, flanked by soldiers and suited ministers, walked towards him, pausing to shake hands and accept flowers.

Grace was at the front of the crowd as Ralf walked past. He shook hands with Horis, then he saw Grace and stopped.

"Can it be?" he said, Grace was too struck to speak, she merely nodded and clasped his outstretched hand.

The uniforms behind him urged him on. "Step lively," one said pushing him forward. "Minister won't wait all day."

Ralf leant forward and whispered in her ear, "Aleksander Hotel, at six, ask for the flyer's suite," he said before moving off.

Sapper pushed his way to them. "Where did you get to? I said we should keep together."

"We are not going to the docks," Horis told him. "Let us find somewhere out of this mayhem and we can explain."

Chapter 23

The Aleksander Hotel was in a quieter and more refined part of the city. Grace, Horis and Sapper waited in the vestibule as a message was dispatched to the suite of rooms that Ralf was using.

"You may go up," the desk clerk said, "in the elevator to the top floor."

Ralf himself opened the door. "Come in, one and all," he said. "I recognised you immediately, Grace, but who are your companions?"

"This is my husband," Grace said. If Ralf was disappointed he never revealed it, merely shook Horis by the hand.

"I have heard of you," he said. "All through her captivity, you were all she spoke of, you are a lucky man, sir."

Horis blushed at that. "Thank you, sir," he said. "Grace has told me of your kindness and help in those dark times, I am grateful."

Ralf smiled. "As I said then, we were both prisoners, merely of differing types; I still am a prisoner in many ways, despite all this." He waved his arm around the luxurious room, with its huge windows looking out over the city towards the park at Brunswick. "As long as I perform and fly. At least I am free up there, with the birds and the Drogans."

"This is my friend Sapper," introduced Horis. "He helped in the events at Northcastle."

"Then you must be one of her rescuers; welcome." Ralf shook him by the hand.

"We have met before," said Sapper, looking him in the eye. "At the fence in Northcastle."

Ralf thought for a moment, in his mind he could see heather and the small band huddled in the gully.

"Ah yes, a moment of sadness, but I believe I did the right thing. Both then, in the heat of the moment, and now, after the luxury of reflection. Fortunately my part in those matters has remained undiscovered. Please sit and we can talk before I am whisked away to some other event where I will be paraded again, like a beast in the circus."

Ralf rang for char and cakes, which arrived almost before he had finished the call. A uniformed waiter wheeled in the trolley and served everyone, before retreating.

They talked of conditions in the camp, Grace's escape and Ralf's plane. Grace remembered most how the number of flyers was reduced every day by crashes and exploding gas tanks, it had always been a relief to her to see that Ralf bore a charmed life and returned each evening.

"Are there still the terrible losses among your comrades?" she asked.

Ralf shook his head. "No, the planes are so much safer now; we seldom lose a pilot unless it is down to his own carelessness. The scientists have introduced many new ideas; it seems that every day there is a better plane than the last. There is a plan to scour the country for suitable landing places. We are to set up a mail service between towns to rival the Rail, without the expense of building lines. And then there are the bigger planes under development. With the new planes that are being developed we may soon be carrying passengers."

Sapper was dubious. "How can that be?" he asked. "Begging your pardon but the weight alone will tax the power of the finest engine, will it not?"

Ralf looked around him. "This is all very secret," he said. "But between us, a discovery has been made that helps with the lift and the speed. I know not what it is, that much is still a secret but I pull a lever and some mechanism makes the plane as light as a feather."

Horis and Grace exchanged glances. "Do you still have it?" she said. In answer Horis pulled the leather pouch from his pocket, attached to the buttonhole by its string.

"What is that?" asked Ralf, and in answer Horis let go of the pouch. Ralf watched incredulously as the pouch bobbed in mid-air, straining to be free of its anchor.

"So that is what all the secrecy is about," said Ralf. "But how did you come by it, this is a new thing that did not happen until after you had... departed?"

"This is one of the first found," explained Horis. "I acquired it in Aserol before I even knew of a plane. I picked this up and my world changed, as did Grace's."

"Fascinating," said Ralf, glancing at the clock on the wall. "I would like to talk all day but I will have to ask you to leave shortly. There are so many demands on me from the government, who bask in the triumphs of others as never before, tonight I am to eat with the First Minister as he launches his new venture, 'The Cavendish Plane Company'. He has a factory making planes and has sold shares in the idea to many in government."

So Cavendish was now making money from the rocks, thought Horis, at the expense of all who had died in the mine. No wonder he needed Terrance out of the way to consolidate his position.

Ralf went on to tell of the grandiose plans of the First Minister, of floating landing places for the navy to take to war and a scheme to draw ever more accurate maps and surveys of the land by plane. "We will be able to identify every hamlet," said Ralf. "Cavendish wishes to bring all into their rightful place in the land."

"Then there will be no place for those who wish for seclusion and freedom from taxation," said Horis. Just as he was about to elaborate, the door opened and a figure in uniform entered. "First Minister Cavendish is nigh," he announced. Horis and Grace looked quickly around for a place to run. Horis put the rock back in his pocket and buttoned the flap. Were they now to be held, caught after everything they had been through by chance?

"Has Cavendish seen either of you before?" Sapper whispered.

Grace shook her head, Horis gulped.

"I met him once long ago," he said. Sapper looked him up and down.

"Ah but I did not recognise you today, you are a shadow of your former self. You will be safe, I think we can bluff our way clear, just do what I do and follow my lead."

More soldiers, with impossible amounts of braid and medals entered the room; they split up and searched the suite. They viewed the three with suspicion and ignored Ralf completely as he stood to attention.

They were faced by an officer. "Who might you three be?" he barked.

"We are family to Ralf, his cousins come to see him in his triumph," said Sapper. Horis and Grace nodded.

"Is that true?" The man was suspicious. "How did you find the place?"

"I spied her in the crowds," said Ralf. "I shouted across to her."

"That was a mistake, and it will cost you," said a voice from the doorway, cold as ice. Ralf turned his head, he snapped to attention and saluted.

"First Minister," he said. "Forgive me, I had not seen them for so long and was desperate to hear news."

Cavendish looked the three over. "Get these bumpkins and turnips out of here," he said. "As for you," he addressed Ralf as they were bundled through the door, "perhaps you had better remember that you only survive because..." The door slammed on the rest of his words.

"Well," said Sapper as they walked away from the hotel, "that was a lucky escape and no mistake."

"I thought I would expire," agreed Grace. "Seeing him standing there, and then relief when he knew not who we were."

"It's obvious that Ralf was right, he is just as much a prisoner as you were."

"Come," said Sapper, "I'll get you back to the ship safe; what a

182

day this has been. Horis, once again you have provided me with excitement and adventure, working on your farm would no doubt be as exciting."

Horis agreed, but he was deep in thought. Cavendish had power now and if not checked could control the country as his personal fief. Whether that was a good or bad thing remained to be seen, as long as he did not become bored and turn his thoughts to settling scores.

Sapper had left them at the dock gate. "You'll be safe enough here," he said. "I must away to the barracks before they lock me out."

"Thank you, Sapper," said Grace, embracing him. "It was so good to see you and your band again."

"I shall send word to you when I get my farm," added Horis. "There may be work if any want it."

Sapper nodded and walked away into the night; he could be a farmer, he decided.

"Did you have a pleasant day with your friends?" asked Hector the next day at the fast-breaker.

"We did, Uncle," answered Grace, making an unusual appearance; normally she enjoyed a late rising and char in bed, courtesy of Horis, but today she was hungry. "We met some old friends, and then First Minister Cavendish himself, although he was not so pleased to see us."

"The First Minister?" said Cuthbert the engineer. "How did you meet him?"

"'Tis a long story," said Horis. "Far too involved for the meal table, let us just say that he is a friend of a friend."

Cuthbert looked impressed, if only he knew the full tale, it was better to let him wonder.

Everyone goes to Ventis

Chapter 24

Maloney stepped from the Ryde in Bingham; he had been released by the Watch the previous day and had spent last night at home with Shirl. Then he had caught the early Ryde north.

Although the Watch were suspicious of his involvement in the deaths at the yard, the workers had all stuck together and no mention had been made of Picton's name. The fact that Picton had carried no identity papers had helped the cause. It was illegal to be unable to produce papers on demand; this alone marked him as more suspicious than Maloney from the start.

"Tell me again, Mr Maloney," said the Watch officer, as they sat in the small room in the Watch House, "why were you in the yard?"

Maloney was relaxed; he could see how this was going. He had enjoyed a leisurely fast-breaker in his cell and this interview felt more like a conversation between friends than a serious interrogation.

"Officer, I saw the man hanging around the yard entrance as I went to visit a friend. It seemed to me like he was up to no good, my suspicions were aroused. I watched as he sneaked into the yard, he waited until the gateman was distracted by traffic and crept in. I alerted Archie, the gateman, and we followed him."

The Watchman nodded. Maloney was known to the Watch as a useful man to have around; he had been helpful to them before. And Archie had told the same, from his bed in the infirmary.

"I see, and what happened then?"

Maloney told him the truth of the events in the yard up to the arrival of the Watch, neglecting to mention names.

"Well it seems the man had a grudge against this Monte, we are trying to find out why. Do you have any ideas?"

Maloney shook his head. "Honestly, no. I knew Monte only in passing."

"That seems satisfactory then." The Watchman made a note. "You may go, Mr Maloney."

He had first gone to the Grand Hotel, pretending to be a relative of Picton come for his luggage. The man had not been at that hotel. Maloney then tried several others before locating the man's things in the Seashore Guest Hotel, a place no more than a flophouse near the docks. For a few notes the porter was happy to let Maloney take the single bag. Maloney was sure its mate had already been sold, along with any items of value. Looking inside, he found only clothes. A more thorough search revealed a secret compartment in the lining containing a stack of papers and a good amount of cash.

He passed a message to Divid and Caln; "If Grace should get in touch, tell her that I have gone to Bingham," he had said. "You must warn them that Terrance is abroad, intent on revenge."

Then, thinking of all possibilities he arranged a speaker call to the barracks in Metropol City.

Sapper was delighted to hear from Maloney. "Hail, sir," he said. "What news from sunny Aserol?"

"Sapper," said Maloney, "I need you to keep an eye for the *Swiftsure* in the port."

"Why so?"

"Our man is not yet clear of danger," he replied, going on to tell of the events since his return. "So if you see the vessel; get a message to Horis."

"I will," said Sapper. "I liked the man, he deserves peace, leave it with me."

Once again Shirl bade her man farewell in the dawn. "When will you stop saving everyone else?" she asked as he went to the door.

"I cannot leave this half done, Shirl," he said. "The fellow needs protecting, and I have to finish what I started, you know that."

Shirl nodded, she was an army wife and daughter, she understood. "Then be careful," she said. "One arm is enough to lose."

"I will, my love," he said. "Tell Permilia and Bess, if you should see them, that all will be well." He hefted his bag and set off for the Rail.

Now, stood on the platform in Bingham, he set out to put his plan into action. He had spent the journey considering the best way to approach things. First he would have to find Picton's offices and the whereabouts of Terrance. Then he supposed that he would have to take events as they came. The papers he had recovered revealed little. Just his name and that of Horis and Grace. There were a few notes from his conversation with Sayrah, and the last thing was a record of a call to Terrance, saying he knew Divid's location and would proceed as he saw fit. There was the address of a legal office in Metropol City and a receipt for papers deposited. That may be of some use later, he thought. Horis deserved to reap any rewards from Picton's death that he could.

The news-seller at the Rail station gave him directions to Picton's place of business. As he walked through the town of Bingham he could see that it was as prosperous as Aserol, though less so than Metropol City. There were many mobiles on the street, the coal yards were full and smoke plumed from the chimneys of the Locals. And the shops were full of the latest goods; the residents were well dressed and seemed happy.

Picton's Investigative Agency was located in a large brick building on a corner of the main street. Clearly it was, or had been a place of importance, although close up the paint was peeling on the window frames. The rooms, once he went inside, were dusty and smelt of a lack of use.

There was a young woman sat at a large desk, papers strewn over it. She looked up as he entered.

"How may I help you, sir?" she said, her eyes red and full of worry.

"Excuse me," he said. "I'm looking for Mr Picton."

She smiled weakly. "I'm sorry, sir; Mr Picton is presently on a case and unavailable."

"I understand," said Maloney. Wondering how to broach the subject, he decided that honesty was the best way; after all, he was a simple soldier and not used to subterfuges.

"I know of the case he is on," he said, "and I know that harm has befallen him in Aserol."

She looked at him in shock, as if he were the harm, now come to visit itself on her.

"Oh not by me," he said. "I seek no advantage, merely to follow a trail. Picton, rest him, was not at the end of it, as I'm sure you know. I wish to find the next piece."

"Oh sir," she said. "I have had no word from him for several days, and now other things have happened. I saw the news-sheet and wondered. Your arrival may help us both."

"How so?" asked Maloney, perhaps this would be easier than he had expected.

"Well," she continued. "Ah, but where are my manners? Let me make you char, then we can continue in comfort."

She was upset over something, that much was obvious even to Maloney, it would be best to let her relax. He waited patiently till she brought the char.

She sat and poured, offered milk and honey. "Now," she said, "tell me of Picton and I will tell you of the events here. I fear that they are connected somehow."

Maloney gave her an account of Picton's demise, it shocked her and she wept. Maloney, being a practical man sat uncomfortably for a moment then offered his kerchief. She applied it to her tears and smiled thanks.

"I feared it," she said, handing the damp cloth back. "I had a feeling of unease when the client presented himself although he seemed normal on the surface. I gave him my sister's address, she takes lodgers, and now I wish that I had not. My sister has gone silent. I tried the speaker just before you arrived, but it was broken. That in itself is not worrying but I went yesterday and there was no reply. The maid had come here and told me that they had gone away, leaving only Mr Ter… oh, I mean the client in possession of their house." She stopped. "I'm not supposed to give the client's name, it's the rules," she said.

"There, girl," replied Maloney. "I know his name and I would go to your sister's house to speak with this Mr Terrance. I would be most grateful if you accompany me, as a witness to my intentions; which I can assure you are honourable." Maloney felt bad saying that but, he reasoned, his intentions were. It was Terrance's that were not.

Viola looked up at him. "I have no key for the house," she said. "I'm frightened to go inside but I know that I must."

Maloney smiled at her naiveté. As if any determined person needed a key. "That will not be a problem. As long as you give me permission I can get us inside and you need not fear. I will keep you safe."

"Then let us go directly," she said. "I will lock up the office." She bustled about for a bit and returned with her coat.

They stepped into the street. "I feel safe with you, Mr Maloney," she said and took his hand. "Why a glove?" she asked. "You don't have one on your right hand."

Maloney rolled his sleeve up, showing the wood and brass of his artificial arm. "A present from the Western Isles," he said.

Her hand went to her mouth. "Oh… I'm so sorry, you poor man," she said. "But I understand; my sister's husband returned a cripple from the same war."

To make conversation, Maloney asked his name. "Walsingham," she replied and Maloney was jolted by the name; how small was the world.

"I knew of a Walsingham," he said, "a fine soldier. Caught in a blast he was and I thought him dead."

She shook her head. "Not so, although sometimes I wonder at the mercy of it. No, he had no body beneath the hip by the time the medics had saved him. A clockwork chair and a changed disposition, not fortune and glory, were his rewards for that adventure."

Maloney could understand the anguish that Walsingham had felt; it would have been so much worse for him than his own fate.

"Poor man," he said, the words feeling inadequate. "In some respects I was luckier. The Institute selected me for its research. My arm is clockwork and can do most things except feel, and it has saved me from harm on many occasions."

He waggled the fingers and she gasped, "I have never seen a false arm with moving parts, normally the wrist and grip are fixed to enable objects to be held."

Maloney nodded. "If I had been given one of those I could not have borne it. This attaches to my nerves by the science of statics, I think, and the wrist and fingers move, just as your appendage. I only have to remember to wind it daily."

After a short walk, they arrived at the house, the gate was undone. "It was not like this yesterday," she said. "Or this morning as I passed on my way to work. Someone has been here since then."

They walked up the driveway. "I thought you said that the door was locked," Maloney said. "See it now stands open wide."

Viola trembled. "It was yesterday, and this morning, and there was a light on in the kitchen last night."

"Stay behind me," Maloney said as he peered around the doorframe. He saw only chaos inside, the paintings were thrown from the walls and the sideboard in the hallway had its doors opened, broken bottles littered the floor.

Viola pushed past him. "Hortense," she shouted. She raced into the first of the rooms. She put her hand to her mouth in shock at the destruction. "The house has been burgled," she said. "We must call the Watch."

"Not so fast," replied Maloney, as he went into the kitchen. It was deserted and in ruins, smashed plates and cups everywhere. "Let me investigate further before we do that. Wait here."

He walked through the house, inspecting every room, then went upstairs and repeated his perusal. He saw the stripped bed in the rear bedroom and the streaks where the lye had dried on partly cleaned walls. Then he spotted a bullet lodged in the doorframe. There was more here than a robbery; that was just for show.

He returned to the kitchen and saw that on the table were the remains of a meal. Viola was sat down by the range in an armchair, her head in her hands. "What has happened?" she said. "Where are my family, and was I right about Terrance?"

"It seems like a burglary," he said, "but look closer, there has been a lot of destruction but little actual theft. There are valuables that are untouched, and one particular bedchamber has received far more attention than the others."

She looked confused. "What do you mean?"

"I can clearly smell lye and soap in that room," he said. "The smaller one at the rear, if you look closer, there are drying smears on the plaster and floorboards. Someone has cleaned the room, and not very well. The bed has also been stripped and remade. The question is, what have they tried to hide?"

Viola was distraught. "Do you think...?"

Maloney had neglected to say that he had smelt blood, under the sharp odours of the lye and soap mixture. He wanted to cause the lady as little pain as possible and keep her from calling the Watch, they might not be so understanding of him here as in Aserol.

"Are there cellars?" he asked. She nodded and pointed to a door on the far side of the kitchen. "Through there, down the stairs."

Maloney found a gas lamp at the top of the stair together with a box of Lucifer's. These were a new thing to him, a stick coated in some flammable substance that you scratched on a piece of rough card on the side of the box. What was the matter with his patent lighter, a gas filled device he had had for years?

He lit the lamp and, holding it aloft in his mechanical arm, ventured downstairs. There was a wine room, which was empty, save for a barrel of ale and a few dusty bottles. He could hear a stream running as he unbolted and opened a stout door. This space must be the cool room, the running water and thick stone walls kept the temperature low for the storage of cheeses and cured meats.

He swung the lamp around the room; at first glance it was empty, save for a water powered clockwork winder in the corner. That was strange for a house that until recently had been inhabited by at least three people and a maid. Where were the provisions?

As he shone the light further he saw that all the contents had been piled into one corner; that was suspicious, the cool air would not flow properly and do its job. He moved closer. There was the smell of blood again. There must be a side of porker or jointed ovine stored here to cure. He shone his light over the boxes, saw the two objects wrapped in red-stained cotton behind the boxes. With a sinking feeling in his stomach he knew what was there. He had to know if Terrance was in one of the bundles. Cautiously he lifted a corner of the bloody sheet, fearing what he would see. Hortense's shocked face stared back at him.

"Is everything alright?" Viola said. She had come silently down the stairs and was stood at his shoulder. Seasoned soldier that he was, it had still made him start. Hurriedly he dropped the cloth, covering the blank stare. "Is that smell meat?" she added.

"Just some over ripe joint of bovine," he said, moving to hide the things he had seen from her. "Can you go and make us some char?"

He meant to distract her, but she would not be moved. "I can see your face," she said. "It's not bovine is it?"

"I'm sorry," he said. Again she pushed past him. She lifted the sheet, her eyes welled up and she staggered in a faint. Maloney held her with his good arm, she was limp and unresponsive. He put the lamp down on a box and managed to lift her up the stairs. He carried her into the front lounge, laying her on an undamaged settee. She was unconscious and breathing lightly. He went back to the cool room and examined the other corpse, finding an unfamiliar face, missing legs and gunshot wounds. It must be Walsingham. That would explain the bullet lodged in the doorframe. If the deaths had been a result of a burglary, then Terrance's corpse should also be here. It was not.

He shut the door as he left the cool room. Murder had been done here, most foully by the look of it and his money was on Terrance having been the murderer. What to do?

If he stayed and called the Watch he would be held up for days, and Terrance, wherever he had gone, would never be found. On the other hand, he could not leave the girl here; to wake alone knowing what lay in the cellar would mortify her. He picked up the speaker handset, there was no buzzing. The connection was broken.

Walking back into the kitchen he saw a scrap of paper on the table, partly hidden under the mess. In a firm hand was written the times of the Rydes to Ploughtown; that was the last stop on the Rail towards Ventis. The Rail line was not yet complete, steam lorries and omnibuses, together with equine-drawn wagons plied the last miles into the town. The word *Swiftsure* was also written down on the paper. Maloney put the scrap in his pocket; he knew now where Terrance was headed.

He checked on Viola, she was still unconscious; he thought again of how he might tell the Watch without being held by them, then he had an idea. He looked behind the speaker, the wire was cut but there was enough slack for him to repair it. He hunted in the kitchen drawers for some tools that he could use to repair the circuit.

It was the work of a few moments to bare and twist the wires together, reconnecting the apparatus. Maloney jiggled the switch to attract the attention of the exchange, with a kerchief over the mouthpiece, damp from Viola's tears he noted, he muffled his voice and asked for the Watch to be directed to the house.

Quickly he shouldered his pack and went outside, through the side gate into a lane. He kept out of sight as a Watch wagon drew up outside the house and several Watchmen entered. A moment later one came out. "There is an unconscious lady, bring a stretcher," the uniformed man called to his mates. Maloney loped away, keeping to the back streets. Viola would be safe now, while he was in the clear and on the way to Ventis. Terrance had quite a start on him but with luck he could catch up before he found Horis and Grace.

Horis buys a farm

Chapter 25

Meantime, while all this was occurring, Horis and Grace were back in Ventis. Having sailed from Metropol City to proceed to a loading port, the *Swiftsure* developed a problem with the pumps that supplied cooling water to the engine. They were closer to Ventis than to Metropol City when the fault became apparent. Hector and Cuthbert had nursed the vessel into the anchorage at slow speed. Now they needed a part that the ship could not repair. On arrival, the agents boarded and Hector explained the problem, they left with drawings and instructions to finds a smithy.

"I feel that Ventis is a better place to settle than Omnipa," Grace said as they watched the boats plying their trade around the anchorage. There were fishers setting off for the day's work and an air of industry. "It has speakers, unlike Omnipa, so I would not be out of touch with my family."

"I understand that," Horis answered. "The property prices are a trifle more here but we can have a good life. I still hanker after raising ovines and growing apples, here is as good a place as any. There are fewer ovines so the price for their meat and wool will be higher. Apple liquor from Ventis is famed and sold all over the country, even in Metropol City itself. Also," he added, "the weather here is as good as it is in Aserol, or even Omnipa itself."

"You can farm what you like," Grace said. "I know you will make a good job of whatever you turn to. As long as the property comes with a stout dwelling I will be contented. At least two bedchambers would be essential for what I have in mind."

"Why might that be that we need two?" enquired Horis. "Surely one will suffice."

She gave him a despairing look. "You will just have to trust that I know of what I speak," she said.

With several days to wait before they could set off again, they took a boat ashore. They planned to spend time investigating the situation with farms that might be for sale. Horis returned to the market, to see if the farmer he had spoken to before was attending; maybe he would have information. Grace went to call Divid on the speaker and look at the other stalls for household items that they would need to furnish a home together.

The stallholder with the apple flavoured ovine was there and he recognised Horis. "Hail," he greeted him. "You have escaped from the lady again then."

Horis joined in the joshing. "I have slipped my leash," he said. "But," and he brandished the whistle, "I can call her back when I need to."

The man looked at the whistle, surprise on his features. "Where did you get one of those?" he asked. "I had you down as a townsman."

Horis smiled. "I am, or at least I was, I was persuaded to buy this thing whilst I was in Tarpitt. I was fooled by the salesman's patter. When I tried to call my wife with it, I found that it does not work. Even so, I produce it when I am vexed with her, we laugh together and forget our quarrels."

The man gave him a strange look and Horis wondered if he had said too much. "We're interested in settling in Ventis," he said quickly. "We seek a business and dwelling to make ours."

The man regarded him with interest. "Have you viewed the properties in the land agents?" he suggested.

"I expect that Grace is there now," said Horis, he should have looked there first, but he had an idea of prices and was eager to avoid paying agents fees. "I thought I would ask around in the marketplace, to see if anyone knew of a concern for sale where I might set up home?"

"So you can avoid fees and having to listen to the agent's exaggerations as well," said the man. He put out his hand. "That's very wise. I'm Everdus Filian," he said. "As it happens I have my farm just outside Ventis. It may be for sale if my price is acceptable. There is goodwill with it, I sell my meats and cydir to many, go to the *Dun Cervine* and try a bowl of the stew for your luncheon, the meat in it is from my beasts. Maybe..." he left the words hanging, "...they could be your beasts."

Yes they could, thought Horis. "I will. I'm pleased that I came to see you directly. I'm Horis Stro– er, Nabbaro," Horis replied, the man gave him another strange look. Flustered Horis added, "Stroman, my middle name, I hate it."

"Ha!" Filian replied. "Mine is Brackenbury and I hate that just as much!" They laughed together and Horis warmed to the man, if all in Ventis were like him, life here would be pleasant indeed.

"How should I get to this farm to view it?" asked Horis. "Should I be interested," he added quickly. "Is it easy enough to find?"

"Just leave the town on the road towards Millingard," he said. "Then take the fork signposted to Hobblehaven. Look for the buildings on your left; the farm is called Heatherfall. I am there of an evening."

Filian turned to serve a lady who demanded that he stop chattering and sell her a leg joint. Looking around, Horis tried to imagine himself in the stallholder's place. He would have to learn animal husbandry, how to care for and butcher the beasts and many more things besides. He had the idea of calling on Sapper or one of the soldiers. Daniel or one of them had said that they were from farming stock; they would know what had to be done.

He walked back to the speaker office, Grace was sat outside. "Have you made your call?" he asked.

"No," she said, "there is a fault on the line. They think that brigands may have stolen the wire."

"I'm sure all will be right," Horis said, seeing her fragile look. "Maloney is pursuing Terrance, it's hardly likely that he would go to Bingham and leave Divid unprotected. No news is usually good news."

"I suppose," she said. "But I can't help worrying, letters are all very well but I have no place for replies to be sent."

"Well then," he said triumphantly, "I may have some good news about that."

"What do you mean?"

"Let me explain over a bowl of stew," he said, "The *Dun Cervine* is over there and I have much to tell."

Chapter 26

Horis and Grace found the farm, just where Filian had said it would be, down a secluded lane yet handy for the town. From the first glimpse, it seemed a fine place and they were hopeful that the price would be within their means. They had a few days to decide; the spare part for the *Swiftsure* had been made and was now being fitted and tested. With luck, Filian would be looking for a quick sale or could be talked into one.

It appeared that the premises included a walled orchard, barns and several fields. There were a large number of ovines, and the best thing, a large stone and thatch dwelling built beside a swift running stream. The flow would be diverted to cool a storeroom in the house for fresh food. Horis could also see as they walked to the door that part of the water's flow was diverted via a system of pipes into the house.

Filian was sat outside, enjoying a glass of cydir in the evening sun. "Hail, you two," he said as he saw them approach. "Have you come for what I hope?"

"We have," said Horis. "You told me you wished to sell; well, we may wish to buy."

Filian set down his glass. "Come inside then and I will show you the house first."

They went into the kitchen, the most important room as far as Grace was concerned. She was pleased to find that, as well as the flow of cool water to the store there was a faucet over the sink, there would be no need to go outside for water on a cold morning.

A large log burning range boiled water for heating the house and the steam that was produced powered a small device that could be used to wind clockworks for the various household appliances that Filian had installed. It also drove a small pump which could direct both hot and cold water upstairs to the washroom. All in all, it was a fine proposition. As good as any house in the city and if the price turned out to be more than Horis was prepared to pay, he could console himself with the thought that it was in a quiet, remote place. There was a fine lounge, well-furnished, and upstairs there were three bedchambers, which seemed more than enough.

The only thing that was missing was a gas supply for cooking but there was a plentiful supply of logs and a small coppice which would be adequate. Horis could see that he would be kept very fit running the place; it would be a change, once he got to grips with the routines.

"The house is excellent," Grace remarked as they left it and walked across to the first barn, the stream had also been diverted into it where it drove a huge wooden wheel. By means of a heavy belt and wooden gears, this drove a shaft running along the ceiling of the barn, other belts led to all sorts of machines. Horis looked at them in their ranks, all he wanted to do was raise ovines and pick apples, now there was all this machinery, how would he ever master the use of it?

"What's all this?" he asked.

Filian laughed. "The joys of a modern farmer. These are machines for threshing grain and squeezing apples. There is also a device which winds springs for the portable clockworks." He saw Horis's face. "Don't worry, the pieces are simple to understand and stoutly made. They will give you no trouble; they all have information sheets to explain the rudiments."

"We can get Divid to visit," Grace added. "That's my brother, sir, he drives an Exo, mechanics are his passion."

Filian was relieved; he had seen the sale slipping away. "A grand idea, lady, I'm sure you will soon have the knack of it. Come, there is more to see."

There was another barn but it was sealed tight and they passed it by. Next to it was a stable with a wagon and two equines in a small paddock. "I will be taking them," he said, "to carry my possessions. You will need to get your own; the farrier in town, Absolom Rexwood, will help you in that."

Another thing, thought Horis, buying a cart and keeping an equine. He could see his money evaporating in front of his eyes. The trouble was, he was set on the place, by her comments he was sure that Grace thought the same.

All that was left was to view the fields and orchards, here Horis was on unsafe territory, he knew little of what was good ground. The apple trees he saw were sturdy and had blossom starting to open, which he took as a good sign. Filian waxed in a most glowing way of the orchard.

"Wait till we return to the house," he said, "you can try the cydir and you will see. I also fortify the brew in the small barn. Over the years it ferments into the most potent liquor. I bottle it and sell it, very popular and profitable it is too. All my stock and equipment will be included in the price."

There were stone walled fields, which had been ploughed. "These are for roots, and one is for grains, I grow and thresh for my own use," Filian explained. "Any excess grains I have can make a fiery spirit."

The pastures contained ovines and a few bovines mixed together, they seemed content as they nibbled at the grass. "I let them in the orchard to keep the grass down," said Filian. "They eat the fallen apples in season, it's where the meat gets its flavour."

"Would the beasts be part of the deal?" Grace asked.

"They would indeed, lady," was the reply. "The bovines I keep not for the meat but for the milk and all I can make from it, butter, cheese and the like. I sell the young males but the ovines and the apples make the bulk of my income."

Horis was about to ask who did the milking and dairy work when Grace surprised him. "I can learn to do all those tasks," she said. Horis felt pride, his Grace was ready to embrace the adventure and throw herself into the role.

"If you have ovines, there must be a canine to herd them, will you take it?" she asked. Horis had not considered that point either, his wife was so much better acquainted with the needs of the country; he supposed that he was really just a city dweller, out of place.

Filian said nothing about a canine. "Come back to the house and we will discuss all the details," he said, marching away.

They discussed the price over a large jug of the cydir that Filian had brewed, it was tasty and Horis could see that it had potential for sale if he could find a way of getting it to market. Then he realised that to do that, he would have to make the brew himself, with the next harvest.

"As I mentioned in the market, you will have all my contracts," said Filian. "I have a local butcher who deals with the animals for me; he collects them and sells the meat on my behalf. We supply several establishments with ovines and a fruiterer with apples, the ones I don't keep for the cydir that is. We must also talk of Barnabas."

"What do you think?" Horis asked Grace.

"It is a lovely concern," she replied. "All things considered I think it would suit us well, we could still see Hector when he passed and there is room for Divid and his family to visit and stay if they wish."

Horis liked the sound of that. "Perhaps Maloney could pay us a visit," he suggested. "That would be good, or one of the soldiers to help me work the fields."

"There is more accommodation in the large barn, the shearers use it in season," Filian added.

Grace had a question. "Who is Barnabas? Is he your farmhand, or a canine?"

The man laughed. "No, Barnabas is my guard; he keeps the fields and the beasts safe, he does a little herding of a sort I suppose."

"Would this Barnabas come as part of the sale price?" he asked.

Filian laughed. "Only if he wishes to stay." With a flourish he produced a whistle.

"When I saw you had one, Horis, I wondered, does he know? And I'm sure that, despite your story of it being a love token, you do. Barnabas is not a canine, although he does a lot of the same things."

Horis felt that he had to come clean. He looked at Grace. "Shall we be honest?" he said.

She shrugged. "Why not, it seems that he knows it all anyway."

"I am a follower of Myganth," he said and Filian looked puzzled.

"A what?" he said. "I know not what you mean. I was passed the whistle by the man I bought the place from. He showed me where to place my fingers. Blow it and Barnabas will come, he said. He took me to the field, called it himself and introduced me; that was all, it seems to be aware of what I want. I guess that the last man trained it well."

They went out into the middle of the nearest orchard and Filian blew on his whistle. After a moment there was the flapping of wings and a large Drogan landed in the field in front of the farmer. It folded its wings and turned its head as it looked at the group. Despite his hours of training and the assurances of Seph, Horis felt rooted to the spot, his insides had turned to water, he was unable to move and he held Grace's hand tight. She was not so afeared and gazed straight back into the beast's black eyes.

"Here is Barnabas," Filian said. "He will keep me safe, round up my ovines, as long as I show him what's to be done."

"But can you not control him with the whistle?" asked Horis. "My teacher Hannith, in Tarpitt, showed me that you can order the Drogan to do many things, did you not have the book in your Fenesh?"

Filian looked blank. "In my what? I only call the beast, once it is here it will do what it sees fit. Although," he added, "it seems to have a good grasp of running the place and often I find it has moved the stock or performed some other task unbidden"

"May I presume to converse with it then," said Horis. "As I said,

I learnt the uses of the whistle from a man in the Isles and would like to practise."

Filian shrugged his shoulders. "Do what you will, but I will not be responsible if he bites you."

"But Horis," said Grace, "you will not know his answers without the Fenesh."

That was true. "I will tell him that, if I can recall," he replied. "We will just have to keep it simple."

Horis produced his whistle and tried to remember the tones to make the Drogan understand. But first, he recalled the advice of Hannith; that he should introduce himself. He blew.

Barnabas reared up at the sound, turning his head on one side. Then he took off and flew around the orchard, one full circuit. He swooped and soared, almost as if in celebration. He finally returned to the ground and at a second blast, flapped his wings and squawked loudly. It was plain to see that Barnabas was responding to the notes from the whistle, even that he was pleased in some way to have heard them.

Horis blew a third time; the Drogan waddled forward on its stumpy legs, using the claws on its wings for balance. It bent its head and sniffed at Horis and Grace. After a period of time that felt like several days to Horis, he slowly came to the conclusion that he had said the right thing and that the Drogan was not about to devour him. He reached out and touched the beast's neck; it did not recoil or react in any way.

Grace stretched out her hand and the beast lowered its head and licked her fingers with a red tongue, flicking back and forth like an anguilline's. "It tickles," she laughed and the beast shot its head back, alarmed by the noise. Horis was possessed by a protective urge and moved to stand between the Drogan and his wife. The beast reared up on its legs and beat its wings but Horis was unmoved.

After this display, the Drogan's head returned and butted Horis until he stood aside. Grace moved forward and the beast resumed its licking of her fingers.

"He likes you, madam," Filian said. "And you, sir, that's how it should be. Barnabas will keep you safe, as long as you feed him regular he will not take a beast for himself. Any wild Drogans from the north will not bother you on their migration. You seem to have him more under control than I ever did."

They went back towards the farmhouse. "You go inside, sir," Horis said. "My wife and I wish for a private discussion, we will join you shortly."

Filian nodded. "I will brew fresh char, unless you want more cydir, either way, come in when you are ready."

They stood under the shade of a large tree. Horis knew not what type it was, he could see the Drogan, it was still sat in the field and was watching him. He felt relieved; after his practising, he could now use the whistle in real life.

"I told him that I was a follower of Myganth," he said. "I said that I could not tell what he was saying but that I was a friend. Without the Fenesh I know not his reply."

Grace took him in her arms. "You clever man," she said. "It seems to have accepted us."

They stood in contented silence for a while; the air was filled with the buzzing of bees and the heady scent of fresh earth and new blossoms, at that moment it felt like the best place in the entire world.

"Isn't it just the most beautiful spot," said Grace, taking his hand. "We must live here, and with your skill, the Drogan will keep us safe."

"I agree," said Horis. "Between us, with effort, we can be happy and safe here."

They went into the house.

"Let's to business then," Filian said. "You have seen my farm and its Drogan, and you have drunk my cydir, are you minded to make me an offer for it all?"

Chapter 27

Two days later, Horis and Grace stood on the *Swiftsure*, watching as their few possessions were swung into the waiting boat by the ship's gear. The majority of it was the things that Grace had accumulated over the years of occasional voyaging. Horis, apart from the Fenesh, had little to show; he clutched the box to him and would not allow that item to the vagaries of the ship's derrick. Grace had written long letters to her parents and to Divid, telling them of her new abode and encouraging them to write back or even to visit.

"You are set then," said Hector. "You are to leave me again. At least this time you are not on some mad quest." He paused. "Are you?"

"We are not, Uncle," said Grace, she put her arms around him and held him. "This time we are moving to our new home and starting a quiet life. If a quest came calling, I would send it on its way. Thank you for everything, we will come to see you every time you arrive."

She stepped back. Hector turned to Horis. "As for you," he said, "I don't have to tell you what I did last time, I know you will look after her."

Horis shook his hand. "That I will and we will have a life free from fear in our new home."

Hector could not help but admire the confidence in Horis's tone; he sincerely hoped that they would. He passed a packet across. "Here is the rest of your money," he said. "You will always be welcomed on the *Swiftsure*. Good luck in your new life."

The boat secured to the jetty in the harbour and as promised

Filian was there with his wagon to carry them to their new home. "Have you a wagon and equine yet?" he asked as they rode down the lanes, the sun shining between the trees. To Horis it felt like the first day of a new life, now some practical thing had to spoil it.

"Not yet," he said, "but it's on my list of things to organise, which seems to get longer every time I contemplate it."

Filian nodded. "You will never be short of a task, and that's the truth. Speak to Rexwood, tell him I sent you."

They arrived at Heatherfall and Filian helped them to unload their bags and boxes.

"What is that you hold so tight?" he asked seeing Horis with the Fenesh.

"This is the thing that I thought you had," he said. "The thing that taught me the speech of the Drogan."

Filian looked wistful. "I would like so much to have learnt more from you and maybe to have conversed with Barnabas, there must have been so much that he was saying that I didn't know."

"If you have time," suggested Horis, "I can assist you in that."

Grace stayed in the house while the men went into the field. Filian had made a pile of everything he was taking in the porch, ready to load on his wagon so she had the run of the place. She could arrange the pieces of furniture that he was leaving to her satisfaction. It was wonderful, a home of her own. She had lived in the shared dormitory at the laundry, with her parents, then with her brother's family, never with a private place of her own to set out as she liked. In her mind she pictured more furnishings and newer window dressings; she would have to cajole Horis to provide them for her in due course.

She examined the stove and its water supply; it was so simple to operate, the flow of water was controlled by a sluice and a valve, warm water was produced almost on demand when it was opened. All that was needed was to keep the fire burning, a task familiar to every Norlandian. Grace looked up at a sound, the Drogan had landed in the field and she could see the two men approach it.

She smiled; her man was a constant surprise, as much to him as to her, he mastered every task, despite his initial belief that he would not. Their lives would be happy here, the house felt friendly and welcoming already. She turned from the window and went into the stores to see what provisions there were, she could celebrate their arrival with a meal.

In the field Horis opened the Fenesh and set the paper moving. "Call Barnabas," he said and Filian blew. The farmer was amazed to see the whistle's note on the paper.

"Well I never did," he said. "I understood that it made a sound that I could not hear, to see it is strange after all this time. And you can read the meaning."

"I can," replied Horis. "This call means come and help me."

Barnabas landed at that point and the pen took on a life of its own, dancing across the paper and Horis struggled to keep up with the words.

"What does he say?" asked Filian.

"Greetings-Myganth-Master-Where-Other," Horis said. "It wants to know where Grace is."

"It liked her, what will you say?"

Horis blew. "New-Master-Other-Near." That seemed to satisfy it.

"Tell it that I am going and that you are its new master," suggested Filian. "Then when you are here alone it will not think that you have harmed me."

It seemed like a sensible idea. Horis blew, "Old-Master-Go-I-New-Master." At that Barnabas reared up and flapped his wings, he squawked loudly and was obviously angered. Horis looked quickly at the paper, had he blown the wrong note or said the wrong thing? No, he had sent the correct message; clearly Barnabas was not happy with the idea of a new master.

The Drogan beat his chest and continued its squawking, then it took off and flew into the blue skies, rising higher and higher until it was a mere speck in the distance. Its actions had distracted Horis from the paper; he had to wind the drum back. When he found the message, it said I-Go-Think.

Horis was stunned, he knew not what to say, turning to Filian he repeated the message. He saw a tear in the man's eye.

"He has gone, I know it. I realised that I would not see him again, I could not call him where I was going, it would cause a panic. I wanted to see him one last time and thank him for all his service. I will go, there is naught here for me now."

In silence, Horis and Filian loaded the wagon; Filian took a last look around as he climbed onto the bench seat and took the reins. One equine was in the trace, the other alongside on a halter.

"Goodbye and good luck," he said. "I will be sad to leave the place, even more so now that I know Barnabas has gone from it."

He whipped his equine. The cart, loaded with all his possessions, pulled away down the lane and was soon out of sight.

Chapter 28

As the sound of the wagon receded, Horis took Grace in his arms. "So," he said, "we are farmer and wife; perhaps we should get to grips with our new enterprise."

"Before we do," she said, "I took a look at the Fenesh while you were loading the cart, in among all the squawking Barnabas said one thing before he flew off."

Horis looked at her, excited. "I know I said it right, old master go. I did not provoke his departure did I?"

Grace smiled. "No you did not; you said what you meant to. Barnabas replied I-Go-Think, after that he also said Sad-Talk-Clan-Decide."

Horis was excited. "Then the beasts do show emotion; Hannith and the others were wrong. Do you think he will come back?"

"Who knows, we will just have to call him daily and hope."

For the next week, Horis and Grace set to learning the jobs of a farmer and cydir producer. To assist them in this they found a young man in the town called Baylock. He agreed to give them advice in return for a small wage, topped up with cydir and liquor, which he seemed able to consume all day without effect.

Baylock proved to be invaluable; he took Horis to the town and introduced him to everyone important for his business. He also found them a serviceable cart, together with a small equine, and helped them transport flagons of cydir and liquor to the taverns of Ventis, which made them some money.

Each morning Horis went into the field with the Fenesh and blew for Barnabas, each day he did not appear, and Horis grew more despondent as time passed. Then on the tenth day, this changed, although he had no inkling at the start.

Before Baylock arrived he set out again. "Well I suppose I should try and attract Barnabas," he said and went to put his boots on. "I'm coming with you today," said Grace, her expression resolute enough to halt a Drogan on its own.

Horis went to the centre of the orchard and put the whistle to his lips; would the beast ever return and accept him without Filian here? He blew the call. As every day so far, nothing happened, the seconds stretched into a minute. "Shall I blow again?" he said.

"Give the beast a chance," said Grace.

Then there was the sound of wings, like wind through the trees, and Barnabas appeared in all his glory. He swung in a circle over Horis, the neck twisting as he regarded them. At last he had returned. He must have decided. Horis had a sudden thought, perhaps the beast had only returned to say goodbye.

Barnabas landed softly and folded his wings; the ovines in the field ran into the corner and stood under the hedge, shaking with fear. Horis should have been afraid. To his surprise he realised that he was not. Barnabas had come back and seemed content.

He advanced a pace towards the beast, its weight rested on the stubby feet and the talons at the wing-elbow. On the ground it was ungainly, a different thing to the majestic, soaring master of the air.

Horis advanced another step and the beast moved backwards. Was it afeard of him?

"Barnabas, friend," he said. He blew the whistle again; Stay-Friend, its blast meant and Barnabas stopped retreating and bent his head. The pen scratched, Man-Good-You-Good-Female-Good-Clan-Talk-I-Stay.

Grace read the words with him. "He seems to know you are his new master, and is happy to remain," she said as the Drogan sniffed both of them as delicately as was possible.

When they walked back to the house, Baylock was waiting for his jobs for the day. "I see Barnabas has returned," he said, as if it were the most natural thing.

"You know of him?"

"Oh yes, Barnabas is famed around these parts, as was Filian. If you can control him and he is happy to stay that is good. There was a lot of sorrow in town when Filian said he was leaving. Barnabas regards Ventis as his territory and has kept it quiet for many a year, he allows no other to disrupt us, the local beasts know and keep to the woods nearer to Millingard."

Two mornings later Horis and Grace were awoken by a commotion outside, hurriedly they dressed. Horis grabbed his whistle, they rushed outside.

Barnabas and another Drogan were dancing in the yard, their necks entwined. It seemed violent although neither was trying to bite the other. The sight of the other Drogan brought joy to Horis's heart.

"That is Seph!" said Horis. "I recognise his damaged ear."

"How had he followed us?" said Grace, incredulous at this turn of events.

"I don't know, get the Fenesh, they might be talking to each other."

Grace rushed back into the house and picked up the box, she opened it and brought it outside. Horis had blown his whistle, Stop!

Both Drogans stopped their whirling. They sat, side by side and looked at him. The newcomer was definitely Seph and Horis wondered how he had been found; how had the beast followed him all the way from Tarpitt?

Grace set the Fenesh down on the ground and turned on the clockwork. The pen moved, the Drogans were talking to each other. Horis concentrated on what he wanted to say, his mind assembled the sequence.

"What-You-Do?" blew Horis.

Both beasts looked at him.

Grace studied the paper; she was quicker and more adept than

Horis at reading the line. She called out as the pen drew its line.

"We-Talk," she said. "We-Agree-You-Friend. Then there is another voice, a different pitch, Other-Man-Friend-Him-Gone-I-Go."

She looked at Horis. "What does this mean?" Barnabas squawked and the pen wrote.

Say-Nothing-Read-Later. There was a flurry from the pen. "One or both of them are telling us something," Grace said. "It's too quick, we will have to decipher it later. The line went on for several minutes, then subsided. Barnabas suddenly flapped his wings and lifted into the sky, he rose in a spiral and soon was lost to sight.

The pen scratched again. "There's more," said Grace. "It says I-Seph-Here-Serve-Now-Read-Understand."

Horis blew, "Thank-You," Seph sat impassive.

Grace took the paper. "I will have to study this properly," she said. "There is so much here."

She was ensconced all day in the kitchen, reading and checking what the Drogans had said. Meantime Horis worked in the fields with Baylock. When he had arrived he had told him what had happened.

"There is a new Drogan here?" said Baylock, fear in his voice. "What if he doesn't like me?"

"I know this Drogan from the Isles," Horis told him. "We met there. He has followed me for some reason; Grace is even now deciphering his words."

"I would like to talk to the Drogans," Baylock admitted. Horis remembered what he had been told, teach another to follow you, Salmah had said. He could teach Baylock.

"Grace and I can train you if you wish," he said. "It would mean that I have kept a promise."

Baylock nodded. "Thank you."

They approached Seph. "Seph-New-Friend-I-Teach-Myganth," Horis said and the beast bent to sniff the lad's hand.

"There it is done," Horis told him. "Lessons will commence

once we have finished our work for the day."

At luncheon, which Grace brought out into the orchard, she told him of the message on the paper. Baylock sat apart and ate, he was a good lad, thought Horis and will make a splendid pupil, it will be a joy to teach him after all that he has taught me.

"Baylock wishes to learn the way of the Fenesh," he told Grace as they ate another of her fine pies. She looked surprised.

"Well that was part of what was said, one of the Drogans, I assume it was Seph, suggested it as part of some agreement."

"That's right; Hannith and Salmah both told me to pass the skill on. What else did they say?"

"So much," she said. "I have it in my own words, I cannot read that staccato out for long."

Horis scratched his back against the tree bole that supported him; he was replete with home-made pie and cydir. "Tell me then."

"Well," Grace began, "the two talked at once and it took a lot of effort to untangle but it appears that you have caused a stir. The Drogans in Norlandia know that there are only a few here who can use the Fenesh. There are some who can use the whistle without knowing what it really means, they are tolerated. Never for a long time has there been one who has learnt in the Isles."

"That is interesting," said Horis. "I suppose that the wars and suspicions of our nations have not helped."

Grace nodded. "Maybe, Seph says that he has come to tell all the Drogans of Norlandia to listen to you, that you will help bring them together. And that message will be passed to all, and thence to their masters across the land, that they must band together to survive."

The Road to Ventis

Chapter 29

Terrance stood in the ticket hall in Bingham station; he had a single case and a leather satchel over his shoulder. The case was his, the satchel borrowed from Walsingham's bedroom. He had packed in haste, the case contained food and his clothes and personal items; the satchel the valuables he had purloined from the strongbox. He was agitated and kept looking around for signs that he had been discovered, without realising it he had reached the front of the queue for tickets.

"Yes," said the official, behind his metal grille. "We don't have all day; what destination?"

"Ventis," whispered Terrance, was anyone paying attention to his destination? Why had he said Ventis? He knew that the Ryde terminated at Ploughtown, the last leg was by steam omnibus, over the hills that were still being tunnelled.

"Ventis," shouted the clerk, making sure that every person in the ticket hall knew where he was bound. "The Ryde stops at Ploughtown; they are still building the line to Ventis. And anyway, you have missed the Ryde to Ploughtown. It goes at thirteen and it's after fourteen now, you can come back in the morning for the early service."

Terrance was panicked, how had he done that? He had the times written down; he felt in his pocket, they had gone. In a flash he remembered that he had left the sheet on the table in the Walsinghams'. Now he could be followed, even now the Watch might be looking at it.

"Can I not go towards Metropol City and connect from there?" he asked desperately.

The man looked at him as if he were quite mad. "You may," he said. "But it will cost you more, and you will not get there until after tomorrow's early Ryde has arrived. Come back in the morning."

"That will be acceptable," said Terrance, knowing that he had to depart from Bingham in any way that he could. "Give me my ticket," he produced a wad of notes and pushed them under the screen.

"Very well," said the clerk, he manipulated his clockwork printing press and after a clatter, a ticket emerged from the slot by the grille. The man took the notes and counted some off, he pushed the rest back. "Platform two then, get off at Crowburgh for the service to Ploughtown, this ticket is valid for the omnibus as well."

Terrance took his ticket and the notes, shouted, "Thank you," and pushed his way past the queue. He showed his ticket at the barrier and was allowed through. He had to get out of Bingham, now that he had changed his route it would be safer, the paper he had forgotten gave the times of the Rydes to Ploughtown, he would not be looked for travelling in another way. For the first time in ages he started to relax. Six hours later, he was less so when the Ryde from Crowburgh to Ploughtown was delayed overnight by an accident on the line.

It was another two days before Maloney stood in the same spot. He, by contrast was on time for the Ryde, he had bought his ticket on departure from the house and with a day to spare, had gone for ale and a meal.

He had spent the night in the ale house, sitting unnoticed in the corner. When it was closing time, he had told the innkeeper he could not go home. "A domestic dispute with my lady you understand," he said and the man took pity.

"You may use the bench," he said, and Maloney, who had spent nights in worse places, had a sound sleep, safe from discovery. In the morn he woke early and let himself out. The way to the station was quiet but once he got to the station he found extra Watchmen on duty. He was asked his destination. "Ploughtown," he replied, showing his ticket. "What's amiss?"

"None of your concern," the Watchman said sternly. "We search for a man with a false left arm returning to Aserol and for another man heading to Metropol City. Since you are neither you may continue."

Maloney was glad that he had removed his arm before he had gone to the ale house. He had reckoned that when Gloriana had awoken she would have mentioned his arm as a distinguishing feature. He supposed that most people would assume that once you had such an appendage you would never remove it.

The Watchman had revealed that they were also looking for Terrance, if not by name. But what they were not seeking was a man without an arm. Little did the Watchman know that it resided in the special pouch in his bag.

The Ryde arrived and Maloney boarded. It was a long trip to Ploughtown, about ten hours, and after he had attached his arm again he settled himself to sleep for as long as he could. Maloney, like most soldiers, had the knack of sleep on demand, for they never knew when they might sleep again, and the countryside passed in a blur as he rested.

Terrance stood at the halt in Ploughtown; he could not think of it as a station, it had barely a roof and only plain boards to keep his feet from the mud. He had wasted a day while the line was cleared outside Crowburgh and worse, it was now raining. At least he had the food that Gloriana had made to sustain him, but he had had to purchase char at extortionate cost from the vendors on the Ryde while they waited.

He hurried into the hut by the side of the tracks where his ticket was inspected. Around him, construction proceeded on the Rail to

Ventis, great steam cranes lifted steel rails from a wagon and Exomen put them in position. Other mechanical devices laid sleepers and joined things together, it was a show of the power of modern industry.

Terrance had once wielded that power and in truth he missed it greatly. Perhaps when he had dealt with Horis he could get work on the Rails, they were expanding across the country and there would be positions in management for educated men like him.

Unknown to him, Maloney had overtaken him, passing the hut not an hour before. He was already in the line for the steam-omnibus to Ventis. Terrance braved the rain and walked across to the halt, joining the back of a long line of travellers. Gone were the days when he could use his rank to force his way to the front.

They boarded the omnibus in turn. Maloney got a seat and as he did so he saw Terrance in the line. Quickly he lifted his arm to cover his face, fortunately it was his right arm, the false left hand in its glove might have been recognised.

Terrance did not notice, he was calculating whether he would get a place, there appeared to be little room left as he neared the front of the line.

"That's it," the driver's hand came down two men in front of Terrance. "We're full up; next service is in four hours, providing it gets here safe, the roads are muddy and treacherous."

Terrance was about to plead for a seat, he had his hand ready to offer cash to the driver as the door shut with a hiss of steam. The engine, under the seating floor, rumbled and the omnibus pulled away. Terrance looked up, desolate, straight into the eye of Maloney.

He blinked; surely it could not be the man again? The last time he had seen him was at the gate in Northcastle on that day that was burned into his mind. He looked again, the coach had passed. "Stop," he shouted, the men in the line laughed.

"What's amiss," one said. "Will she not wait a few hours for you then?"

A uniformed official came to the line; he handed out numbered tickets to the men waiting. "Come back after lunch," he said, "you will be sure of a place on the next service. We will call around the town square when it arrives."

Terrance headed for the ale house he had spied across the muddy square. Did they not have sealed roads in this backwater? he thought as his clothes became more and more splattered with mud. He was starting to look less like the important gentleman he thought himself, more like some sort of yokel. Appearance had always been important to him, a sign that he was better than the unwashed rabble that he considered the general population to be. That was another thing that had been taken from him by Strongman and his friends.

He sat in the ale house with a plate of bread and cheese to go with his ale. While he ate, he nursed his grievances. He was descending rapidly down the social ladder and he could see of no way to arrest his fall. Now it looked like that blasted soldier was ahead of him, so Horis and the woman must be in Ventis. He had paid Picton and lost his apartment for naught. At least he had recovered some of his losses in the Walsinghams' strongbox. The jewels alone were worth a good amount; he knew a little about their value from the things he had bought Isabella. All that seemed like another life to him now.

The steam omnibus wheezed as it climbed the hill; the road was a mass of churned mud. Logs had been laid in an attempt to stabilise the road in places but they were wet and rotting. Only the weight of the omnibus kept its wheels anchored and turning. Finally, at a pace slower than a crawl, it reached the crest and descended in a semi-controlled slide. This was the fourth such hill in a row, each steeper than the last. It was no wonder, thought Maloney, that Ventis was not yet connected to the Rail.

"Is the journey always like this?" he asked the man sitting next to him.

"It's worse than I can remember this year," the man answered. "The government should hurry up and get the Rail finished before the commerce of the whole town suffers, instead of fighting each other in their opulence."

The coach reached the flat between the hills and its motion settled. "Rest stop in a short while," shouted the driver. "The waystation at Millingard is just down the valley, there will be soup and the chance to stretch your legs."

The coach passed between tall trees, there was a shout of, "What the..." and the squeal of brakes hastily applied. The coach skidded and started to turn, Maloney had a sight of a Drogan sitting in their way, feasting on some animal it had caught, then the coach tipped up as it left the road and plunged down a bank. There was panic inside, the passengers were thrown from their seats and Maloney heard the crack of bones. He had braced himself automatically as the vehicle started to turn, becoming again a soldier, time slowed for him as he watched people falling and heard their screams. His companion in the seat tried to hold on but was unable and toppled down the aisle. There was a crunch as the front of the coach hit a large tree, then twin thumps as something landed on the roof, shaken from its branches by the impact.

Silence reigned in the coach for a moment, then the moans of the injured started. The coach had come to rest at an angle, its rear wheels were off the ground, its nose buried in the tree. Steam escaped from a fractured pressure line, whistling angrily. There were scrabbling noises from the roof as whatever it was slid forward.

"Is everyone alright?" shouted the driver, who had been strapped into his seat, unlike the passengers. "Are there any medics on the coach?" he asked.

Maloney was not qualified but had seen his share of casualties on the field of battle. He came forward to the pile of humanity at the front of the bus and did what he could. There were broken bones and cuts aplenty, rather less to those on the top of the heap, the poor passengers underneath had cushioned their fall. Together with the driver he separated the tangle of limbs into people and assessed their injuries. At the base of the heap were two with broken necks. "These two poor souls have had it," he said. "They're beyond our help."

There was much blood and Maloney worked quickly at the worst, he put folk in pairs, uninjured and injured, and showed them how to apply pressure to staunch bleeding. He pulled the shirts from the dead and tore them into bandages. Many of the others regarded him apathetically, or resisted his efforts, he knew that they were in shock and needed firm leadership. He had seen this reaction in people before, but under more trying conditions. At least here they were not being peppered with arrows and darts.

As they worked, more recovered their senses and joined in to help. The noises from the roof continued, a clicking and scratching that became more frantic, then there were a series of heavy thumps that bowed the roof inward. Maloney looked at the driver, who had been glancing at the roof with a worried face. "Is that what I think it is?" he said.

The driver swallowed, his neck twitched. "I'm sure of it; we have hit a tree with a Drogan roost in it. The impact has dislodged the chicks; they are tangled in the netting over the luggage rack. The noise is their parents' claws as they try to free them." The passengers looked nervously at the roof, as if they expected to see the beasts drop through it at any minute.

Maloney understood. "Then we are stuck, the parents will guard the chicks and if we try to leave they will see us as a threat."

The driver nodded. "When we are missed, the waystation will send a search party, there will be gas guns and they will chase the beasts away. We only have to sit tight."

But the Drogans will smell the blood, and try to get inside, he thought, though he said nothing.

Several hours passed, another man and a woman had succumbed to blood loss, despite the aid given by Maloney. The Drogans still wrestled with the net on the roof, their squawking becoming more desperate and the inside of the coach was now like the inside of a drum. It rocked to the efforts of the parents to free their offspring.

Several of the unharmed passengers were getting restless. "We don't want to sit here," they wailed. "The Drogans will attack us."

"You're more likely to be attacked if you step outside," said Maloney. "You're safer in here."

"They are distracted," said a large man, he had fallen and his weight had probably broken one of the necks. He stood, with difficulty. "I'm off," he announced. "You can all stay here and be eaten, or starve."

He pushed past Maloney and the driver, opened the door and jumped out.

Two things happened almost simultaneously, a Drogan casually leant over the side of the coach and plucked the man's head clean off. His body fell, twitching and spurting hot blood over Maloney before he could get the door shut. The passengers screamed and rushed to the opposite side of the coach. But there was no safety there, the second Drogan had dropped to the ground and was banging at the windows with its beak. Several cracked but none were breached.

The second was the noise of an engine, coming from the road above them, its growl was cut off by the door's slam. Maloney debated whether to tell the others that he had heard it. Even though it was only a few yards away, with the marauding Drogans to get past, it may as well have been on one of the moons. And it would be gone before they could reach the road.

Terrance was on the coach that passed. He had been contemplating a third ale when the call had gone out, "The omnibus is arrived, if you have tickets take your places."

In the event it was less than half full and he had a double seat to himself. He was able to stretch out and relax, as much as he could with the painful jarring motion as it bounced over the rough roads.

The whole country seemed to consist of switchback hills and small valleys, he hoped they would reach a waystation soon, his bladder was starting to complain. He should not have had that second ale.

"Millingard waystation shortly," sang out the driver as they entered a wooded area.

"Will there be char and vittles?" shouted an old woman on the left, everyone laughed and the driver took his eyes off the road to turn and speak to her. Terrance glanced out of the window; he had the briefest glimpse of what looked like the rear of another coach. It appeared to have crashed into the trees, and there were Drogans around it, several of them. He thought that he saw a body on the ground but they were past so quick. No-one else had noticed; surely, Terrance thought, it must be the coach with Maloney aboard. He would say nothing and see what occurred in Millingard.

The coach pulled to a halt in Millingard. Dark was falling. An official ran up to the door. "Where have you been, are you the morning service?" he shouted.

"We are the second of the day, why is that?" answered the driver.

"The other has not arrived. Did you see aught on your way?"

Terrance kept quiet but listened intently; the omnibus with his adversary on was the one he had seen.

"We saw nothing," said the driver. "Any of you good folk see a vehicle in distress on the way?"

Nobody spoke up, except the old lady. "Can I have my char yet?" she cawed.

"It must have gone over the cliffs somewhere," the official said. "I will have to mount a search party and work backwards from here. But we can do little until morning's light."

Terrance smiled to himself; his omnibus would travel on overnight, its way lit by the gas lamps on its nose. They were past the worst of the hills, it was mainly flat ground, pasture and wheat fields from here to Ventis. He would arrive in Ventis at noon tomorrow, long before Maloney was even rescued, if he still lived.

The char would taste especially good in Millingard, he thought, as he descended. It appeared that his luck was changing, if the Drogans dealt with Maloney, that only left Horis and Grace.

An hour later, they were on the way again. As the coach carrying Terrance left, the service from Ventis pulled in, the driver was instructed to carry on and soldiers from the small garrison were embarked, armed with gas guns and lamps. The passengers were all led into the eatery and the coach became a searcher, it crawled away into the woods, all eyes alert.

Maloney was fighting a losing battle, despite the fact the every time a person had ventured outside the coach a Drogan would kill it, there were still those who wished to try. After the first death, another man had opened the door, waited for a second then ran towards the road. He had got ten paces when the beast swooped. Now there was a third keen to try his luck. "If we throw a body out, it will distract the beasts," he said.

There was horror among the women passengers. "They deserve respect," one said. "Just because they are dead, doesn't mean they should be Drogan fodder so you can live."

"Well I'm doing it anyway," was the reply. "If you think it wrong, well you'll just have to try and stop me." Maloney and the driver grabbed the man as he tried to push a body through the door, it swung open and the head of a Drogan appeared, causing screams. The man, less brave now, changed his mind and turned back inside, he tripped over the body and sprawled, just as the jaws of the beast snapped shut where he would have been. Maloney was caught behind the door and tried to push it closed as the Drogan dropped to the ground and forced its way into the coach. Everyone ran to the back, desperate to avoid the snapping jaws. The second Drogan also dropped to the ground and forced its way in.

Now Maloney was behind them both; he could hear the battering on the glass as the desperate passengers tried to break a window and escape. The Drogans were finding it hard going clambering over the seats, there was little room for them to move and it hampered their efforts to get to the humans.

The rear window opened to the driver, he had the key for it and people jumped through, Maloney left the coach and shut the door behind him. He ran to the back of the coach as the last of the survivors climbed through the window. "Is that all?" he said to the driver, who was still inside behind him. The Drogans were ten feet away.

"I hope so," he said, heaving himself through the opening. He pushed it shut and it locked as a head thumped into it.

"Come on, up the hill to the road," Maloney shouted as the Drogan chicks set up a fearsome squawking from the roof. Their parents threw themselves against the glass but had not enough room to build up the momentum necessary to break out.

As the party straggled through the last of the trees and onto the road, they saw the gas lights from the searchers approaching from Millingard. They stood in the road, a bedraggled bunch as the omnibus pulled to a halt in front of them. Soldiers descended.

Chapter 30

At last in Ventis, Terrance stepped off the omnibus; he was saddle-sore, hungry and weary. He was in desperate need of a bed, but first he had to find out if the *Swiftsure* was expected. He collected his case as it was thrown down from the rack on the roof.

He went towards the harbour, guided by the sight of the sea and found the harbour office.

The official looked at his worn clothes and stubbled chin. "What can we do for you?"

"I seek a vessel and have travelled a long way," said Terrance, brushing at his clothes.

"Which vessel would that be?" he was asked.

"The *Swiftsure*," he said and the man nodded.

"She calls here but why do you seek her?"

"I seek one of the crew, it's a personal matter."

The official nodded. "Just how will you get to the *Swiftsure* when she arrives?" he enquired. "Swim to her?"

Terrance did not understand his meaning; the man saw his blank look and explained. "The *Swiftsure* is too large a vessel to get into our harbour, she anchors in the roads and we service her by barge."

That was a setback, Terrance knew not how he could get aboard; he would have to think.

"In any event," the man continued, "you've just missed her. The *Swiftsure* only departed a few days ago, it will be six weeks or more till she returns."

Another problem; he had missed his quarry by the merest of margins. "I need to see a man on the vessel," Terrance said. "Can I take lodging hereabouts until it returns?"

The man nodded. "Try the *Dun Cervine*, a tavern near the market, go back past the coach terminus and it will be in front of you."

Terrance thanked the man and retraced his steps. Six weeks in this awful place; perhaps he could get a job with lodgings as part of the wage. The thought of physical labour disgusted him but he needed to be practical now, two of his targets were within reach, it would be worth it. If he got a job with some fishers he would have access to a boat, that would solve one of his problems.

With ease he found the *Dun Cervine*, it had a faded sign of a cervine hanging outside and was opposite the entrance to the marketplace. Terrance stood upright and squared his shoulders. He went inside. The place was packed and he had to push his way to the bar, then wait while ale and food was dispensed to several others. His stomach growled. The serving girls ignored him and flirted with customers, it irritated him to be ignored as he stood and waved a banknote. Couldn't the stupid provincials see he was important? At last he attracted the attention of a male steward.

"Good day, sir," he said. "I seek lodgings until a certain vessel arrives."

The man looked him up and down. "If you can pay," he said.

"I can," he replied. "Do you have food as well? I have been travelling a long while."

Terrance tucked into a hearty stew of roots and chunks of ovine; it was flavoured with apple in a delicate way. Together with a thick slice of warm bread it was the best meal that Terrance had tasted for a long while. Indeed it was as fine as any of the high priced eateries in the city would have provided, and considerably cheaper too. He saw that at least half of the patrons had similar bowls to his in front of them.

Terrance had hoped to find Horis sooner, his store of cash was dwindling, it had been augmented by the content of the Walsinghams' strongbox but now it needed to last him a longer time. Perhaps if he could not get work he might find a place to sell the jewels.

Finishing his meal, he returned to the bar and the man. "May I see my room?" he said. "I'm weary from the journey."

"Of course, my potboy will show you. Jed," he called. "Get here and show this man to the top guest room."

A young lad, no more than ten years, appeared. He grinned, showing black teeth, then he turned and scampered away, Terrance following. The boy went down the passage and up a flight of twisted stairs. "Come on, mister," he squeaked. "Rooms are up here."

Terrance found him in a sparsely furnished room, just a bed and a washstand under the eaves. He sat on the bed, the mattress lumpy and thin, he could feel the springs beneath it. It made the seat on the coach seem like an easy chair at home or a padded stall at the theatre.

"I'll take it," he said. "Tell me, Jed, are there any jobs in Ventis for willing men?"

"You might try in the market," the boy shouted as he ran down the stairs again at the innkeeper's call.

Terrance shut the door and lay on the bed, he was almost instantly asleep.

Maloney arrived in Millingard as day broke; the survivors were taken inside the company rest-stop. There they were fed and given char and blankets. There was an official from the Rail-Ryde company who was waiting to welcome them all.

"A steam crane will be dispatched to haul the wreck back to the road," he said, when asked about their luggage. "But first the soldiers will have to attend to the Drogans."

Then he took the driver into his office while they ate and sat. After an hour or so the driver emerged to face them.

Maloney saw that he was sweating profusely. "I've been given a grilling and no mistake," he said, "about the deaths. My manager says that I should have kept the fools on board. But I told him that I tried. And he is sore about the damage to the omnibus. I said that perhaps I should have struck the Drogan, then I would have missed the tree. Mr Maloney, he would like to see you, if you will."

"Of course." Maloney rose and went into the office.

"Are you the soldier?" the manager asked.

"I was once," Maloney said, waving his false arm. "Now I am just a passenger."

The manager, suited and fat, looked like he had never done a hard day's work, nor had even faced a danger.

"Thank you for your aid," he said. "My driver tells me that you helped him and tried to prevent the loss of life."

Maloney smiled. "The driver is too kind," he told the manager. "In truth, he acted in exemplary fashion. He cannot be blamed for the accident; he was trying to avoid one. Once we had crashed, he set a fine example by his actions. He gave orders but they were ignored. What was he to do? Even after one man had forced past him, others sought to chance escape. I tried to help him keep order; he should be commended, not admonished. And I will tell anybody from your company that, in his defence."

The manager looked pleased. "From what he told me you performed well, giving aid to the wounded and trying to keep order."

Maloney blushed. "I have faced worse. I merely tried to prevent a panic."

"Well you succeeded in that, the thanks of the company are due, your bags will be along presently and then you may continue your journey, have you a ship to catch in Ventis?"

"In a manner of speaking," said Maloney, "I have."

Terrance awoke in the dark and for a moment forgot where he was. He stood and banged his head on the low ceiling in his room. He felt stiff, muscles he never knew he possessed were complaining at the treatment they had received on the journey. He crossed to the window. It was morning, he had slept for much longer than he had meant. Still, it mattered little; he had six weeks to kill, six weeks to keep out of Maloney's way, should he even arrive. There was always the chance that the Drogans had finished him off in the forest. If he were to appear, he could dispose of him before the *Swiftsure* returned.

He needed to look around, get his bearings; the lie of the land would be useful if he had to hide again. He decided to go to the market, he may learn of a way to get to the *Swiftsure*, even of employment. He washed and dressed and went downstairs, carrying his valuables in the satchel; there was no chance of him being parted from them.

"You're too late for fast-break," called the innkeeper as he appeared. The bar was full of farmers, drinking ale and cydir.

"No matter, I'm out to the market," he said.

Before he went into the market hall, he saw a jewellers shop and went inside. But the place had nothing anywhere near the quality of the jewellery that he carried; to try and sell them among this pile of rubbish would be impossible. After pretending interest in a few items, and under the suspicious eye of the shopkeeper, he departed.

Another avenue was closed. He was avoiding the market, he knew, as he walked to the harbour. There were a line of small boats drawn up, the skippers shouted their trade. "Fishes for sale," sang one and, "Transport to the anchored vessels," another. This was a real relief to him, he could just go out to the *Swiftsure* in one of these, he could do the deed and return, for small change.

Heartened, he finally went into the market, here was another version of the chaos that the country seemed to be to him. People milled and the air was thick with the smell of butchered meat. It reminded him of the Walsinghams' house after his killing spree, he wondered what the reaction to that had been in Bingham, maybe it had awoken the sleepy place.

He was swept along by the throng of buyers, past stalls with cuts of meat on blocks, bunches of dirt-encrusted vegetables, eggs and dairy goods, all displayed openly for the flies to wander over.

He happened to stop by a butcher selling ovine meat and Terrance remembered the stew he had eaten in the ale house. The stallholder offered him a sample of cooked meat on a skewer, which he declined. Then seeing the fellow's face, he thought it more diplomatic to accept. He tasted and it was delicious, but not as good as that he had eaten the day before. "It's very nice," he said, attempting to strike up conversation.

The farmer smiled, hearing a cultured voice in all the provincial hubbub. "Thank you, sir. We don't see many from the city in here," he remarked.

"I'm waiting for a vessel to arrive," said Terrance. "Yesterday I had the most delicious stew in the *Dun Cervine*. It was ovine not unlike yours, but tasted more of apples, I have never had the like before, is it some local delicacy?"

The man nodded. "If you had it in the *Cervine* than it was old Filian's meat," he said. "He was the first to sell it, now he supplies many places. His ovines graze in the orchard, as do mine but there is something about his apples, they give a different taste to the meat. We all wish for his secret ingredient, he has cornered the market."

"This Filian must be a rich man," said Terrance automatically, he was making small talk, his mind on Maloney; he must keep alert.

"I suppose that he might be," continued the stallholder. "Enough to leave here anyways. I hear that he has recently sold the farm and moved back to be near to his family. He had owned that farm and the goodwill of his customers for many years, I suspect he made a good profit. They do say that the purchaser was a newcomer to Ventis, not a farmer but a sailor from one of the regular traders. Like as not he has tired of travelling and decided to settle. Or perhaps he did so to please his wife; Grace is her name, or so they say. We will have to see how he fares, whether he can keep the quality."

A new arrival from a ship, and his wife was called Grace; Terrance was suddenly alert.

"Please tell me, where might I find this farm?" he asked innocently.

Chapter 31

Horis set out early like he did every day; it had become a sort of ritual. Each morning before Baylock arrived he went to check the livestock for any that had taken ill overnight. Also, he had several of the season's agnina to check. Baylock had been instructing him on birthing and he had assisted at several, yet not one on his own so far. He had learned so much from the man that he felt guilty to want to employ some or all of the soldiers who had helped him. That was a decision he had been putting off. Baylock was also learning the whistle in his luncheon breaks and was progressing well. He had the basic notes and would soon start on the combinations.

Grace had also got into the habit of rising early. She rose when Horis left and had the stove raked out and relit in a trice. When it was burning well, she set char to brew and put the pan to warming for the porker rashers. We should keep the odd porker, thought Grace, they would eat all the kitchen scraps and one or two a year would be enough to supply meat for our fast-break and a few pies.

She was excited, later today she would go back into the town, it would also be a chance to see if the speakers were repaired and to call Divid. With luck they could all come and stay here for a while, it was a long journey but Divid would make it, she was sure. Maybe Hector could bring them, she thought. It would be good to catch up on all the news from Aserol.

Baylock was walking the mile from his parents' house to the farm, he was enjoying his job. Mr Horis was quick to learn and not frightened to make mistakes in the pursuit of knowledge. And the new Drogan, Seph or whatever he was called, was just the same as Barnabas, it treated him with respect and never made a hostile move towards him. Now that he was learning the whistle, he would soon be able to converse with it, he relished the idea. There were those in the *Cervine* who remembered tales of folk talking to Drogans, he longed to shout out, 'I will be one soon,' but dared not.

Maloney arrived in the town at sunrise; he had travelled overnight from Millingard, after being reunited with his luggage. His first job would be to find Horis and warn him of Terrance's presence in the town. Then he could find Terrance and deal with him before he caused any trouble. There was a tavern across the street from the coach halt; that would be the best place to start his enquiries.

The *Dun Cervine*. He recognised it from the last time he had been here, with Horis and Grace, when they had found Grieve wandering. Hefting his bags he walked across the road.

Terrance was up and had rested well; he had found the location of Horis and Grace by asking the innkeeper where the ovine had come from. The man still referred to it as 'Filian's farm' but Terrance knew it was the place. It was not too far to walk, he would go there directly. But first he would enjoy a decent fast-break; he was paying for it after all. He looked up from his plate as the door opened.

Horis wanted to call Seph; he had need of him to move some of the livestock to a different field. He reached into his pocket for his whistle, it was not there. In a frenzy he patted all his other pockets, where was it? Had Baylock not returned it after the last practice? Then he remembered, he had left it in the large barn, it was in the pocket of his other overalls. Sighing, he turned and trudged back towards the farmhouse.

Maloney peered through the glass. The inside of the *Dun Cervine* was dingy, he had stopped and let another enter before him, perhaps Terrance was inside; caution was in order. As he looked he saw a man get up from a table and move towards the door, it was Terrance, he turned away and made for the alley between the buildings.

As the farmer passed Terrance and moved to a table with his friends, he got up and went into the street. Revenge would be his; he was on his way at last. The gas pistol bulged in his pocket. Today was the day, the culmination of all his efforts. He was so busy thinking of revenge that he would not have seen Maloney, should he have been in front of him.

Maloney peered around the corner of the alley, Terrance was striding off in the direction of Millingard, there was little cover but he had to be followed. He gave him a fifty-yard start and set off. Where was he going? What to do with his luggage? There was nowhere to leave it.

As Baylock came through the last of the trees and entered the lane, he was surprised to see a man peering over the wall at the farmhouse, immediately he was angered. Some robber was up to no good and his new employer was the intended victim. The impudent man had even brought a bag to fill with booty, the cheek of it. He picked up a fallen branch and crept closer.

Horis had found the whistle and was on his way back to the field, as he came around the corner of the barn he saw Grace being led by a man holding a pistol. The man was unshaven and dressed in muddy rags, a robber no doubt, and it looked like they were heading towards where Grace thought he would be. Keeping to the wall, he followed them, holding the whistle.

Maloney put down the bag and rested against a stone wall. Terrance had not looked behind him as they left the town and turned off the road down a lane. Terrance had entered the yard of a farmhouse; he had seemed all along to know exactly where he was bound. Was Horis here? He peered over the wall at the dwelling; he could see a woman at the window.

Maloney never knew what happened next. One moment he was looking over a low wall at a farmhouse, the next there was a rustle behind him and before he could turn, there was a savage pain in his head, then everything went dark.

Baylock stood over the prone body; he had saved Mr Horis from robbery or worse. He should run and tell him, reaching the gate he skidded into another man, who was in the act of closing the gate behind him. "What are you doing?" he asked. In answer, the man pulled a pistol from his pocket.

"Quiet," he said. "Go into the house and call Grace out here, I wish to speak to her."

"No," said Baylock. "I will not. And it will do you no good shouting; your accomplice will not come to your aid." Baylock moved to grab the pistol.

Grace paused; she had heard a sound from the yard. She put down the kettle and went to the door. There was a man lying on the ground, fearing it was Horis, she ran to him.

Terrance was confused, what had the man meant? He had no accomplice. It was too late to ask him now, they had wrestled and Terrance had fired his pistol into the man, who now lay still on the ground. He moved towards the door, hiding behind the porch.

He grabbed Grace from behind as she ran past him. "Got you," he said as she kicked back at him. He threw her to the ground, she turned and was about to rise when she saw the pistol. Her thoughts went back to Metropol City and Grieve; she knew what the pistol could do. She kept still. She looked at her assailant, under the whiskers and the muddy clothes, she remembered the man. She had to play for time, and how to warn Horis?

"Sensible girl," said Terrance. "You remember me?"

The voice confirmed it; he had found them, but how? The letters could not have got to Aserol and anyway, Terrance had been in Bingham, she knew no-one in that place.

"How could I forget you," she said. "It's impossible…"

Terrance smiled. "Nonsense, it was easy, now get up and take me to Strongman."

"What have you done?" she pointed to the prone figure. As she lifted her hand Terrance aimed the pistol at her face.

"Careful now, I'd hate to shoot you here. I want your man to watch when I do it."

Grace could see that it was Baylock on the ground. She recognised the dark jacket that he wore, darker now with blood. She wanted to tend to him but Terrance waved her away. "I suspect he's past help, I've had to kill and kill again to get here, one or two more will make no difference. Now take me to Strongman."

"He was in the fields, he said he was moving livestock," Grace was trying not to sob, she didn't want to give Terrance the pleasure of seeing her fear.

"Take me to him THIS MINUTE," shouted Terrance.

Horis had got to the field and was behind a tree not twenty feet from Terrance. He peered round the bole; saw the pistol pointed at Grace. He would have to do something.

"Strongman, where are you? Come out and face me," Terrance shouted. "I have your woman here, come and talk and you may save her."

Horis took a deep breath. Then he moved around the tree. "I'm here," he said. "Do not harm her."

Terrance smiled. "Ah, there you are, my erstwhile ex-employee, come and stand here, next to Grace. Don't try anything rash, one has today and he was not faster than a bullet."

"He has shot Baylock," said Grace. "I know not if he lives."

"Don't concern yourself, soon you will not care," said Terrance. "Now both of you, stand over here, and do it quickly."

Horis did as he was bid. Grace clung to him and he smoothed her hair, whispering, "It will be alright." She looked at his hand. "The whistle," she said. He nodded.

Terrance spoke. "I'm sorry to interrupt your reunion," he said in a voice devoid of any sorrow. "You have a fine farm here; I think I may take it on. But there is business to attend to first and a reckoning. I have a choice, which one of you two do I shoot first?"

Horis, with his new found courage and strength was no longer cowed by his old superior or his threats. He had seen behind his façade and was pleased that he had been instrumental in bringing him to Earth. He put the whistle to his lips and blew. "Come-Help," was the message in the blast.

"What was that?" asked Terrance. "Another useless gesture; a whistle that does not work. Who will answer that call?"

Horis said nothing; he just hoped that Seph was in range of the call.

"You ruined me," Terrance began, "with your inability to follow a simple plan."

"You mean your plan to make me the blame of Aserol?" Horis asked. "Your plan to hide your deeds, and what of the miners you killed? Were they also not following your plan?"

"Fool, you were supposed to die with them, and hide all the evidence; it was a matter of national importance, far above your grasp."

"How can the death of many be in the interests of the country?"

"The rocks had to be kept secret. Obley telling you of them was a mistake, who else might he have told? If our enemies had got the rocks they could have found a use for them, maybe they would have been tempted to invade us for them. When I learned what he had done from Grantham, I had to secure the mine. And you spoilt it all, running and telling everyone. Look where I have ended up, my house is gone, my wife and children, I have nothing."

Horis laughed at that. "You have it so wrong," he said. "I have been to the Western Isles, and they have the rocks there, they call them Yanneh and know all of their properties."

That was not strictly true but Terrance would not know, and it gave more time for Seph to arrive.

"The rocks would have cemented my fortune and power," Terrance continued, he was getting more agitated, staring at them both. "You took my chance at greatness."

The pistol wavered in his hand and Horis considered trying to grab it. He was no longer the overweight and unfit man that Terrance remembered.

But he did nothing, for he saw over Terrance's shoulder that Seph had arrived. The beast landed and moved silently until it was close behind Terrance, who had not heard its approach.

"What do you hope to achieve by killing us?" asked Grace. She too had seen Seph, seen the need to keep Terrance distracted from what was going on behind him. "Will it restore your wealth?"

Terrance laughed. "Regrettably not. Cavendish has made that clear. Revenge is what I want, pure and sweet. After I have finished with you I will have a farm to keep me alive. I imagine I can sell the ovines and apples in your stead."

Seph was within reach of Terrance now.

"That's enough talk," he said. "Pay attention, madam. I think that I will wound Horis first, and you can watch him expire. Then it will be your turn." His voice was harsh and threatening. Terrance pointed the pistol.

Horis could see Seph had recognised it as a weapon and Terrance as a threat to his master. His scales rippled in the sunlight, blue-black and red, mainly red now as his anger flared.

"Put the pistol away," said Grace. "You should leave, whilst you may."

Terrance laughed, it was a manic sound that had Seph's scales turning darker red, with beautiful shades of gold. "Why should I do that? There will be no gallant rescue this time, you are alone, your one-armed friend is stuck on the road and his tame soldiers are not here. I have you at my mercy."

He paused. "Or shall I do it the other way? Kill you first?" He wrestled with his dilemma, now that it was here, he could not decide how to cause the most anguish. Time seemed to stand still as Seph moved closer.

He made up his mind. "No, Horis will be first, you can watch, madam, then it might be time for a pleasing interlude before it is your turn."

Grace gazed impassively at Terrance, like her man, the threats meant little to her, she had heard them all before. "We are not alone," she said quietly. "Look behind you."

Seph reared his head above Terrance, he waited, perfectly poised.

Terrance smiled again. "What, and be distracted whilst you run, surely you don't expect me to fall for…?"

His words stopped. There was a crunching sound as Seph struck.

THE END

A New Life in Ventis is the sequel to The Rocks of Aserol.

At first glance it was a simple enough job, go to Aserol and find out what's happening at the Waster mine. For Horis Strongman it's the start of an adventure, there are things that don't add up and he stumbles upon a secret. It's enough to kill for, but can he stay alive to expose it?

In a world where Coal is King, where machines of Metal are powered by Steam and Clockwork, those in power want him silenced by any means.

Accused of a terrible crime, Horis is forced to run, aided by those who can prove his innocence, and unsure of whom he can trust.

From the mines to the skies, on the oceans and rivers, The Rocks of Aserol could change the world.

Sample Chapter

As Horis walked away from the Rail-Ryde and down the hill, his case bumped against his leg with every step. The crowds thinned as he got further from the terminus and he wondered why the omnibus halt was so far away.

He was starting to perspire, and he felt as though people were watching his discomfort when he found himself at the halt. There were several long queues for the various routes, and no obvious means of telling which one he should choose to reach the hotel arranged for him.

He asked a man standing close to him, but the answer was delivered in such a thick provincial accent that it left him none the wiser. Politely he bowed and thanked the man anyway, all the time looking for an inspector.

As in the capital, the omnibuses were guided by a metal shoe at the front, which was held in a single track laid in the cobbles. There were wheels to steer across the intersections and provide stability. Unlike in the capital, the omnibuses in Aserol had a single deck and were drawn by pairs of giant equines, blinkered and resplendent in leather. As soon as one arrived, the crowd swarmed towards it, jostling for spaces. There was a number on the front, but no details as to the places on the journey.

With his bags and his small stature, Horis quickly realised that any journey would not be pleasant.

Hoping that Terrance would understand the extra expense, he turned away. He felt very out of place, a stranger in his own land.

In desperation, Horis made his way to the mobile stand, where he soon found himself at the head of the much shorter queue for a steam-mobile.

The latest adaptation of technology, it was a form of equineless carriage, driven by a coal boiler heating water to drive pistons, much like a Rail-Ryde locomotive, only much smaller. The driver sat outside at the rear, atop the boiler and furnace, with a coal bunker behind him.

Gravity and a belt fed the powdered coal into the furnace, where water was heated to drive the pistons and propel the mobile.

The passenger compartment was at the front, below the driver, and above the water tank. They were still only used over short distances, or in urban areas; for no decent roads connected towns, and there were few places to refuel with either coal or water. The machine vibrated with an alarming motion as the pressure was vented from the boiler, as ready as a racing equine to do his bidding.

Its brass and steel frame and fittings were dulled and grimy, and the wheel rims caked with mud and coal dust, which did not inspire confidence, but he was next in line and for good or ill, this was his conveyance. Horis opened the door and placed his bags inside, then looked up at the driver, masked and leathered, sitting hunched over the controls; he turned to Horis and grinned, showing a set of metal false teeth that shone. "Where to, Guv'nor?" he asked.

"Provincial Hotel, good sir," Horis answered, and almost before he had a chance to seat himself and shut the door, he was swept back into the deep velvet cushions of the seat as the machine accelerated away, scattering the urchin children that played and begged around all such places. Horis squawked into the speaking tube that connected him to the driver, "Have a care, man!" but there was no answer. Horis remembered tales of the first of these machines, how in the rush to make ever smaller boilers the thinner construction had resulted in explosions and deaths. Also, the dry coal dust was known to be particularly combustible. He hoped that this one was well built and maintained.

Opening the grimy window, Horis could see the mountains that encircled the town, mountains that were covered with tall trees, and which contained the reason for his visit. The summons had come the day before, and as the most junior in the Ministry of Coal he had been singled out for the job. In truth, it was close to the public holiday, and none of the others had wanted the disruption; as Horis was single he had been everyone else's choice for the journey.

He had left his lodgings early this morning for the long Rail-Ryde to Aserol, with no knowledge of how long he might remain away, and only a vague notion as to his purpose.

His superior, Terrance, whose family owned the mine, had given him little intelligence. "See what Mr Obley is up to," he had said. "I would go myself, but…" He waved his arms about. "…It's Harvest and I am required at official things. Reassure him and solve his problems, you have my authority to do what is reasonable. He has called like this before; it will probably be a trivial matter. And see if there is any talk of the mine in town, Obley has strange ways of dealing with his 'problems'."

As he was carried along the cobbles, the mobile bucked and rattled and Horis thought of his fast-breaker, a rather splendid piece of haddock and boiled new potatoes eaten on the journey. It was more than he would normally break his fast with but was included in the price of the ticket. At the time it had seemed a shame not to indulge. The springs on the mobile were tired and gave a motion like a ship in a squall, and Horis silently prayed to Bal that the meal would not make a reappearance.

Buildings and people flashed by, and the machine tilted violently as it cornered. It overtook many equine-drawn vehicles, and Horis wished that he had taken the more sedate option of a carriage ride. He noticed that the equines seemed unperturbed by the machine, even though in many ways it would be their nemesis.

After what felt like an hour, although it had only been a few minutes, the mobile wheezed to a halt. Horis could see that he was outside a somewhat faded building that was barely clinging onto past grandeur. It was one of several joined in a long curving terrace, facing the harbour. The driver's voice squawked through the speaking tube.

"Provincial Hotel, sir, I hope you enjoyed the Ryde, the old girl does her best, but spares is hard to come by."

"It was fine," gulped Horis, his stomach was still fighting with gravity for control of his haddock. He looked at the fare shown on a clockwork and opened the door. Climbing out onto the pavement, he rummaged in his pocket for coins. Handing the driver half a Sol, he muttered, "Keep it," and started to drag his belongings from the mobile, which shuddered and spluttered, dripping steaming water into the drain ditch. There was a rattle from the coal bunker as more fuel was fed into the furnace down the belt.

"Bal blesses you, sir," said the driver, looking at the coin. He touched his cap in salute, and Horis saw that his hand was made of polished wood, the fingers frozen in a claw-shaped position that fitted the controls of the mobile. "I hope you enjoys it here in Aserol."

"I'm on Ministry business," he replied, but with a roar the machine had gone; only a wisp of steam remained.

I hope that you have enjoyed this book

If you've enjoyed reading this story, please would you consider leaving a review on the website where you purchased it, even if it's only a few words, it will be appreciated and might just help someone else discover their next great read!
Thank you very much.
  Richard.

www.richarddeescifi.co.uk